To *Live* Again

For Lori,
Wishing you
God's full life. John 10:10
Love Rosemary Morton

Rosemary Morton

Inspiring Voices®
A Service of Guideposts

Inspiring Voices books may be ordered through booksellers or by contacting:

Inspiring Voices
1663 Liberty Drive
Bloomington, IN 47403
www.inspiringvoices.com
1-(866) 697-5313

ISBN: 978-1-4624-0654-8 (sc)
ISBN: 978-1-4624-0653-1 (e)

Library of Congress Control Number: 2013909854

Printed in the United States of America.

Inspiring Voices rev. date: 06/19/2013

To Dan for your patience and support. To Michelle, Noelle, and Helga for your prodding and encouragement, and LaVonne and Murna for your belief in me. Thank you, Sharon Hinck. I couldn't have done it without you.

"Now comfort me so I can live, really live;
Your revelation is the tune I dance to."
Psalm 119:77 The Message

Chapter 1

"Why doesn't Anne try to rehabilitate someone else?" Katie picked up her cane and limped around the living room while muttering to herself. "I haven't played the guitar in ages, not to mention my voice. I haven't sung anything except hymns in church for the last three years. How does she expect me to perform?"

Katie looked at the letter in her left hand and sighed in frustration, then stopped at a picture of John on the fireplace mantle. Setting the letter down and leaning her cane against the bricks, she picked up the picture and stroked a finger down his right cheek in a caress. How she longed to feel his flesh again.

After replacing John's picture, her eyes moved to a photo of their son, J. J. He'd been almost nine and laughing when it was taken, so his dimples were prominently displayed. Her finger touched the glass shielding that dimple, and her heart longed for the husband and son who'd been stolen from her. How she missed them. Tears slid from her eyes. She wiped them on her sleeve, then picked up the letter and cane and headed for her studio.

Katie walked to the desk and forcefully tossed down the letter from her best friend, Anne. With a shake of her head, she sat down and stared at it, then read the words aloud.

"Katie, I'm in a bind and need your help. The vocalist for Senator Harvey's fundraiser on March 18th has had to cancel, and I brought your name up to the committee as the perfect substitute. Obviously there isn't much time, but since I know how good you are, I'm sure you can be ready to perform by then. I'll call when I get a minute."

Katie knew the senator slightly from some political work John had done but not well enough to feel badly about saying no to the invitation.

Leaning back with a big sigh, her eyes wandered toward the case holding her guitar. The phone rang and Katie reached for the receiver.

"Hello."

"Hi, Katie. Did you get my letter?"

"Yes, Anne. It came today and . . ."

"I wanted to be sure you had it before I called. You're not mad I asked, are you? You know you have to get out and start doing things, and this is a good way to start—with a bang." There was a moment of silence. When Anne spoke again, tenderness colored her voice. "Katie, you're so good. You'd be the perfect performer for this event. Please say you'll do it."

Katie ran a hand through her hair and closed her eyes as she leaned back again and tried to stifle the rising panic. "How in the world could you think I'd even consider doing something like this? I love you dearly, but even for you, it's a little much to expect me to perform in public."

"Hmph. What do you mean, 'perform in public?' For goodness sake, I know you're self-conscious about your leg, but you're much more aware of it than anyone else. You've been hiding there in your tower long enough. Some of us miss you terribly, and if we don't start pushing, we'll never see you, and the world will lose a grand talent."

Katie fiddled with her cane and looked down at her right leg with a grimace. She could picture Anne in her law office wearing a sophisticated suit, sitting behind a desk with shoes off and hair a mess from pushing fingers through it while thinking.

"What do you mean, 'miss me'?" she said finally. "Don't we see each other all the time? Oh, Anne! What am I going to do with you? Will you ever give up?"

"No, I won't, so you might as well say yes and be done with it. You know me, just like a dog with a bone. I never let go and usually get what I want if it's important enough. And this is very important. I've already hinted I have the most wonderful musician all but lined up. You wouldn't make a liar out of me, would you?"

Katie sighed and glanced again at the letter, noting the date of the event.

"No, I wouldn't make a liar out of you. You've done that yourself. And besides, this is only a month away. How in the world could I be in condition to sing and play in such a short time? You're impossible. Loveable, but impossible." Katie heard Anne's phone ding softly, indicating she had a call. "Do you need to take that? We can talk later."

"No, whoever it is will leave a message. Look, anyone with your ability can just practice a little and be ready in a month. It's not as if you're being asked to do a tour of the country. If you don't commit yourself to performing soon, then you never will." Anne paused, and in the quiet Katie could almost hear her own heart beating. She knew Anne believed in her talent, but it didn't make this any easier.

"Anne, please . . ."

"Listen up, girl," Anne interrupted. "I think you're wonderful, and I'm not just saying this because you're my friend. I know talent when I hear it. You could have made a name for yourself in the music world, only you weren't interested when John and J. J. were alive. Your life centered around them. I understand that. I accepted it then, but I think the time is right for you to start using your talents. You need this as much as I need you to do it for me."

Katie rubbed her eyes. "I don't know. I'm scared. Part of me wants to jump at the chance to sing and play and then—what if I can't do it?"

Anne's voice became gentle. "Oh, my dear, don't worry. You're still you. Talent doesn't vanish."

"It didn't die with John and J. J.?" Katie struggled to keep her voice steady and took a deep breath.

"Listen, don't say no. Let's do this. Get out your guitar and play some scales, sing a little, listen to yourself, and think about it. I'll come over tonight with some Vietnamese food, and we'll talk about this over dinner. What do you say?"

"You're trying to soften me up with food. Okay, you win. Come over, but don't expect me to say yes." She could picture Anne smiling and knew her friend thought she'd won.

"I'll be there about seven. Gotta run. I have an appointment in five minutes."

"Fine. I'll see you at seven, and that'll give me a few hours to get over this strange killing urge."

Anne laughed, and Katie's spirits lifted as she hung up.

Now I'm in for it. If she gets past the door, she'll have me committed. What if I can't play anymore?

Katie twisted the diamond in her left ear. The piece wouldn't have to be anything very difficult. Suddenly, an urge to touch the strings again washed over her. She moved to the case holding her guitar and lifted the cover with slightly trembling fingers. The familiar scent of old velveteen brought a scene to her mind. She'd argued with John about something. She couldn't remember what, but she'd played her guitar out of frustration. When she'd calmed down, her fingers had picked out a simple love song. When she had finished, John was leaning against the doorframe smiling at her. He'd walked over, kissed the top of her head, and apologized. She could hear John's voice in her head even now. He'd found it easy to apologize. She'd been more stubborn.

She sighed, took the guitar out of its case, and sat on the floor to check the strings. It wasn't badly out of tune after being left alone so long. Why hadn't she used it to help her through this difficult time?

With head bent over the strings, she picked out a gentle melody and smiled in delight at recapturing the joyous feeling of making music. Occasionally she stopped and went over a phrase to correct mistakes or fingering. Eventually Katie started to hum, then sang softly "My Favorite Things" from *The Sound of Music*. J. J. had loved putting his own words to it, like "snowball fights" and "mud pies." They'd always ended up laughing.

Next she sang one of her own compositions, a ballad about the healing touch of a smile. John told her once that if she would sing it to his patients, they'd heal much faster. After she finished singing, her fingers softly picked out the melody. If only she could sing it for him again.

Tears welled up. Katie clutched the guitar and let them flow. This time they brought healing instead of grief. After grabbing a tissue, she glanced down at the letter on her desk.

Anne, you amazing friend. What would I do without you?

The rest of the afternoon was spent on the floor of her studio exercising both instrument and voice. Finally, the hardness of the floor and uncomfortable position forced her to move. A hot bath would be just the thing to remove the kinks.

Cane in hand, she moved down the hall. She loved this huge old house and was so happy that she'd bought the second floor and turned it into a beautiful home. As Katie passed the guest room, she thought of her mother who needed to come for another visit, then proceeded through her room to the bathroom. After turning on the taps, she straightened, walked back into the bedroom, and looked around with fresh appreciation.

The old-fashioned watercolor wallpaper spilled over into the fabrics. Everything appeared soft and comforting, both to the eye and touch. Masses of pillows were thrown on the bed and on the overstuffed antique loveseat where she liked to curl up and read.

Katie sat on the window seat overlooking the back garden where beautiful old oak trees stood bare of leaves. The snow sparkled, fresh and clean in the twilight. Chattering squirrels chased one another across the white expanse and up the trees.

That oak, with its wide spreading branches, would have been the perfect tree for John and J. J. to build a tree house. She could have helped too and it would have been such fun. Why had God let them die? Would she ever know?

Katie sighed, and a few minutes later, walked back into the bathroom, turned off the faucets and shed her clothes. After sinking into the hot water, she groaned, and leaned back to soak out some of the stiffness.

Her fingers felt a little sore but not unpleasantly so. It meant she could still make music. Scenes floated through her mind of other practice sessions when her fingers had become tender. None of them had been as satisfying as today's had been.

The cooling water brought her out of her reverie and back to the present. Katie looked at the clock and gasped. Anne was due in half an hour. She'd better hurry or she'd be in a towel when Anne arrived.

Quickly she lathered with bath gel, then let the water out of the tub, and ran the shower to rinse off. The doorbell rang just as she pulled on her robe.

Wouldn't you know—early! If that isn't just like Anne. First, she turns me into a mass of nerves. Then, when I'm relaxed, she stirs things up again.

The bell rang again as she reached for her cane.

"I'm coming. Hold on." Katie hurried to the door and flung it wide.

"Could you just once not . . ."

There on her threshold, slightly behind Anne, stood a man Katie had never seen before.

Chapter 2

"Are you going to let us in, or do we picnic out here?" Anne grinned and moved forward. "I know I didn't tell you I'd bring a friend, but I didn't know it when we talked. This is Seth Prentice. Seth, Katie Nelson."

With all the dignity she could muster, Katie stepped back slowly. "I'm pleased to meet you. Come in."

Anne headed toward the kitchen. "Don't be upset with me. I ran into Seth and invited him along to discuss the fundraiser. I had no idea it would be quite so informal." She looked back with a sheepish smile, and Katie couldn't help laughing.

"All right, you win. Mr. Prentice, make yourself at home while I finish dressing. Hang your coat in the closet." She indicated the door to the left of the front entrance and swept a quick glance up his tall form to the tanned face.

The man shed his coat and chuckled. "Please, call me Seth. I had no idea Anne hadn't called to tell you I'd be coming. With Anne, however, anything's possible."

"Is someone talking about me behind my back?"

"Behind your back, in front of your face, you deserve every bit of it," Katie said as she headed for her room. She stopped briefly after entering to lean against the closed door, placed her hand over her pounding heart, and took a deep breath. She told herself to get a grip and make the best of it.

Going into the closet, she quickly searched for something to wear. Her hand came to rest on an Asian-styled jumpsuit, a favorite for at-home dining. She tossed her robe on the bed, found fresh lingerie, and dressed.

After redoing her makeup, Katie stepped back and looked in the mirror. She'd do. She reached the door, then realized she didn't have shoes on. With a sigh, she turned back and found ones to complement her outfit. She glanced again into the mirror and wished her appearance wasn't always spoiled by the cane, then bowed mockingly at herself and a twinkle appeared in her eyes. She told herself to use it with grace, or maybe beat Anne with it.

Katie chuckled and headed toward the living room, moving slowly enough so her right leg could keep up.

Seth set aside the paper he'd been perusing, ran a hand through his beautifully cut dark hair, and rose from the couch as she entered the room.

"Tell me how you fit into this, Seth." She walked to a chair by the fireplace, motioned for him to sit again and did so herself. She tucked up her left foot, folded her hands in her lap, and leaned back.

"Everything's ready. Save this discussion until we're at the table," Anne called from the kitchen. "Come on, Seth, you can carry one of the trays."

Katie smiled at Seth, shrugged, picked up her cane, and moved to the table. The candles hadn't been lit. She retrieved matches from the sideboard, lit them, and moved to the chair at the head of the table. Seth placed his tray on the table, pulled out her chair, then walked to Anne's chair and did the same.

"A candlelight dinner for three." Anne smiled as he pushed her chair in. "I should have had you bring one of your numerous bachelor friends to even up the numbers."

"What? Then I'd have had to share you two beautiful women."

Katie felt her heart skip a beat. She hadn't heard a compliment from a man's lips for three years. Even though she knew it was in jest, she could feel her cheeks flushing and looked down to smooth the napkin on her lap.

They covered a variety of subjects as they ate. While Anne and Seth discussed the advantage of one computer brand over another, she studied him.

"So, enough beating around the bush. Why are you here, Seth?"

Anne opened her mouth to say something, but Katie turned purposefully to Seth, waiting for his answer.

He raised his right eyebrow. "She told me how talented you are and I thought I'd hear you for myself."

Katie's eyes shifted to her friend. "Anne, how could you? You know I haven't sung since John died. You expect me to sing now? Tonight?" Katie's hand shook slightly as she picked up her teacup, so she wrapped both hands around it. She could see love on Anne's face, but also determination, and knew Anne wouldn't give up easily.

"Katie, really, running into Seth seemed like a miracle. You said you'd consider the gala." Anne slid her hand toward Katie. "He didn't have plans for tonight, and on the spur of the moment, I invited him. He knows a fine musician when he hears one, and I couldn't resist—because you might not be in the mood to sing again for a long time. So there!" Anne drew a long breath, picked up her fork, and continued to eat.

"Listen you two," Seth said. "Let's finish dinner, and if Katie feels like playing or singing, great. If not, then we've had a pleasant evening, okay?"

They finished eating and moved to the living room with a fresh pot of tea. After refilling teacups, Katie once again curled up in her winged-back chair by the fireplace. Seth sat on the sofa, and Anne chose the floor. Stretching her long legs out, Anne sighed and patted her stomach. "I could eat those wonderful vegetables every day."

The warm glow from the fire and soft lights from the lamps softened the planes and angles of Seth's prominent cheekbones. He looked relaxed and amused. However, Katie suspected he could be quite forbidding when crossed. A tropical vacation could have accounted for his deep tan. Judging by his looks, he could certainly afford to take one. From his well-groomed hair to the soles of his Gucci shoes, he emanated a feeling of wealth and power.

"Well, what do you think—friend or foe?"

Katie's eyes rose to meet his, completely unruffled by being caught looking him over.

"Was I staring? I like seeing a man with a plain gold watch instead of the big multi-function ones so many wear these days."

Seth tossed his head back and laughed. "That's a new one. No one has ever told me they're fascinated by my watch." He waggled his eyebrows. "Now if you'd like to come closer, I'll show it to you in detail." They all laughed this time.

Anne rose from the floor and walked down the hall. Katie assumed she'd gone to the bathroom, but Anne came back carrying the guitar. Katie wasn't going to get out of playing. Anxiety gripped her. She took a deep breath to stifle it.

"I'll enjoy the fire while you tune this thing." Anne handed the guitar to Katie then returned to the floor.

"You really are determined aren't you? I'm warning you. I'm rusty." Katie glanced at Anne then Seth.

"It's okay. You're among friends." As Seth spoke, his cell phone rang. He looked at the number and made an apologetic gesture. "I need to take this."

Katie directed him to her office down the hall for privacy.

After he left the room, Anne turned from looking at the fire with her eyebrows raised. "I think you've made a hit. He's usually very slow in giving his approval. What do you think of him?"

"Not now, Anne. You'll have to come back tomorrow to tell me who he really is, and how you know him. I don't remember you mentioning him before. Have I missed something here?"

"No, you're right. We can discuss it another time." Anne turned back to the fire, and Katie tucked up her left leg and checked the tuning of her guitar.

Seth soon returned to his corner of the sofa and no one said anything while Katie finished tuning and started to pick out a melody line. She tipped her head to the side, listening intently and soon forgot her audience.

* * *

Her beauty and vulnerability struck Seth. He hoped she had more strength than appeared on the surface, because Anne didn't seem ready to back down regarding the performance.

Katie started playing more intricate melodies, and Seth raised his eyebrows in appreciation. He wasn't listening to an amateur, but to an accomplished classical guitarist.

As the strains from a familiar Spanish piece died away, she played a ballad, and softly added her voice to the music her fingers created. He nodded in appreciation as the song ended.

Katie looked up. "Well, do you want another style? I don't do hard rock, but I can do a little of what they're calling soft rock." She rubbed the fingers of her left hand. "I take my offer back. Practicing this afternoon has made my fingertips really tender. The calluses are gone after three years of not playing. Do you want to give me a verdict now, or do we go on until I bleed?"

Seth looked at his watch and reluctantly rose. He came over to Katie and reached down to take the guitar.

"Oh, I think you know the verdict. I'd like to talk again and hear more. I need to be on my way since it's getting late, and I have an early appointment tomorrow. Where should I put this?" He held up the guitar.

"Just prop it here by the window. Thanks." Katie rubbed her left foot then reached for her cane. "Did you ride together?"

Anne nodded and looked at Seth. "I should have brought my car so you wouldn't have had to go out of your way to take me home."

He shook his head. "It's hardly out of my way, and I don't mind."

Anne laughed. "Take note, Katie. He's not always so amenable. Your music must have soothed the beast in him." She walked to the foyer and found their coats. "I'll be so thankful when the weather starts warming up. Our Minnesota winter has been especially long this year."

Seth helped Anne into her coat and agreed. Turning back to Katie, Seth took her hand in his. "Thanks for a lovely evening. It's been one of the nicest I can remember in a long time."

Anne gave her a hug. "Thanks from me too. I'll call tomorrow."

Katie opened the door and stood in its opening as they walked the few steps to the elevator. "Good night. Thanks again for the food, Anne. Yummy as always. Drive safely."

* * *

After the elevator door shut, Katie closed hers softly, went to stand in front of the fire for several minutes, and then used the remote to turn the gas in the fireplace off. Instead of cleaning everything up now, she'd do it in the morning.

While getting ready for bed, her thoughts wandered over the evening's events. Why hadn't she felt more uncomfortable, playing and singing in front of a relative stranger? Then again, he hadn't felt like a stranger. Where did that thought come from?

Chapter 3

Anne shivered as Seth started the engine then glanced up at Katie's window.

He touched a button to set the heat temperature. "Sorry. Warming the car slipped my mind until we walked out the door."

"It's okay. It'll be warm soon. Well, what do you think? Did you like her?"

Seth started driving. When he didn't answer immediately, Anne glanced at him and waited. Finally he spoke. "Very much. You need to tell me more. I knew you had a friend named Katie, but had no clue she was so special. Why haven't you talked about her if you're such close friends?"

Anne remembered the lost look she'd seen on Katie's face these last years. She tugged on her seat belt to get more comfortable, and shoved her hands into her coat pockets. "She needed privacy while healing. Somehow I've felt disloyal talking about her. Lately I've gotten the impression she's ready to live again."

"Why?"

"She's been acting restless. The timing seemed right." Anne turned toward him. "She has talent doesn't she?"

"Oh, yes! Where'd she study?"

As they drove, the glow from the street lamps shed enough light into the car for Anne to catch Seth's slight smile and nod. She wondered what his smile meant.

"She went to St. Olaf, then to Rice University's Shepherd's School of Music in Houston. She studied both voice and guitar."

They stopped at a red light and Seth shook his head. "Why in the world didn't she make it a career? She obviously has both the natural talent and practiced skills."

Anne shrugged. "She's always loved music, but for enjoyment, not a profession. John and Katie started dating during our sophomore year in college." Anne pushed her hair back and looked out the window. Stately houses lined the street as they drove toward her home on the river.

"Ultimately, marriage to John held more appeal than pursuing music. Once they married and had J. J., she felt complete."

"How long have you known her?"

Anne thought a moment. The first time she'd seen her friend, Katie had been stamping her foot, demanding one of the school bullies quit tormenting a scraggly cat. Anne smiled at the memory. "High school, so about twenty-four years."

Seth turned to look at her with raised eyebrows. "How old is she?"

"She'll be thirty-nine in August. Why?"

"She looks younger."

"She always has, but now there's an elusive touch of something in her face. I can't explain it. I suppose genuine sadness shows no matter what. On her it seems to add an extra beauty."

Seth maneuvered his car carefully down the hill.

She spoke. "I don't take this street when we have heavy snow or it's icy. I've ended up in snow banks several times trying to maneuver around the curves. The lower river road is longer but not so curvy."

He nodded. "I can imagine. I love it here on the river, but having a home right downtown has its compensations." He pulled into her driveway.

Anne touched his arm. "Thanks for going with me. Oh, here's Katie's phone number." She opened her purse, found a business card, and quickly wrote the number on the back.

He thanked her, put it into his breast pocket, and started to open his door.

"No, don't get out. I'll see myself to the door. No need for you to freeze too." She jumped out and ran up the steps to her porch where she'd left the light on. After fitting her key into the lock and opening the door, she turned and waved to Seth. He blinked the headlights, and pulled out of her driveway.

* * *

As Seth drove away, he flipped on his CD. Music by Segovia poured out of the speakers. Even though he was one of Seth's favorite musicians, it didn't stir him as much as the simple ballad Katie had played earlier that evening.

He realized that Katie had no idea how good she was nor how beautiful. Had he ever met a person as talented with no conceit regarding her abilities? Probably not. This ought to prove interesting.

Katie's former husband must have been selfish not to have encouraged her talents. She clearly had a lot of drive to study as extensively as she had. Well, he'd know more soon. She piqued his interest.

He pulled into his building's underground garage. Removing his coat in the elevator as he rode up, he savored the warmth of the building. Although winter vacations to someplace warm were a welcome break, it made the cold seem worse when he came home.

He unlocked the door, tossed his coat over a chair in the foyer, and walked directly to his office. The day's mail waited on his desk, and he flipped through it. An envelope with flowing handwriting caught his attention. He picked it up and shook his head.

Sylvia. Will she never give up?

He sat down and wrote a note to call her. Seth preferred to do his own pursuing, and Sylvia didn't seem to understand that their relationship had ended. In fact, there had never been a relationship to begin with. He'd dated a number of women, but he had yet to meet one who could hold his interest very long. They all seemed alike. Out for what they could get, and willing to play at being in love. He didn't mind their little games as long as it amused him. He wished she'd get the picture.

Seth unbuttoned his shirt as he walked toward his bedroom. Getting to know Katie Nelson would be a very interesting experience.

Chapter 4

Seth picked up his keys from the bench in the noisy locker room of the athletic club. His friend, Jim, said something that he couldn't make out. "What?"

"I said, you didn't concentrate on your game today. What's on your mind?" Jim hoisted his athletic bag onto a shoulder.

Seth glanced into his locker to make sure he hadn't forgotten anything, then turned to Jim. "You're right. Something happened last night. Do you have time for lunch?"

"Sure, great. I'm starved. Let's eat here."

The elevator was full and neither one spoke as they rode to the third-floor restaurant. They left their bags at the coat check and only had a moment's wait before being seated. Subdued music and softly murmuring voices coaxed Seth's muscles to relax and he settled into the chair with a deep breath. Their server arrived and asked if they'd like a drink.

Jim looked up. "I'll just have ice water, thanks."

"Mineral water for me. And I'll have the turkey club with a cup of whatever soup is being served. Thanks."

"I don't need a menu either. I'll have the hamburger special." Jim smiled. The server left. Jim leaned back and stretched out his legs. "Okay, let's hear it."

"Do you remember Anne Dunbar? I think you've met her."

Jim nodded. "Tall, blond, beautiful, and a partner in her dad's law firm? Is she the new woman in your life who spoils your concentration?"

Seth drew his finger across his throat in a cut-it-out gesture. "Hey, I'm trying to tell this story."

Jim laughed. "I'm all ears."

"Yesterday, after a meeting at her office, Anne said she wanted me to meet a special friend of hers. On a whim I went along. Before we got there, she said her friend was a very fine musician who had suffered a major tragedy."

Jim raised an eyebrow. "Oops. Another musician hoping to be launched? Did you keep your cool?"

"I was disappointed, but yeah, I kept my cool. I might own a recording studio, but I certainly don't recruit talent. I made the best of it." The server brought their water and Seth paused to take a drink. "We arrived a little early at one of the converted mansions up on the summit."

Jim's eyebrows rose. "I've heard some of the owners have done a very nice job on them."

Seth nodded and waited while the server set their food before them, then went on. "Hers is certainly beautiful. She owns the top floor. Anyway, when we got there, she opened the door wearing a robe, and obviously just out of her bath. Anne hadn't called to tell her about me."

"Uh, oh. I think I see where this is going." Jim took a big bite of his hamburger and motioned for Seth to go on.

"She was obviously shocked to see me standing there, but invited us in and excused herself to get dressed." Seth drank some water and ate part of his sandwich. He swallowed. "Her name is Katie, by the way."

"Okay, her first name's Katie. What's her last name?" John reached for the ketchup and poured a mound on his plate.

"It's Nelson. Her husband was a John Nelson."

"Was? Are you talking about Dr. John Nelson's wife? The one injured when her husband and son were killed a few years ago?"

"Yes. Did you know him?"

"Barely. I met him at a political function. The accident happened shortly after that. I remember his wife's name was Katie. She hadn't been with him that evening so I never met her."

Seth stirred his clam chowder, then ate a spoonful.

Jim put his elbow on the table and rested his chin on his hand. "What a tragedy, for both her and the medical community. If I remember correctly, they were hit by a drunk driver. Didn't Anne tell you all this?"

Seth put his spoon down and shook his head. "Tell me all you know."

"Are you accusing me of being a gossip?" Jim chuckled and went back to eating his burger.

"Yup. Don't stop now. I love it when you gossip. It's so unmanly of you." Seth laughed at the look of horror on his friend's face. "Just kidding."

"That's all. I'm done talking if you're going to make fun of me." Jim filled his mouth with fries. After a short silence, he went on. "Anne was probably protecting Katie's privacy."

"Um, hm. Well, whatever her story is, her talent all but knocked my socks off! She's an accomplished classical guitarist, with one of the finest voices I've heard in a long time. And she has absolutely no idea how good she is. There's one flaw. The accident left her with an injured right leg, and she uses a cane to walk."

"Flaw, huh. What does she look like? Does all this talent come in an attractive package?"

Seth hesitated and looked at his friend. "Not my usual style. My preference has always been tall women."

"Like Sylvia."

"Well, yes. Katie's hardly over five feet, but she's a stunning little thing. I guess it's the eyes you notice first. They're huge and very green. She has all the right curves too, just more subtly packaged."

Jim's jaw dropped. "You sound smitten."

Seth looked down at his plate, picked up the remains of his sandwich and shrugged. "Impressed yes, smitten, no." He took a bite and after swallowing looked up. "What I witnessed last night appeared to be some sort of rebirth for her."

Jim finished off his fries and leaned down to pick his napkin off the floor.

Seth reached for his mineral water. "How can you eat all that grease and not get fat?"

Jim laughed. "Genetics. Don't change the subject. What do you mean rebirth? I'd like to meet this incredible lady."

"Are you going to the senator's fund-raiser next month?" Jim nodded. "You'll meet her there. I hope. Anne wants her to be the musical entertainment, and I suspect her persuasive powers might do the trick."

"Can she have a program ready in a month? There'll be some important and talented people attending. They won't appreciate a second class show."

Seth ran his hand through his hair and leaned back. "Nothing second class about her. She can do it. I hope she chooses to."

Jim's face spread in a knowing grin.

Seth tossed his napkin on the table. He'd revealed more than he intended, but he'd needed to talk to someone.

* * *

"Isn't this athletic club in the greatest old building? I'm glad they didn't destroy it during the seventies when the city planners thought new was better." Katie smiled at Anne and leaned back so their waiter could refill her coffee. "Did you know that this used to be a men's club? No women allowed."

Anne nodded. "Dad said Grandpa had a membership back then. I guess lots of deals were made here. I love this place for lunch. They never hurry you. I don't come here during the week because it's too busy. I'm glad you suggested this."

"Me too. I'm happy I kept our membership up. Well, my membership. I came here quite often during the time I needed physical therapy. The pool did wonders for my wracked-up body." She sighed.

Anne touched Katie's hand, then plopped her chin on her fists. "Your body looks great now. And by the way, you impressed Seth last night. He thought you'd be dynamic on March eighteenth. Say you'll do it. Please."

"Talk about changing the subject, girl. You know I can't make a quick decision." She stopped and smiled at Anne. "But I did buy a new dress today. I can wear it on the eighteenth if my answer ends up being yes."

Anne choked on her coffee and grabbed her napkin. "You'll do it?"

"I'm telling you I'll *think* about playing, but you need to give me time."

"All right, I won't press for an answer. Tell me what you thought of Seth. Were you impressed?"

Katie rolled her eyes and pushed her plate away. "I had a feeling at the beginning of the night he'd rather be almost anywhere than my house. Especially when I answered the door. Good grief, Anne. You could have called."

Anne crossed her arms and sat up straighter. "I know, but you'd have told me not to bring him. You didn't answer me. Were you impressed?"

Katie wanted to laugh. "Who is this wonderful Seth anyway?"

"Wonderful? You're calling him wonderful? You were impressed."

Katie grinned, picked up her coffee and rested her elbows on the table. "Okay, get on with your story."

"He is one of *the* Prentices of Prentice Advertising. You know, billboards, television. Any type of advertising. He also owns Prentice Recording Studios. I met him through Dad." Anne held up her hand when Katie tried to speak. "Hold on. He came to the firm one day several years ago because Dad's his lawyer, and I got introduced. We've met at social functions and gradually become friends. Nothing romantic. He usually goes for the glamour girl. His latest one is named Sylvia."

Katie's head jerked up. "Sylvia? A tall redhead, about thirty-two, with practically perfect everything?"

"Yes, do you know her?"

Katie shook her head. "It just so happens, a woman of that description walked into Farrow's when I picked up my shoes today."

"New shoes and a new dress. Oh, my."

"Stop it, Anne. Let me finish."

"Sorry." Anne added cream to her coffee and sat back. "Go on."

"Well, I was waiting for the sales person to find my shoes when two women walked in. You know how small Farrow's is. You can't help but overhear people." Katie pursed her lips and twisted her earring.

"And? You just blatantly listened?"

"Yup."

Anne tapped her fingers on the table. "Come on, girl. Don't make me drag this out of you."

Katie smiled teasingly. "You're so impatient. When the salesperson brought my shoes out she called the redhead Sylvia. Then the two shoppers stood right behind me while I paid, and I couldn't avoid hearing what they talked about." Katie paused, remembering the jolt her heart had made when she heard the name Seth. At the look of impatience on Anne's, face Katie laughed and went on. "I wasn't really listening until I heard the name Seth. I wanted so much to turn around and get a good look at her. Oh, boy! If they were talking about Seth Prentice, he's going to get caught if Sylvia has anything to say about it."

Anne rolled her eyes. "It sounds just like her. If it was Seth she was talking about, and she really hopes to snare him, she'd better be more careful. He seems to know how to avoid matrimony."

Katie rubbed her forehead.

"Do you have a headache?" Anne sounded concerned.

"No. I was just thinking that we don't even know if the person I saw is the Sylvia Seth has been dating. Let's change the subject before I start disliking that person even more than I did in the store." Katie stifled a yawn.

"What were we talking about? Oh yes, I was telling you about wonderful Seth."

"Stop it."

Anne laughed and made as if to zip her lip, which made Katie giggle. "Now I understand why he seemed reluctant to hear me play last night. Does he have anything to do with the studio, other than ownership?"

"No, not anymore, but the studio produces most of the music for several large national accounts their advertising company holds. He said he shows up for some of their brainstorming sessions. He's respected in both the advertising and music worlds."

"Owners always get respect, don't they?" Katie knew she sounded a little cynical.

"Yes, I suppose so. There's more to his story, though. Seth could have been a nationally recognized musician, but developed nodules on his vocal cords. After their removal, I don't think his voice was ever the same."

"Oh, Anne. How can he bear it? I noticed he had a little rasp in his voice. Can he sing at all?"

"I don't know. He doesn't talk about giving up his musical career. I asked my father about his background. A very interesting and private man, our Seth." Anne had to lean back so the server could remove her plate and gazed around the room. "Hmm. Speaking of Seth, he's here with his best friend, Jim Carlisle. I wonder when they arrived. I can't believe we didn't see them come in."

"Where are they?" Katie turned her head searching for them.

"Over on the north side, at a table for two." Anne raised her hand in a wave.

Katie grabbed for her arm. "Anne, don't."

"Too late. Seth saw me. It's okay. I know them both. Look up and smile sweetly."

Katie crinkled her nose and laughed at Anne as she turned their way.

Chapter 5

Seeing Katie brought Seth a rush of joy. "Do you want to meet Katie Nelson? She's here with Anne Dunbar."

"Yup. Where are they?"

Seth chuckled at Jim's quick reply. "Across the room. Anne just waved."

Jim motioned for the check. After he signed, they stood and walked toward Anne and Katie's table. Anne said something to Katie. What kind of reception would they give him? His pulse quickened. Could he actually be nervous?

Katie's back was toward them as they approached the table. Anne smiled and Seth laid his hand lightly on Katie's shoulder. She glanced up. "Hi, Seth."

"Hi. I have a friend I'd like you to meet." He left his hand on her shoulder as he introduced Jim. She smiled and held out her hand, forcing Seth to remove his.

"I'm please to meet you, Mr. Carlisle."

"Likewise, Mrs. Nelson," he said as they shook hands. "Seth has been telling me about his evening at your home." Katie glanced quickly at Seth, then smiled at Jim.

"Only nice things I hope. We had a slightly unconventional meeting." She bit the inside of her lip and a slight blush stained her cheeks.

"Are you kidding? Dinner with two beautiful women is pretty hard to top." Seth touched her shoulder again, and she smiled up at him.

Sunlight streaming from floor to ceiling windows revealed her delicate beauty and vulnerability. He felt a fierce urge to protect her.

This is crazy, I hardly know Katie Nelson. She means nothing to me. It must be pity.

"Is something wrong?" Anne asked suddenly.

"No, why?"

"You look so stern. I'd hate to be the one you're thinking about."

Quickly he glanced at Katie who also looked puzzled. He grinned. "It must be something I ate. Do you suppose the turkey is pecking on the clams? I shouldn't have had the soup and sandwich combo."

They all chuckled and Anne invited them to sit down. "Did you have coffee? We could order more."

Jim shook his head. "None for me, thanks. I have to get home. My wife wants me to watch our son, Tommy, this afternoon while she spends time at the library. I'm tired after my work out with Seth. Hopefully I can get away with nothing more strenuous than reading with him or playing on the Xbox." He ran a hand through his short hair.

Katie smiled. "You have a son named Tommy. How old?"

"He's five."

"Is he in Kindergarten?" As she spoke she reached up and twisted her left earring. Seth had noticed this mannerism before and had begun to watch for it.

"No, his birthday's in September. We decided to not have him tested. Beth taught third grade until we had Tommy, and knows how immature boys can be." Katie nodded but didn't respond. He went on. "We thought he'd do better being one of the older ones instead of the youngest in his class."

"We had a son born in September too, and chose to do the same thing. He did very well." Katie looked down at the table.

Seth wanted to comfort her but didn't know what to say.

Jim cleared his throat. "Katie, I'm sorry about your loss. I knew your husband slightly. What a horrible tragedy, losing both of them."

She looked up with a sweet smile and tilted her head to the side. "I surprised myself. I haven't talked about J. J. so naturally since he died. Especially on my own initiative."

Anne reached over and touched Katie's hand. Seth wished he could do the same. He shook his head. What was he thinking?

Jim took a step back. "Well, I better get going. I'm happy we got to meet today, Katie."

"Maybe sometime I'll meet Beth. And Tommy too."

Seth entered into the conversation. "How about on the eighteenth? Of course, Tommy won't be there but Beth will, won't she?"

"I haven't said I'll participate." Katie moved her hand to her lap and pleated her napkin.

Seth didn't back off. "No, but you could go even if you don't perform."

Katie turned her head toward Anne and then back to him before she spoke. "Well yes, I could. Maybe. Yes, I think I'll be there no matter what."

Seth spoke before either of the other two could. "I'd like to take you, if you'd accept me as your escort."

"Thank you. I accept. It'll be nice to have someone to go with. I've hardly been out in public since John died, and it will be easier with a friend." She smiled at everyone.

Seth, who had been holding his breath, let it out slowly.

"Great. We'll talk to finalize the arrangements." Seth stepped back while Jim echoed his goodbye and they turned and left.

* * *

Katie watched them leave, then turned back to Anne. "Go ahead. I can see you're bursting to say something."

"Humph." Anne leaned back and crossed her arms. "You've been a hermit until last night and all of a sudden you have a date with one of the most eligible bachelors in the city. I'm flabbergasted."

Katie stared into her cup. The coffee had turned cold so she took a drink of water instead. "Oh, come on. You can't call this a date. Even

I could see his surprise when he asked me. I thought I'd call his bluff. Besides, it'll be easier to have an escort. There'll be people attending that I haven't seen since John died. Seth will be my buffer. You'll be with Kent and busy with organizational stuff."

Anne motioned to their server then turned back to Katie. "I guess you can wear your new dress no matter what happens. I hope you decide to play and sing though."

"I'm seriously considering it, and I'll tell you in a few days. I'll only do it if I feel it will be done well." Anne started to speak but Katie shook her head to stop her. "Give me until next Wednesday. I know you need to make final arrangements. By the way, why hasn't everything been finalized for months?"

"Actually, we had Edward Bradbury coming but he cancelled because of a family tragedy. I think it has something to do with his son. It's all hush—hush."

"Oh, dear. Poor man. You mentioned him last night, but you didn't go into details."

Anne signed the check and added her club member number. "That's all I know about it." She pushed back her chair and stood. "Where are you parked?"

"In the City Court ramp. Where are you?"

"I'm just two block down from there."

Katie picked up her cane and they stopped at the coat check to pick up their coats and Katie's packages.

Anne reached for the bags. "I'll help carry your stuff since your car is on the way to mine."

"Thanks. I want to stop at the Art Gallery to pick up my watercolor. I hoped you had parked near by so you could help me." Katie smiled at Anne.

They walked at a leisurely pace, checking out the shop windows along the way. Their images were reflected in the glass. Katie observed the difference in their height. Anne was so tall compared to her own diminutive frame. She'd always thought it would be nice to be tall.

They entered the gallery and Anne browsed while Katie picked up her painting. "I'll trade you burdens now, Anne. I can't manage the picture and my cane, but the bags have handles so won't be a problem."

"So why didn't you carry them over here?" Anne teased as they traded.

"You picked them up, and I appreciated your kindness to an old crippled lady."

Anne made a stunned face and Katie burst into laughter. Anne reached for the painting. "Oh, goodness, give me your picture. This isn't dignified behavior for such a posh place."

After they left the gallery Katie stopped and turned to Anne. "Did my mentioning my injury cause that stunned look?"

"Shocked is more like it. I've never heard you do it before. All fooling aside, things are better aren't they? You seem almost lighthearted this weekend. Life's improving isn't it?"

Katie nodded as they turned and walked down the skyway toward the parking ramp. This morning was one of the first days she'd awakened with a feeling of anticipation. "Yesterday, when I sat in my studio and played, I felt as if John gave me his approval and blessing. It's hard to explain what happened, but I played and cried, and cried and played, and had wonderful memories. Tears and music washed away more of the hurt. The timing is right." She stopped and faced her friend squarely. "Thank you, my friend. You dared to love me enough to push."

"You're important to me. I've felt you might be ready to start living again."

Katie tilted her head. "What do you mean?"

"You've been here in person, but your thoughts would drift away, and you'd seem disconnected. Don't misunderstand me. You've not been rude or anything. It seemed as if you were just existing, not really living. Lately, you've become aware of little things." Anne shifted the painting slightly to get a better grip on it. "I'll give you a silly example. I've had three new cars since John died, and this is the first one you've noticed. Do you understand what I'm saying?"

Katie nodded but didn't speak, and her friend went on.

"You haven't been conscious of the world around you. The other day you mentioned how happy you are you kept the oriental carpets when you moved. I insisted at the time that they be kept. Now you're enjoying and appreciating them. See what I mean?"

Katie swallowed the lump in her throat and took a deep breath. "Anne, you're such a special friend. Did you get tired of waiting?"

Anne shook her head. "No, but my heart ached for you."

They arrived at the City Court Ramp and took the elevator to Katie's parking level. After a heartfelt goodbye, Katie pulled out of the parking ramp and maneuvered through downtown traffic.

It looks like I'm finally back among the living. Terrifying, really. I'll practice tonight. Even if I don't participate on the eighteenth, it'll feel good to be proficient again.

Intense joy at being alive, and great thankfulness that she once again felt life had meaning filled her heart as she maneuvered through downtown and up past the Cathedral district. She drove home with her spirits feeling as bright as the sun shining through the windows. Everything seemed more beautiful.

Chapter 6

Seth arrived home early in the evening with his mind in fast forward. There had been several matters to take care of at the office so he'd stopped in, cleared his desk, and left instructions for his assistant regarding Monday. Now he could relax, but he felt restless. Usually after a busy week, sitting down and watching the news with his feet up appealed to him. For some reason, home seemed quiet and lonely tonight.

Sylvia's note lay on his desk where he'd tossed it the night before, a scrawled reminder to call her on the outside of the envelope. He felt guilty for not bothering to open it. He picked it up and moved to one of the inviting, comfortable leather chairs in front of each window. Lamps cast a warm glow over the room and Seth relaxed. He had several bestsellers sitting on the table by his chair. Maybe he should spend Saturday evening reading. His bookshelves were jammed with books he never seemed to have time to read.

He opened Sylvia's note, read it, and raised his eyebrows in admiration.

Smart gal. Zuckerman and Perlman. This should be a great concert. She knows I wouldn't want to miss it.

He reached for the phone and dialed her number. She answered on the first ring. "Hello, Sylvia."

"Hi, Seth. Did you get my note?"

"Yes, that's why I'm calling. How'd you get tickets? I heard this event sold out hours after they went on sale."

She chuckled. "I have my ways. So do you want to go with me?"

"Yes, please," he said. "Dinner before the concert?"

"Are you inviting me to dinner, Seth? If you are, I accept"

"Good."

"I'm happy you can make it." She didn't say more, and Seth waited a few seconds before he broke the silence by telling her he planned to catch up on his weekly reading and then asked what time would be convenient for him to pick her up Thursday.

"Let's see, the concert starts at eight, how about a little before six? We'll have time to be leisurely."

"Perfect. I'll see you then." They said goodbye.

As Seth hung up, he thought of Katie.

I bet she'd enjoy this concert. Now why did she come to my mind? I have to stop thinking about her. She'd love the good music though. I wonder if she's been to a concert since her husband died. Maybe work kept him too busy to take her. She probably had to go with a friend. I know how doctors treat their wives. Haven't I met lots of lonely ones at important functions without their husbands? Most of them with too much to drink and making excuses for being alone. He didn't encourage her to use her talents, of which she has plenty, so he probably didn't think concerts were important either.

Seth got up and stalked down the hall. He pulled the card Anne had given him last night from his breast pocket. Katie's phone number. Sighing, he shook his head.

He needed to get a grip. How could he be annoyed with a man he'd never even known?

He fingered the card while walking toward the kitchen. What was she doing tonight? Was she watching TV? Feeling lonely? After turning on the light, he absently opened the refrigerator to see if there were fixings for an omelet. Closing the door without removing anything, he glanced at the card in his hand and reached for the kitchen phone. Seth dialed her number and contemplated his kitchen. Why did this room feel like a sterile hospital kitchen with every conceivable appliance, but no warmth?

Why hadn't he used a touch of color? And why didn't she answer her phone? It rang eight times and her voice mail didn't come on either. Even though she couldn't move fast, she should have answered by now. Disgusted, he hung up.

Going back to the refrigerator, he took out the makings for an omelet. Once the omelet was in the pan, he reached for the phone again and surprised himself by remembering her number. Again it rang eight times. Again she didn't answer.

She must be out. He shook his head at himself. She could go out if she wanted to.

He plopped bread into the toaster and checked the setting before pushing it down. Why did he always check the setting even though it never changed? Was he was getting set in his ways? Could he permit a woman into his life permanently and be able to adjust to the changes?

What was he thinking? Only two encounters with her and he kept thinking of her all the time. This had to stop.

After he set a place at the table, he flipped his omelet, poured some milk and turned on the kitchen television. The evening news had started. He listened with half an ear while serving up his food.

"No one severely injured," he heard and swung around to the television. There had been an accident. Maybe she'd been in an accident on the way home today and couldn't answer. Seth grabbed the phone again and dialed Anne's number.

"Hello."

"Hi, Anne, it's Seth. Is Katie with you?"

"No, I haven't seen her since this afternoon. Why?"

"Well, I've called her several times and there's no answer. You said she doesn't go out much, so I expected her to be home. You haven't gotten word—um, you wouldn't get word if something happened to her, would you? I mean, who would be contacted if she had an accident?"

"Are you serious? You're wondering if Katie's been in a car accident? She's a good driver, and, as far as I know, didn't have evening plans. She said something about practicing. I got the idea she could hardly wait to get her guitar in her hands again. She probably isn't paying attention to the phone."

"Well, she should. And what's wrong with her voice mail? It didn't come on, so I couldn't leave a message. Doesn't she realize a person trying to reach her could worry?"

Anne didn't say anything for a few seconds, then he heard her quiet answer. "No, I don't suppose she would. She's been alone for more than three years with no one to worry. When I called this morning, her cleaning lady finally answered. She'd unplugged the phone in her bedroom because she didn't want to be awakened early. I think she said she'd call the phone company and find out about her voice mail. Is something wrong? Do you need to reach her?"

Seth took a deep breath before answering. "I thought I'd see if she had plans. Maybe there's a movie she'd like to see. Since you gave me her number, I tried to call."

"But why did you think she had a car accident?"

"I tried calling twice and she didn't answer. I turned on the news and heard about an accident, but didn't catch the details. I thought I'd check with you."

"Seth, what's going on?"

"I got worried. I'm sorry I bothered you. Forget I called."

"It's okay, I don't mind, but I'd be careful if I were you. I'm not sure she'd appreciate anyone keeping tabs on her. She hasn't been accountable to anyone for awhile and is a very private person. Take it easy. Don't rush into anything."

"I'm not rushing anywhere. I thought a movie might be a welcome break. She'd probably like someone to go with. No big deal."

"I'm sure she's fine. She's not unhappy with her own company. Her independence sometimes frustrated John. He would have liked for her to be more dependent on him."

"Do you mean he didn't make the decision she stay at home and be a homemaker instead of doing something with her music?" Seth knew he was badgering her, but he couldn't seem to quit asking questions.

"John had finished medical school when they married. Since money wasn't a problem, they chose not to wait. Katie had her music degree. She wanted nothing more than to get married and become a mother."

"Huh? Are you serious? She didn't want to pursue a career in music? I find that hard to believe." He sat down at the table, happy that Anne was answering his questions.

"Believe it. Katie delighted in being a mother. John went on to do his residency in surgery at Mayo in Rochester, then they moved here. He'd been offered a partnership in a practice before he finished his residency. Even then, he had an impressive reputation." Seth grunted, but to his relief, Anne didn't comment and went on.

"They wanted more children, but she had a very difficult pregnancy. She spent the last three months on total bed rest and her doctor recommended they not have more children. As a result, her life centered around John and J. J. She did a lot of volunteer work at J. J.'s school. When they recognized the extent of her talent, with both children and music, they started inviting her for special events. Word got around, and other schools asked her to give mini workshops."

"Did you ever attend one?" Seth could imagine Katie sitting on the floor surrounded by eager children, smiling and encouraging them to make music.

"Yes. What an experience. The children adored her. I can imagine many guitars were sold at the music stores after she'd been to the schools."

"Or at least how many children begged their parents for one." Seth chuckled.

"You're probably right. Anyway, take it from me, she's independent." Anne stopped talking and Seth knew she'd said more than she intended, so he didn't ask any more questions.

Anne spoke again. "So you see, she can take the phone off the hook or unplug it and not give it a second thought. She'd run very fast from anyone who tried to control her life. Go easy!"

"I'm not going anywhere. I had an urge to be neighborly, and now I'm getting a lecture."

"Seth."

"No, I'm sorry. I didn't mean it. I'll let you go. I have a cold omelet sitting here and colder toast. I don't suppose you'd be in the mood for a movie tonight?"

"Thanks, but Kent's coming in a few minutes and we're going to one. I'll go with you some other time though, when you need some more information about Katie." She chuckled.

He smiled. "Hey, girl, don't give me a hard time."

"Kent's here. Gotta go. Take care."

"You too, Anne. Thanks."

Seth hung the phone up and looked at the table. The omelet he'd heat in the microwave, but the toast went into the garbage and he made new. After turning up the sound on the television, he caught the next day's weather report. Sunday would be nice. Maybe he could pick Katie up and take her out for lunch or brunch. Brunch sounded better, probably around ten thirty. He'd call her in the morning.

He wondered if she'd like The River Side restaurant, which had a beautiful Sunday brunch buffet. It was elegant, not too crowded, not rushed, and they could get to know each other.

What was he doing? He had to get the lady out of his mind.

After finishing his light meal, he went back to his office to actually do some of the reading he'd told Sylvia he wanted to catch up on. His thoughts kept going back to Katie, but every time they did, he made a conscious effort to change them.

When he finally went to bed, he couldn't remember a more unsatisfying evening. He looked at his watch.

I'll call her at eight thirty in the morning.

Chapter 7

Katie came out of church still wrapped in the afterglow and peace of the service. Someone touched her arm and she turned. Her eyes widened at the sight of Seth. "Hi. What are you doing here? Were you in church today?"

"No, I'm waiting for you. I called Anne when I didn't get an answer at your house. She told me you usually go to the early service on Sunday mornings so I'd probably find you here."

Katie's hand tightened on her cane. "Seth, what's going on? I talked to Anne last night. She said you called and asked about me."

He put his hands into his coat pockets and shrugged. "She told you, did she? I should have guessed she would."

"I'm not used to having someone keeping tabs on me." Parishioners were backing up behind them. "We have to move." She headed for the steps, and a gust of wind pierced her coat. She shivered.

Seth took her elbow. "I'm not keeping track of you. I thought it would be fun to go out for brunch." He guided her down the steps and turned toward the side street.

She stopped. "My home's the other direction, Seth."

"Did you drive?" She shook her head. "Well, if you won't go to brunch with me, at least let me take you home. The wind is really picking up."

They walked to his car and he opened her door. The car's interior was warm. He must have been sitting here in the idling car.

He slid in, put his left arm over the steering wheel, and raised his eyebrows. “How about that brunch?”

Katie laughed and adjusted her seat belt. “I suppose you waited a long time, and since I only had a cup of coffee while getting ready this morning, I’m hungry. Okay, I’ll go to brunch with you, but no more surprises. I’m not against surprises, but I don’t really know you.”

“Yet.” He had his face turned away and spoke in an undertone, but she heard him. Her heart sped up. She didn’t like this vulnerable feeling.

He swung out onto the avenue. She forced herself to relax and sat in silence as they headed toward downtown. Let the morning take its course. Seth had taken over, and right now, she’d let him have his way. What could happen? Conversation and a good meal. He’d take her somewhere nice, and Katie hoped it wouldn’t be too crowded. She felt drained and longed for some quiet, easy-going conversation, and no more stress. She sighed.

Seth head turned her way. “Are you okay?”

“I’m relaxing and enjoying the ride.” She patted the leather upholstery. “Nice. Is it new?”

“Fairly. I bought it last fall. I don’t trade cars often. I’ve gotten used to driving a Mercedes so usually stick with them.”

“Hmm.”

Downtown was quiet, and Seth found a parking spot in front of the restaurant. When he gave his name at the entrance, Katie frowned.

He shrugged and offered a lop-sided grin filled with boyish mischief. “I hoped my powers of persuasion would be working overtime today.”

Katie had a hard time keeping her face straight as they follow the hostess. It was hard to be annoyed because his charm disarmed her. They removed their coats and were seated in a quiet booth overlooking the river. She fiddled with the silverware and blurted, “I haven’t been out with a man since John died.” Her voice broke slightly and she took a deep breath. “I only came so I could tell you in a warm place, instead of on the church steps, that I don’t need looking after. And I’m hungry.” She bit her lip and gave him a crooked grin.

"I simply wanted to see you again, Katie." He rubbed the back of his neck and smiled ruefully. "You've been on my mind since we met Friday night. I'm sorry if I've made you uncomfortable. I've made myself uncomfortable." He shrugged. "We're here, so let's have a nice meal in good company, okay?"

Katie agreed. Sundays could be lonely. She seldom made plans to spend it with anyone. Eating out was an unexpected treat. And if she was honest, the company of a good-looking man was fun. Besides, she could pry a little more personal information out of him. He deserved it since he'd barged into her life this way.

After they had leisurely gone through the buffet and were settled, she picked up her fork and pointed it at him. "What do you usually do on Sundays?"

He drank some juice before answering. "It's the one morning I sleep in a bit, have as many cups of coffee as I want while reading the Sunday paper, and maybe watch one of the news shows. Sometimes I cook." He looked down at his plate and pointed. "Not like this. If my parents are in town, the family often hangs out at their house."

"How many siblings do you have?"

"One brother, one sister, both married and each, W. C."

She raised her eyebrows. "What?"

"W. C., 'With Children.'"

She chuckled. "Go on."

"I enjoy football if it's football season, or a good game of tennis or racquetball at the club if anyone wants to play. Nothing very stressful. Can I eat before telling you more?"

She laughed. "If you make it quick."

They concentrated on their food for several minutes. Seth polished off his everything omelet, laid down his fork and picked up his coffee. "I usually bring work home. It's always a temptation to get an early start on the week, but I try not to work on Sundays. Doesn't sound exciting, but I enjoy Sundays. I love listening to classical music while reading the paper. How about you?"

Katie swallowed her strawberry and licked the juice from her fingers. "I can't imagine not going to church. It gives me the greatest sense of peace and rejuvenation. I love the music and the feeling of closeness to God. It's my time to get things into perspective." She hesitated, glanced down at her plate then back at him. His blue eyes watched her intently. "There are times I wonder if God has been whispering to the pastor about me. So often the sermon is just what I need to hear."

"Scary."

She laughed. "I know it isn't true, but sometimes I allow myself to feel as if God is talking just to me. It's a bit presumptuous, but even so, I cherish it. Don't you go to church at all?"

"Once in awhile. I'm not against it. I don't think about it."

"Seriously? We always went to church. It's not something I have to think about. To me, Sundays are for worship."

Seth shifted uncomfortably and signaled the server for more coffee. He picked up his refreshed cup. "I thought God created it for a day of rest."

"You're right. But a week never seems complete if I don't spend time with Him. I loose track of the days and feel restless if I don't worship my Creator."

"But you can worship at home or wherever you are. Many people say they reflect, or meditate or whatever, while in nature and have the same experience."

"I know." Katie nodded and broke a muffin in half. "But making the effort to get ready and actually go to church, seems like I'm telling God He's an important part of my life." He nodded, and Katie wasn't sure if he was agreeing with her or acknowledging that he understood.

He held his cup in both hands and leaned his elbows on the table. "I think I understand where you're coming from. For most people it's a duty and a show they're putting on. You sound as if it's a privilege."

"You're right. I'm not putting on a show. It's a necessary part of each week. Because I enjoy the musical part of worship so much, it's probably harder for me to get the same feeling when at home, or somewhere in the mountains, or other natural setting." She picked up a piece of bacon, tipped her head to the side and smiled at him. "Occasionally I have a feeling of worship when I'm at a concert. Do you ever get so moved by an excellent musical performance you get a lump in your throat?" Katie popped the bacon into her mouth.

"Yes. I'm more inclined to feel moved by beautiful music than anything else. I had musical aspirations at one time." A dark expression flashed across his face.

She'd been hoping there'd be an opportunity to ask about his music. Here it was. "What happened? Why didn't you pursue a musical career? Is it something you don't share with anyone?"

* * *

Seth narrowed his eyes. Katie was staring at him with innocence and openness, tempting him to pour out his heart. How could he convey the overwhelming joy experienced when blending his voice with another, or watching the crowd's emotions during an especially moving segment of an aria? The power of an orchestral accompaniment has to be felt to be understood.

"I'm from a family with ties to the music world. I realize you know this, but I don't know how much detail Anne has given you."

Katie put down her fork and leaned forward. "Not much."

"My dad owns an advertising firm and recording studio." He smiled at the memories. "I loved being in the recording studio. While I was in high school, I finagled my way into many commercials. That's when I determined to make music my career. I didn't like studying the theory part much, but loved music history and performance. I had no idea how difficult voice lessons would be."

Katie nodded. "I know exactly what you're talking about. Being a professional vocalist takes more commitment than I ever wanted to give it. I remember forcing myself to practice for my voice lessons. One of my instructors could tell almost to the minute how much time I'd spent at it. Did that ever frustrate me!"

"We must have had the same teacher. Was her name Mrs. Rossi?" Seth laughed, leaned against the back of their booth, and crossed his legs. "How she could tell when I sloughed off, I'll never know. Anyway, my family encouraged me, and my teachers seemed to think I could do it."

"Dad would have preferred for me to take advertising and business, but he never complained and just kept encouraging me. I even spent several summers out east at music camps." He rubbed the back of his neck. "Are you bored yet?"

"Heavens, no! How could you even ask?"

"I feel like I'm droning on. Wave your napkin when it gets tiresome."

Katie laughed at him and shifted a bit on her bench of the booth. "This is your punishment for abducting me. You have to tell me your life story."

"All right. But remember, you asked for it." He paused a moment and went on. "After getting lots of encouragement, I went to New York to study. Things seemed to be going my way. I worked hard, but enjoyed every minute. My name started appearing on the billboards in ever more important roles, and I felt honored. My hard work was paying off."

"Oh, Seth. I can imagine the thrill." Her eyes smiled as she soaked up every word.

Seth enjoyed having her across the table from him. "Mother gave me her total support and loved it. The production companies assured me parts would keep coming my way." He shifted and frowned. "But then I began to have slight problems on certain notes. My coach recommended a throat specialist." He took a deep breath and looked into her eyes. "I can't explain how I felt when the tests results came in and the doctor said surgery. I had nodules on my vocal cords. The biopsy revealed no cancer, but they needed to be removed. We knew the odds were high that surgery could end my career. As you can tell, it did." Just talking about it thickened his throat. He cleared it and reached for his water.

Katie reached over and touched his hand. He turned his up and clasped her fingers. "It's a long time ago, and I seldom talk about it."

"Do you sing at all? Can you? How could you endure giving it up?"

"I can sing, but as you can tell from my speaking voice, I couldn't proceed with a musical career. When it's been your life's dream, anything less doesn't seem enough." His stomach clenched and heaviness entered his chest at the remembered agony. He took a deep breath to ease it and gripped her fingers. Their clasped hands gave him unexpected comfort.

"I came home and started learning the production end of the advertising business. I must have been difficult to live with. Both my parents were wonderfully patient and encouraging. Mother had always been more enthusiastic about the performing arts than Dad. I think he'd always hoped I wouldn't be so passionate about it all."

Katie gently removed her hand from his and took a drink of juice. "I know what you mean. I watched the intensity of my friends, but couldn't get serious myself. I just loved being surrounded by the atmosphere of making music. I'd like to hear you sometime."

He leaned back and chuckled. "I've got a secret. Occasionally my voice is still used in a commercial, so you've probably heard me already."

"Oh, Seth, how fun!"

The smile on her face was worth giving up a bit of privacy. "You're the first person I've told. I actually get a kick out of it when I hear my voice. I've never admitted that to anyone either. I don't know what it is, but you bring out the deep dark secrets in me."

"Did I tell you I work for the Daily? I can hardly wait to get home and call in my latest contribution to the gossip column."

Seth laughed at her look of feigned innocence. "Better not, or I'll hold you for ransom."

Katie flounced back against the booth. "Oh, all right. My lips are sealed." Then she became somber. "You never know when you look at someone what they've gone through, do you? Almost everyone is touched by pain sometime in their life. We make decisions when we're young, thinking everything will be wonderful 'ever after', and then life deals its blows."

Her eyes filled, but she blinked the tears away. This time he was the one to reach across the table and cover her hand. She smiled mistily. "Sorry, I didn't mean to get so serious. Don't worry; I'm not going to become a watering pot."

Their waitress came over to refill coffee cups, then asked if they needed anything else. When they said no, she wished them a lovely day and left the check.

Seth pulled out his wallet. "What are your plans for the rest of the day? Do you need to get home? We could go to the Fine Arts Museum for the Impressionists exhibit. I haven't been to it, have you?"

He could feel Katie's immediate retreat and felt a flash of irritation with himself. He'd planned to go slower.

"Thanks, but I need to get home. I plan on seeing the exhibit while it's in town, but not today. I hope to get over there sometime this week."

"But not with me?"

"This has been special, but I'd like to go home now please." She started gathering up her belongings.

He couldn't seem to help himself and pushed a little more. "If I'm free, and you're free, what's to stop us from spending the afternoon together?"

"I have things to do." She twisted her left earring as she spoke. "Please, Seth. Don't press the issue and spoil a lovely morning."

He nodded, stood up, and reached for her coat. At the same time, she leaned over to pick up her cane and purse. His out-stretched hand accidently touched her cheek. He apologized but the warmth from her skin lingered on his fingers for several moments.

Seth held Katie's coat while she put it on, then kept his hand lightly on her back as they left the restaurant. He wasn't pleased with himself for pushing, and was torn between admiration and irritation with her for sticking to her decision. He wished she'd change her mind, but he wouldn't ask again.

In the car, Seth saw her shiver. Without thinking, he reached over and touched her hair. "Another month and it'll be warming up."

She turned and his hand moved from her hair to the back of the seat.

"I'm not fragile. I can handle the cold. I've lived in Minnesota most of my life."

He tapped the steering wheel. "Sorry. I don't know what's come over me. You're a very special person and I'd like to be friends. What do you say? Friends?" He put out his hand. She put hers into it.

"Friends."

* * *

As they drove toward her home, Katie couldn't help thinking he'd be great to go to the exhibit with. She'd love to share opinions on the different artists. However, things were moving too rapidly. It frightened her. She knew she'd be missing a wonderful opportunity to get to know more about this unusual man, but she needed to catch her breath and evaluate what was happening between them.

Seth pulled into the driveway and immediately got out to open her door. After helping her, they faced each other. "Thanks for coming. I don't remember enjoying a Sunday this much for a long time. May I call you? Will you go to a concert or movie with me soon?"

Katie tilted her head slightly to the left and smiled. So much for time to catch her breath. A small bubble of excitement welled up in her chest. "Give me a call. Thanks for the lovely brunch. I thoroughly enjoyed it." The smile vanished. "And thanks for sharing part of your life story with me." She placed her hand on his arm, then turned and walked away.

Chapter 8

Warm air, scented by the flowers sitting on her foyer table, greeted her as she entered her home. Katie smiled as she removed her coat. Who'd have thought she'd meet such an interesting person? Everything seemed brighter and fresh today. Her heart felt light with anticipation and eagerness.

She changed into a well-worn sweat suit and ambled to the kitchen to make tea. She added shortbread to the tray, in case she got hungry later, and carried it carefully into the living room. She got comfortable and picked up the paper, starting with her usual ritual of reading the Sunday Morning section first.

What did Seth like to read first? Good grief, was she really thinking about him again? She shook her head, sighed, and tried to put him from her mind.

Still feeling restless, she inserted several favorite CDs into her sound system. The first one was the Brandenburg Concertos, given to her by a German friend who loved Bach as much as she did. As usual, she turned the volume up, giving thanks for soundproofing. Sinking back into the couch she picked up the paper again. This time she concentrated.

Katie's legs were getting stiff and she checked the time. Goodness. It was already after five. As she uncurled her legs, the phone rang. Her feet touched the floor and she looked around for her cane. Oh yes. She'd left it in the kitchen. While passing the sound system, she turned the volume down. The phone stopped ringing before she reached it. Her voice mail hadn't been fixed yet so she checked caller ID. Anne's number came up and she returned the call.

"Hi, Anne. I'm here, but couldn't make it to the phone fast enough."

"Your voice mail not fixed yet?"

"Nope. What's up?" Katie sat on a kitchen chair.

Anne chuckled. "Oh, I've been listening to Bach. Knowing how much you love his music, I always think about you when I hear something by him."

"You're right on. Bach's been my main source of entertainment this afternoon. The majesty of his music can make me forget everything else."

"Plenty of things make you forget everything else. Reading a good book, cooking a great meal."

Katie laughed. "I don't cook much any more, but still love to read."

"Yeah. Well, it's not much fun cooking for one is it? Anyway, I'm really calling about the Impressionist's Show. Do you want to go? It's over next Sunday. I don't want to miss it and thought we could go together."

Katie was glad Anne had reminded her. "Yes! Just say when. Seth asked me to go with him this afternoon. I didn't want him taking up the whole day, so said no."

"What? You saw him today? Oh, my. And why in the world would you turn him down?"

Katie sighed. "When I came out of church this morning he was waiting for me. He practically forced me into the car and took me to brunch. He's moving too fast, Anne. I'm not jumping into a relationship just because I find the man handsome, artistic, thoughtful, and practically perfect in every way."

"Hmm. I suppose you know what you're doing. Now, about the show. I don't have a heavy load this week. What do you say about lunch on Thursday, then the museum?"

Katie bit her bottom lip. Why hadn't Anne nagged her about refusing to go with Seth? Too bad they weren't talking in person so she could see Anne's expression. "I have a doctor's appointment in Rochester one day this week, but which day slips my mind. Hold on a minute." She grabbed her cell phone and checked the calendar. "My appointment's Wednesday morning so Thursday's great."

"Why are you going to the doctor?"

"Dr. Hanson called and asked me to come in and have an MRI of my leg. It seems there's a possibility of another surgery. I'd love to be able to walk without my blasted cane! He told me he doesn't know if it'll be workable with my situation, but I'm going to check it out."

"So would I. Oh, Katie I hope something can be done. Maybe some of the pain will be relieved too."

"The pain comes when I'm too tired or have been sitting wrong. I don't notice it much anymore." Katie looked at the pictures of John and J. J. sitting on the fireplace mantle. Her physical pain didn't compare to the pain of losing them.

Anne's voice brought her back to the present. "I'll pick you up about eleven thirty on Thursday. It's not out of my way and we might as well ride together. By the way, where'd you go for lunch today?"

Katie laughed. Anne was more curious than she'd let on. "The River Side. Of course, he couldn't have chosen a place I like more. I wonder how he guessed it would be a favorite of mine."

"He probably picked one of his favorites. The guy has good taste, you know. He's interested in you, which in my opinion, is having good taste."

Katie could hear a smile in Anne's voice and settled back into her chair. "Oh, you're biased 'cause you like me!"

"Maybe, but don't tell him 'no' too many times or I'll be thoroughly annoyed, and you know what I am like when annoyed."

"Right. You have to have your way. That's why you've turned into such a competent lawyer. Manage, manage, manage."

"Wait a minute. I'm much more than competent. I am extraordinary. Speaking of work, I have a new case you'll be interested in. It's a medical malpractice suit and I'm representing the doctor. From all the evidence I've seen, I believe he's innocent."

Katie sat straighter. "Have you ever represented a doctor in a malpractice suit?"

"Actually, it's been an interest of mine for some time, but I haven't taken any cases up to this point. The intricacies are almost overwhelming. I've spent lots of time doing research, so when Dad asked if I wanted this one, I said yes."

Had Anne mentioned this interest before? And, had she been so wrapped up in her own sorrows that she hadn't paid attention? "When's it coming to trial?"

"The family's trying to push it through, but hopefully I'll have three to four months before we're actually in the courtroom. I just got the assignment Friday afternoon. I haven't met with Dr. Browne yet, but plan to do so as soon as possible. I'll know more after our meeting. You know, the personal stuff."

Katie laughed and pushed her hair back from her face. "He's probably sixty, short, round, bald and the grandfather of ten. Is that the kind of personal data you're talking about?"

Anne giggled. "I'm always on the lookout for an eligible bachelor. From the little Dad said, he sounds like an interesting, dynamic person, who's very involved in people's lives. I agreed to take him on as a client because of who he is, not to meet an interesting man. However, all joking aside, things are going nowhere with Kent."

Katie heard a touch of agitation in Anne's voice. "Really? Did something happen last night?"

"Nothing happened, either good or bad. I'm in the mood for an adventure and he's not very adventuresome. I'm restless, in a rut, and in need of a new challenge."

"That doesn't sound like you. Maybe you need a fresh outlook. Get away or something. Where've you been this winter? Nowhere. Just here working." Katie heard Anne sigh and, once again, wished they were talking face to face.

"You're probably right. I feel as if Kent's taking me for granted. There's a certain amount of 'for granted' in a permanent relationship, but I don't see our relationship becoming permanent at this point. I feel guilty too. I appreciate Kent and all his good qualities, I just don't see us having a long term relationship."

Katie could tell that her friend was struggling. "You've been seeing each other for almost three years. It sounds to me as if you need to make a decision. I'm available whenever you want someone to listen." She heard Anne sigh again and wished she could touch her.

"Thanks, Katie. I didn't mean to blurt all this out. I know it has been in my subconscious, but I haven't wanted to think about it. I'll take you up on the offer soon."

"Good. An outside observer sometimes sees things we don't. I'm sure you have it happen in your work all the time."

"Yeah. You know, I've missed the old you."

Katie heard Anne sniff. She leaned her head against the back of her chair and closed her eyes for a moment. "Thanks for your patience. Together we'll manage our complicated lives."

"It's a deal. Now I need to finish reading my case notes, and I'll keep you posted on this grandfather of ten. I'll see you Thursday. Oh, one more thing. Do you by any chance have tickets for the concert at Orchestra Hall that night?"

"No, but don't I wish I did! Pinchas Zuckerman and Itzhak Perlman. It'll probably be the best concert of the season. I might have access to a person with a private source, if I can find his number. I've never called him myself, but John used to. He could get tickets to most things. He's an Irishman and I think his first name is Sean. He'd probably remember John, even after three years. Do you want me to get you a ticket, too?"

"You bet. It sounds funny for you to be talking about 'private sources.' I'm surprised John knew someone with those connections." Anne chuckled. "Let me know. Tickets to Orchestra Hall would make Thursday a perfect day."

Katie agreed and said she'd do everything in her power to make it happen.

After she hung up, the thought of going to the concert with Seth flitted through her mind. She ran her fingers through her hair and with a laugh and a shake of her head sang, "I'm gonna wash that man right out of my hair."

Chapter 9

Katie spent most of Monday morning at her desk. She paid the bills that weren't on auto pay and took care of correspondence she'd been putting off. After several hours of focused work, she had a neat stack of envelopes ready to go and an empty inbox. She reached for stamps, and her gaze landed on the notation she'd made about the senator's fundraiser. A rush of eagerness and anticipation filled her. This was something she wanted to do.

After picking up her cane, Katie walked to the elevator and rode down. How many times had she been thankful for the elevator? It was one of the reasons she'd been able to buy the place. Too bad the old stairs had been removed to put it in. It must have been a grand entrance hall. She stepped outside to put the letters in the box by the door and breathed in a lungful of crisp, clean, fresh air. The sun shone, but a brisk breeze blew. She shivered and didn't linger.

Back upstairs, she stood in front of the living room window and lifted her face to the light. Soaking up sunshine during the winter made her heart glad. She smiled and walked to her bedroom and sat on the window seat. The beautiful old oaks would have new buds emerging soon. Time went by so fast.

She leaned on the windowsill and rested her head on the glass. From this distance the sun sparkling on the snow made it look clean and neat. She knew how dingy it actually was, but enjoyed the fantasy of the pristine picture. Life was like that too. It seemed better from a distance. She'd been existing instead of living. It was time to have the courage to leave her secluded tower and deal with reality, in all its cold, grungy, messiness.

Katie's fingers toyed with the chain around her neck. Her father had given it to her when she'd had her tonsils removed as a senior in high school. Tears came to her eyes as she remembered the missing pieces, and people gone forever. Not only John and J. J., but her father too. She still missed him, even though it had been seventeen years since he'd lost his struggle with cancer. He'd been the greatest father. He would stand back and smile if she did something grand, and when things hadn't gone according to plan, he'd always managed to say something positive, and often funny too.

He'd made painful things hurt less. Maybe that's why she'd struggled so hard during this healing time. Her dad would have been a source of strength and he hadn't been here to help.

Well, life really does go on, and there are many who are worse off than you, Katie.

Later, as she sat down to eat lunch, her phone rang. She picked it up and said hello.

"Hi, Katie. It's Seth. I'm wondering if you've reconsidered going to the Impressionist's exhibit, and if you'd go with me."

Katie's heart skipped a beat. "Hi, yourself. I didn't expect to hear from you so soon. Thanks for the invite, but Anne and I are going on Thursday. It should be wonderful."

"Why didn't you expect to hear from me?"

She felt breathless and knew she was blushing. Even though he couldn't see her, it made her uncomfortable. "Well, we were together yesterday. I didn't expect you'd call so soon."

"Am I interrupting something?"

"No. I'm just sitting down to lunch."

"I had a break in my schedule and decided I'd try one more time to see the exhibit with you." She heard papers rustling and pictured him at his desk.

She ignored the exhibit comment. "Actually, I'm glad you called. I've made up my mind about the fundraiser. I'm going to perform, and I'd really like your opinion about musical selections. Do you know what they want?"

"I'm not sure. Let me talk to one of the committee members about this. I'll find out what they expected of Edward Bradbury. If I were you, I'd assess the political climate."

"What?" Now she was going to have to do research?

"You know, find out what kind of music the senator enjoys, choose some you enjoy, and practice. If you'd like, I can swing by in the next day or two and we can look over your list together. Between the two of us, we'll come up with a good selection."

She heard someone speaking to him in the background, but he ignored them and continued. "The crowd will be fairly diverse. The senator appeals to a broad spectrum. High school students work for him and people far past retirement. I'll try to get in touch with Al sometime today and get back to you. Will you be home this evening?"

Katie felt as if she'd gotten caught in a whirlwind. "Seth, I didn't mean to give you extra work. I just wanted your opinion."

"No problem. I want to help. I'm glad you asked."

"Okay, thanks. I'll spend time this afternoon going over selections and hopefully have some ideas when you call. There isn't much time and I need lots of practice."

"I'll call around seven thirty. My five o'clock meeting might run a little late."

Katie hung up the phone and took a bite of her sandwich. Talking about music reminded her of the concert on Thursday. She made a mental note to call about tickets as soon as she finished eating. Would Seth be there? He seemed the type to have season tickets.

Oh, good grief, quit thinking about the man. He's been on your mind constantly since Friday night.

After cleaning up the kitchen, she went looking for the Irishman's phone number. It had to be in her desk somewhere. She rummaged in the middle drawer, found an old address book and opened it to 'S.' There was no one named Sean under 'S.' Where else could it be? John had his own unique logic when recording phone numbers.

Did he go by name? First name? Last name? Subject? It might be in the 'T's' for ticket.

Sure enough. Under 'T' she found the name and phone number. Sean Sweeny. Hmm. Sounded Irish to her. She dialed and waited for an answer. It went to voice mail. An Irish brogue. This had to be it. "Sean, this is Katie Nelson. You knew my husband, John. I'm looking for two tickets for the concert at Orchestra Hall on Thursday evening. I know this is late notice, but you came to my mind, and I thought I'd give you a call." After leaving her number, she thanked him for his help and said goodbye.

She tapped her pen on the address book a few times. Anne would be thrilled if she managed to snag some tickets. Who was she kidding? She'd be thrilled herself. It would be great to go to a live concert again.

Time to practice. She turned to her music cabinet and flipped through a stack of music. Several would be appropriate. She set them on her music stand, then reached for her guitar. Today its patina felt like silk against her hands. She nestled it into her side and gently caressed the strings.

Practice started with scales and arpeggios then segued into some casual, just-for-fun music from the fifties. Her dad had loved music from the fifties. After warming up she opened the first piece of music by Bach and dug deeper into her skills. Several times she stopped to make a fingering notation on the score. If only she had the piano playing the counter melody. She loved how the theme wound in and out, almost as if she were moving through a maze.

The afternoon light was waning when she finally put the guitar aside. Her shoulders were stiff and fingers tender from practicing so long. Satisfaction over how much she'd accomplished overshadowed the discomfort.

This was a great start. She'd probably do the Bach piece. The first movement was just long enough to hold people's interest, and yet leave them wishing for more. What else would be appropriate? It would depend on how much they wanted.

Katie glanced at the clock. There was time to watch the early evening news in her bedroom and relax before thinking about dinner.

She turned lights on while walking through the living room. Summer's longer days would be so welcome. The pictures of her men sitting on the mantle drew her attention and she stopped to smile at them and brush each cheek with her forefinger. With a sigh she continued on to the bedroom.

The doors of the entertainment unit were open so she picked up the remote, turned on the television, and sank gratefully into the soft comfort of the loveseat. Leaning back, she stretched. A cup of tea would have been a good idea but she didn't want to move.

The World News had just finished when the phone rang. It was too early to be Seth.

"Hello."

"Katie, it's Seth. My meeting's over early. I haven't had a minute all day to contact someone on the committee. Did you find out anything?"

She grabbed the remote and hit the mute button. "No, I just looked over some of my music and did a lot of practicing. I think I might do a movement from a Bach concerto and I need help choosing something else." She didn't want to feel joy when she heard his voice, but couldn't seem to help herself.

"Bach sounds good. And maybe one more?"

"That's what I thought too. Do you know his topic or is it politics as usual?"

"Sorry. I'm not much help. Right now I know nothing. Some days are crazy. I think I have them in control and away they spin."

"I know what you're talking about. My life hasn't been eventful lately, but I certainly remember those days." Katie had an enlarged picture of one of the music sessions she'd done at J. J.'s school hanging on the wall across from her love seat. What a busy day that had been.

"Have you eaten dinner? I could swing by and pick you up. We could go someplace simple and discuss this further."

Oh, dear. Here he goes again. "Thanks Seth, but I'm weary after practicing and want to make it an early night. I'll take a rain check though." Katie bit her lip. Had she really said that?

"I'll hold you to it."

"Great. If you have a free evening soon, you can come over and critique the music for me." Some monster had control of her tongue.

"I'll call and we'll set up a time. Take care."

"Thanks, Seth. Bye." Katie hung up the phone, turned off the TV and flopped against the pillows. A giggle escaped her and she cradled her warm cheeks in her hands. She needed to catch that monster and strangle it before she got into more trouble. She laughed again and then her stomach rumbled.

She picked up her cane and headed toward the kitchen to see what she could find in the fridge or freezer for a quick meal. What had people done before microwaves?

While leftover lasagna heated, she made herself a salad, set the table, and lit the candles. Katie always lit candles, even when alone. She'd set the table especially nicely when serving the simplest meals to John and J. J. Ambience turned hot dogs into a feast.

The phone rang again just as she was ready to eat. She rolled her eyes.

"Hello."

"Katie, it's Anne. Sorry to bother you right at dinnertime. I would have called you before, but my day has been crazy."

"No bother. I talked to Seth earlier. Did he talk to you?"

"Yup, and I talked to one of the men on the committee. We think one classical number and one other one. Something you could both play and sing? A show tune maybe? Something patriotic?"

"Hmm. I wonder. Do you think Seth would sing with me? I've asked him over to critique the music. It'll be a good way to get him to sing a little without knowing my motive. What do you think? Is my idea way out of line?"

"Don't hold your breath, because I don't think he'd even consider it. I dare you to try though. If you could get Seth to sing, it would be a miracle."

Katie looked at her tender fingertips. "As much of a miracle as getting me to take out my guitar again?"

"Oh, yes, my friend. Maybe even more of a miracle."

The doubt in Anne's voice fueled Katie's determination. "When Seth comes over, I'll run through some numbers he won't be able to resist."

"Humph."

"Hey, girl, don't be so skeptical. If he still loves music as much as I think he does, he won't be able to keep himself from singing with me." Katie once had longed to sing with John. She'd coaxed and teased, but he'd claimed he was tone deaf and never even hummed along with her. "I'll let you know what happens. I need to get this settled quickly so I'll invite him over tomorrow or Wednesday if he's free."

"Sounds great to me. I'd love to be there but it's probably not a good idea. Call and let me know. I'll be dying to hear. Don't wait till we see each other on Thursday either. My curiosity won't be able to stand it."

Katie promised to call. What a productive and stimulating day she'd had. Much better than any had been for a long time.

Later, while getting ready for bed, she smiled at John's picture through misty eyes.

I think I'm going to live after all, John. Life takes over, and some friends don't give up. I miss you and J. J., but I'm learning to go on.

Chapter 10

At six thirty Tuesday morning, Seth rolled into his parking spot in the ramp of the building where the Prentice Advertising offices were located. He was early enough to clear up a few things on his desk he hadn't gotten to yesterday. Music was blaring from the security booth. A young man in uniform watched the monitors and nodded his head to the beat. Seth wondered if he'd be able to hear a page over the system with so much noise. He smiled when the attendant looked his way and waved.

In the building's lobby, he switched elevators and went on up to his office located on the thirty-seventh floor. The smell of coffee greeted him as he entered. Someone else was already in and his message light was blinking. Instead of checking voice mail, he turned on his computer to check the day's schedule. Other than a daily seven forty-five meeting with his assistant, most of the day would be taken up with issues from the accounting department. It couldn't be put off now that he'd returned to town.

He moved his curser to the eleven thirty slot on his calendar. His lunch hour was free. Maybe he could call Katie and see if she could meet for lunch. He actually laughed out loud at himself. What was he thinking? Katie was playing insistently in his thoughts like a tune that he couldn't shake.

A co-worker walking past stopped and stuck his head in the door. "What's so funny Seth? Get a good joke in your email?"

"No, I just remembered something." He looked at his computer, then back at his co-worker. "How does your day look, Glen? Do you have time for me later this afternoon? I'd like to go over the new layout you're working on for the car dealer."

"As a matter of fact, I do. Would three fifteen work?"

"Fine. Three fifteen it is."

Glen walked away, and Seth turned around to add the meeting to his calendar wishing he could add lunch with Katie too. How long would it take before he'd feel free to call her "spur of the moment?"

Who was he kidding? He was already doing it. Maybe he should call her now and find out if they could get together tonight or tomorrow night.

He checked the time. Too early. Did she like to rise early or stay in bed? He didn't know much about her. Yet.

He added a reminder on his Outlook to call her at eleven thirty so he wouldn't forget. Not as if he'd forget. He'd probably be watching the clock, waiting to make the call. Oh, boy. He was acting like a teenager again.

Next, voice mail. He reached for the phone. The first one was his mother. She'd called from St. Thomas to say they missed him already and to call if he had time. The next came from Sylvia. She asked him to call and didn't give a reason. He'd better call her back and get it over with.

He accessed a line and dialed her number at home. She answered quickly and thanked him for calling her back.

"No problem. How may I help you?"

"I'm wondering if you're going to the senator's benefit next month and if you know if there are any extra tickets. I'm sure I told my assistant to order them, but somehow it fell through the cracks."

"Let me see what I can do. How many do you need? Anne Dunbar said it's a sellout, but I'm sure I can track down a few."

"Two would be great. You're going aren't you?"

"Yes, I'll be there. I'll let you know as soon as I have the ticket information. Otherwise, I'll see you on Thursday evening."

"Okay, thanks. See you."

Seth grimaced at the phone. If he hadn't met Katie, he'd be taking Sylvia to the fundraiser. He laced his fingers behind his head and leaned back in his chair. His grimace turned into a smile.

Chapter 11

Katie woke on Tuesday with a feeling of purpose and energy she hadn't had in a long time. It was seven and she'd had one of her most refreshing nights in years. Work, and something to look forward to, was good for her.

Throwing back the covers, she swung her legs over the side of the bed and buried her toes in the thick carpet. The sky was getting light and she felt energized. She reached for her cane and walked toward the bathroom. After flipping on the lights, she peered at herself in the mirror—leaning close to check out the wrinkle situation.

She turned her head from side to side. It would be several years before she needed to check the yellow pages for a cosmetic surgeon.

Katie giggled at herself and moved to the shower and turned on the water. She hummed a little good morning ditty by Agapeland. She'd loved those records when she was little. Hmm. What would it take for her to persuade Seth to sing with her? Provided he really could still sing. As she quickly lathered her hair and showered, she planned her day and could hardly wait to get back to practicing.

The sun had totally risen by the time she entered the kitchen. She fixed coffee and turned on the TV. Good Morning America's topic for the day was friendship. How appropriate. She polished off her first cup of coffee. The paper should have arrived by now. She headed for the front door. Just as she reached it, the doorbell rang. Puzzled, she checked her peephole and there stood Anne. She opened the door wide in welcome.

Anne held up a bag from Bruegger's in one hand and her paper in the other. "How about breakfast?"

"What a great idea. Aren't you working today?" Katie moved back so her friend could come in, and then reached for the paper and bag. Anne took her coat off and tossed it onto the couch as they walked toward the kitchen.

"My first appointment cancelled. Bagels with you seemed a great way to start the day." As they entered the kitchen Anne glanced at the TV. "Since when did you start watching morning TV programs?"

Katie turned it off. "Well, some days I like to watch GMA. In a weird sort of way they've almost become friends." She smiled sheepishly. "Silly I suppose, but it helped with loneliness. I know it's a crutch, but it's been a way to get in touch with the world around me again without having to venture out the door."

"Oh Katie, I'm . . ."

"I know what you're going to say. No, it doesn't take the place of actual friends, but it has helped me to get involved in a passive way." She turned away, set the bag of bagels down on the counter and reached for a knife.

Anne slipped up beside Katie and gave her a brief hug, then stepped to the counter and opened the bag. "What kind do you want? I bought cranberry/orange, cinnamon/raisin, multigrain, onion and plain. I only bought plain cream cheese though."

Katie handed her the knife and pulled the toaster out of her appliance garage while she considered her choices. "I think I'll start with the cranberry/orange. If I'm really hungry, I'll have a multigrain too. And my favorite cream cheese is plain, anyway. How about you? Do you want it sliced and toasted?"

Anne reached up for plates and looked over her shoulder. "I'm having cinnamon/raisin and don't want mine sliced or toasted. I like to break off a piece and scoop up the cream cheese. You seem mighty perky this morning." She set the plates on the counter and turned around.

Katie looked down at the bagel in her hand. "This is like old times. You started eating them that way in college because the toaster never worked right and you couldn't stand it if they got too dark." She sliced the bagel Anne had given her and plopped it into the toaster.

When they sat down at the table, Katie bowed her head. "Thank you, God, for a forever friend. Thank you for blessings that are new every morning. Guide our steps today so we'll walk where you lead. Amen."

Katie picked up her coffee and cradled it in both hands. "What's going on?"

Anne shifted in her chair. "For some reason, my car turned in your direction. I honestly didn't plan this, but since I'm here, can we talk a little about Kent? Maybe if I talk to you, I can look at my relationship with him more clearly."

Katie nodded. She'd been hoping Anne would seriously take stock of where she was going with Kent.

Anne blew on her coffee. "Doesn't it seem significant I'm not at all excited to see him? I enjoy our time together but don't wait for his calls or think about him at unusual times. He's so nice. I should be more excited over him."

"You can't force it."

Anne broke her bagel into pieces and moved them about her plate. "I've wondered several times if what I felt could be love, but I can't see myself spending the rest of my life with him. Maybe something's wrong with me. Maybe I'm supposed to be single all my life. My heart longs for a relationship though, so I don't think that's true."

Katie listened with both mind and heart. "I don't think you've met the right person. I'm sure there are other men who would love to ask you out, but you've been dating Kent so long they feel you're off limits. Are you ever asked out by men at work or men you meet there?"

"Well, sometimes in the course of a case or project I'm working on, I feel one of them is interested, but I've always tried to keep work and play separate. I don't give them any encouragement." Anne took a bite of her bagel and shrugged.

Katie refilled their cups. "Do you think they're a little intimidated? You're bright, beautiful, and successful, so the men you meet probably think you don't need anything from them. I don't see you that way, but then, I know you. I also don't have any answers." She sighed. "I think I've been a very selfish friend, only thinking about myself for the last few years." She reached over to touch Anne's hand. "I'm going to be a better friend and life is getting better."

Anne raised an eyebrow. "Does Seth have anything to do with it?"

"No. Maybe. I don't know. I just met the guy. I think you're to blame."

Anne laughed. "I'll take that kind of blame."

Katie swiveled in her chair and pursed her lips in mischief. "Maybe we should draft an ad in the Personal section of the paper to find a man for you. Or better yet. What about an online dating service? You know—we could say, "Beautiful, bright, sort-of-wealthy, professional woman of younger-than-middle-age, looking for dynamic, attractive, sort-of-wealthy, professional man of younger-than-middle-age."

Anne burst out laughing. "Any man who considered himself dynamic and attractive would probably be in love with himself. I think we should enjoy the progress you've made Katie, and let my love life come about naturally. Let's just look forward to Thursday and get past the senator's benefit. Speaking of Thursday, have you heard from your Irishman?"

Katie shook her head. "He hasn't called back. I'll probably hear today. I'll let you know right away when I do. I want to go to this concert more than anything. Remind me to buy season tickets for one of the concert series next year. I didn't realize how much I missed going until lately."

Anne checked the time. "Oops, I need to run. Let me know how it goes with Seth, you know, over choosing music. Boy would I love to be a mouse in the corner and hear him sing. He also plays the piano. I heard him at a Christmas party several years ago when everyone wanted to sing carols. He got pushed onto the piano bench so didn't have a choice. He's very good, but he didn't sing along."

They left the kitchen. Anne grabbed her coat off the couch as they walked to the front door. "See you soon."

While Katie cleaned the kitchen, the phone rang, and she grabbed it. "Hello?"

"Sean Sweeney here. I found you those tickets you were askin' for. And great seats they are, me girl."

"Oh, Sean. I'm so happy. How much are they, and where can I pick them up?"

"I'm headin' to downtown this afternoon. Just tell me where you live and I'll stop by and drop them off, love."

"Are you sure? I'd be happy to meet you. It's not a problem."

"I don't know the time darlin'. Just give me your address."

Katie told him. "You can call from your car and I'll come down." After she hung up, Katie laughed and ruffled her hair. She hadn't smiled this much or felt this happy in a long time. She made a quick call to Anne and left a message telling her they had tickets for the concert.

Back in the living room, she picked up the newspaper, kicked off her slippers, and curled up on the couch. As she read, her mind kept wandering to the events of the last few days.

It hadn't even been a week since she'd picked up her guitar and started practicing but it felt like the most natural thing in the world to be working on music.

Thank you, Anne. Thank you, God.

She gave up on the newspaper, put her slippers back on, and headed for her studio. As she walked down the hallway she turned the heat up because she wanted to take her sweater off while practicing. Her purse was on the desk. She pulled out her checkbook and wrote a check for the concert tickets, put it into an envelope and wrote *Sweeney* on it.

She snuggled the guitar into her arms and ran her hand over the silky patina. It all seemed so normal and comfortable. Her fingers gently plucked the notes of a Strauss waltz. In her mind she pictured herself dancing with John. Tears filled her eyes and she let them fall. Someone had said 'tears wash our insides'. That's what she experienced. After drying her eyes and blowing her nose, Katie lost herself in the music.

The doorbell rang while Katie was singing "Amazing Grace". She couldn't imagine who would be dropping in for a visit. Anne had already been there. She wasn't expecting anyone and hadn't ordered anything to be delivered. Her watch showed it was two o'clock. Had the phone rung and she'd somehow missed it?

She picked up her cane and hurried to the door. Leaning against the doorjamb was a gentleman she'd never seen before. He wasn't much taller than her. His eyes sparkled mischievously and he wore his hat tilted at a rakish angle.

"Sean?"

He nodded.

"I'm sorry. Did you call and I didn't hear the phone?"

He straightened and took off his hat. "And why should I make a pretty lass come all the way down to my car in this cold? Me mother raised a gentleman."

Katie laughed, stepped back so he could enter and closed the door. "I'll get the check. It's in my studio."

She came right back and exchanged her envelope for the tickets. "I'm so happy to get these."

He twisted his hat in his hands. "I'm sorry, lass, for your loss. I know it's been awhile, but I'm sure it's still very painful for you."

Katie nodded. "Thanks, Sean. I appreciate it. Some days are unbearable, but lately I've been learning to live again. This concert will be one of those special times for me. Thank you for finding the tickets."

"I only hope you've found a bonny young man to go with you."

She laughed. "I have a bonny woman friend to go with, and we'll enjoy every minute of the evening."

After she closed the door behind him she kissed the envelope. "Yes!"

Chapter 12

Katie badly needed a cup of something hot. It was four in the afternoon, her fingers were tender, and her back was sore. She set aside her instrument and gathered up the music spread around. With slippers back on and cane in hand, she headed for the kitchen. She passed the phone. Should she invite Seth over for a music session tonight? She'd love to get together as soon as possible. She filled the kettle and turned on the burner. No, if she called, he could get the wrong idea. Would he be critical? Surely he'd hear all the small errors she made. She'd sure like to hear him sing. What made him so appealing? Thinking about him had to stop.

When the teakettle whistled, she made hot chocolate and took it into the living room to curl up with a book. Her mind needed a change of pace. She went to the library weekly and also spent time in Barnes and Noble or on the Internet looking for a good mystery or thriller.

Today's thriller was by one of her favorite authors. She settled into a comfortable position and soon the story totally captivated her. The phone rang and she glanced at the clock. Over an hour had passed. No wonder she felt stiff. She reached for her cane and moved as quickly as possible before voice mail picked up.

"Hello?"

"Hi, Katie. It's Seth."

Her heart jumped. "Hi, Seth. I wondered if you'd call." Oh, dear. There went her wayward tongue again.

"That sounds encouraging." He chuckled. "Would tomorrow evening be a good time to brainstorm over music with you?"

"Sure. Tomorrow's Wednesday, right? Sometimes I can't keep the days straight. Can you come for dinner?" She shook her head. Now what had she done?

"Dinner sounds nice. You don't have to cook. I can bring something from a deli."

"No, I'd love to cook. I haven't spent much time in the kitchen lately. Please come, and I'll feed you. My payback for your help. What time is good for you?"

"I'll be done at work no later than six thirty. How about seven?"

They agreed on the time and said goodbye. Katie stood by the phone for a moment and bit her lip. Now she had to feed him. Oh dear. Was he a meat and potato guy? Probably. Most men were.

She found a prime rib in the freezer. A vegetable medley and salad along with the meat should be safe. Did he like dessert? Personally, she thought it was the most important part of any dinner. She rummaged a bit more in the freezer and found several unbaked apple turnovers she'd made previously and frozen. They'd be great served warm with ice cream.

With that settled, she ate a light dinner and cleaned up the kitchen. She went back to her book, but her mind wandered. She kept hearing Seth's voice in her head.

After fidgeting for fifteen minutes, she marked her page and tossed her book aside. She had to get out of here and get Seth out of her mind. She'd go to Barnes & Noble. Their travel section was calling her name. She used to love traveling. Looking at the latest Rick Steves European travel book would be fun. She also needed to buy some cards and notepaper. She could do it all at the same mall.

The wonderful smell of coffee greeted her as she walked in the front door of Barnes & Noble. John had always said that if coffee tasted as good as it smelled, he'd drink it too. She'd never been able to convince him that it did. When they had come here, John would spend lots of time looking for a biography he wanted to read. When he finally found just the right one, he'd always known he could find her contentedly sipping coffee and reading or idly watching the crowd. The memory was sweet.

She turned left, took off her tam and ran her fingers through her hair as she made her way toward the travel section. She rounded the corner and stopped in surprise at the sight of Seth. He stood engrossed in a thick book. Her hesitation must have caught his attention because he glanced up. A smile lit up his face. "Hi. This is a surprise. Are you planning a trip?"

Katie's stomach clenched. Was this joy? She didn't want the sight of him to bring her joy. She leaned on her cane and tilted her head to the side. "No, I felt restless and needed to get out of the house." She swept her hand at the books. "I used to love planning trips and just came to browse. Maybe a trip would be what I need to . . ." She shrugged. "I don't know what I need. This seemed like a good idea. What are you studying so intently?"

He closed his book, but left his finger in the page and turned the cover toward her. He'd been looking at Frommer's book on Spain. "Spain appeals to me. What country calls you?"

"I don't know. Rick Steves newest book on Europe is a good place to start. I enjoy watching his travel programs. He's so practical and makes every trip a possibility." It was right in front of her and she reached for it.

Seth was quicker. He already had it off the shelf and handed it to her. "How about a cup of coffee while we browse through these and decide if we want to purchase them?"

She nodded. "Sure, why not. It always smells great in here doesn't it? I'd love a cup of coffee."

They walked over to the coffee bar and up the steps to order.

"You choose a table and I'll bring the drinks. Do you want regular or decaf—or something flavored?"

"Just a small decaf please." She pointed to the top shelf in the display case. "Would you like to share one of those great looking brownies?" She raised her eyebrows.

"Perfect." He stood by the counter and watched while she chose a table, took off her coat, and set down her book. She came back and took

Seth's book then stopped to get napkins and a knife on the way back to their table. Seth brought the tray.

Katie picked up the knife and carefully cut the brownie in half. "I don't suppose you have a tape measure in your pocket do you? I wouldn't want you to get more than me." She licked the frosting off her fingers and checked them to make sure she hadn't missed any.

Seth shook his head and chuckled. "I'll tell you what. If you want more, we can get another when we're done with this one."

"No, I'm teasing. I love chocolate though, so watch your piece."

Seth took a drink of coffee and settled back in his chair with his legs stretched out to the side. He touched his book. "If you could go anywhere in the world, where would you go?"

"Heavens, I have no idea. I haven't considered traveling for several years." Her gaze wandered over the crowded tables and back to Seth. "I love studying the history of the place I'm going to visit. When I'm on a trip, the country I'm in at the time is my favorite place to be. However, I think I'd like to have an extended trip to England. I'd take in all the sights, not hurry, and go where the spirit leads me." She reached up and pushed her hair behind her ear. "I've driven in England and found it a bit intimidating, but I'd be willing to do it again."

"I know what you mean. I drove quite a bit in England."

Katie picked up her mug. "When were you in England?"

"The last time? About two years ago. My brother and I went. He was going through a rough patch in his life and we took a month and traveled together. Before we left, I struggled about being gone so long from the company. I've never regretted going. My brother Peter and I rebuilt our relationship."

Katie watched his face soften when he talked about his brother. She was torn. Did she want to get to know this person sitting across the table? Could she ask about his family? Why not? He was the one who'd brought up his brother. "Do you have any other siblings?"

Before he could speak she rushed on. "Sorry. I'm being nosy." Katie set her coffee down. "My mother loved traveling, but Dad dragged his feet. He'd give in and be a good sport, but I know he liked to be home more than anything. After Dad died, Mom went with me several times. I haven't traveled in the last three years, but that's going to change." She flipped open her travel book and laid her hand on it. "I'll call and ask her to start doing research on where we should go. She loves to get on the Internet to 'see what she can see.'" What was it about this man that made her babble? She licked her lower lip and then bit it in confusion.

He spoke. "I have a sister. Sarah. Do you have any siblings, Katie?"

She glanced up and shook her head. "No, I'm an only child. I know my parents were disappointed over not having more children, but they didn't make me feel smothered because of it. Personally, I'd have loved a brother or sister. Anne has been my closest friend and probably very much like a sister to me." Now at least she knew he had a sister. Was there something wrong with Sarah that he didn't say more than her name? Didn't he want to talk about his family?

He reached for his half of the brownie and took a big bite. "Don't expect to get any of this. I love chocolate too. My mother couldn't keep anything made of chocolate in the house more than a day or two. She used to call it our addiction. I remember Sarah making chocolate chip cookies at a very early age. She ate half the dough before they got baked. Yuck. I never could understand why."

Katie laughed in relief at the change of subject. "The fun of baking cookies is eating large chunks of the dough. Anne and I bought cookie dough in tubes from the dairy case and we'd take it back to our dorm room. Yum."

Seth shuddered and took a drink of coffee. He reached out and touched her book. "Where do you think your mom will want to go?"

"I don't know. It will depend on the time of year. Before my dad died, she wanted to visit the Scandinavian countries. My father was Swedish and it would be interesting to see where his family came from. His grandmother and grandfather both emigrated from somewhere in Sweden." She picked up her coffee and drank.

Seth opened his book and started leafing through it.

Another rebuff? Two could play this game. She pulled her book closer and read the index. Spain started at page . . . What was she doing?

She ran her hand through her hair and turned to Germany. That was safe. They sat in silence reading.

Without looking up, she reached for her half of the brownie and encountered Seth's hand. She pulled hers back. "Hey, you. Were you going to steal my half of the brownie?"

Seth laughed. "Well, you weren't eating it. My piece disappeared." There was chocolate on his fingers and he licked them clean.

"You have no shame." Katie tried to keep a straight face as she picked up her half. She took a bite. "This is a pretty good brownie, but I make ones with nuts and caramel. Anne used to say they were to die for."

Seth raised an eyebrow and looked directly into her eyes. "Can we share one of those sometime?"

"Um, sure. Sometime." She nodded, reached for her coffee, and returned to her book. She couldn't concentrate. Why did he keep making her uncomfortable? What was wrong with her? Couldn't she have a conversation with light banter without feeling he was making a move on her? Of course he wasn't making a move on her. Was he? She needed to get a grip. She forced herself to focus on the book in front of her.

Katie chuckled and looked up. "He still says Americans are easy to pick out of a crowd because they wear white tennis shoes. I know it's silly, but because of his comments, I refuse to bring them along on a trip even though they're comfortable." She lifted her booted foot slightly out in front of her and put it back down. "Europeans are such a fashion conscious culture. They have the latest fashions long before we do. I love Italian shoes."

"I don't notice shoes much. Do you have to be careful what kind you buy because of your leg?" As soon as Seth finished speaking he flinched. "Katie, I'm such a dolt. Forgive . . ."

Katie cut in. "Imagine a person who wears Gucci loafers saying he doesn't notice shoes. Don't deny it; you were wearing Gucci the other night. And yes, I have to be careful what shoes I buy. It's disappointing because I love high heels."

He looked down at his outstretched feet, the right one crossed over the left. "I didn't say I don't like good shoes or nice looking ones to wear myself, I just haven't made it a practice to notice what other people are wearing on their feet. Oh, I notice if they're really atrocious or unusual. Do you like these?" He wore waterproof Timberlands.

"Are they warm? Do they keep your feet dry? If they do, I like them. I can't believe we're having a conversation about shoes."

He shifted in his chair. "Well you started it. What do you wear when you travel? Can you do much walking? Oops—sorry."

"It's okay. I haven't traveled since the accident so I'll have to go somewhere to find out. I'm not opposed to taking cabs, and I can find a bench when I need one. The more I think about it, the more I want to take a trip. I'm glad I came tonight." She smiled, closed her book, and pushed her chair back. "I'm going to buy this and start planning my trip as soon as I've read it."

"There's just one little problem Katie. If you think your mother will want to go to Scandinavia, this travel book on Europe won't be helpful. Scandinavia isn't listed as one of the countries it covers."

She shrugged. "You're right. But I'll take it anyway."

Seth also closed his book and gathered up their empty cups and paper and carried them to the trash container. He came back and wiped the crumbs from the table into his hand with a new napkin and went back to the trash container.

Katie liked the fact that he didn't wipe them onto the floor as she'd watched another man do earlier. He'd made her smile often in the short time she'd known him.

She stood up and he took her coat from her and held it while she put it on. She turned. "Thanks."

"You're welcome. See you tomorrow around seven."

She nodded, picked up her cane, and walked to the checkout line. Seeing him tomorrow sounded kind of like a date. She glanced over her shoulder. He was watching her. She raised her hand in a casual wave. At least she hoped it looked casual. Her nerves were tense. Was she crazy to think she could do this?

Chapter 13

Wednesday was very cold, but the sun shone and made it seem warmer. Katie's home was spotless. Ethel had been there during Katie's trip to the doctor in Rochester and done her magic with duster and cleaning supplies. Gerbera daisies made the dining room look like spring. The green plants had been given a touch of plant polish. Now she needed to practice. No, this wasn't a performance, but playing for him again made her somewhat apprehensive.

Katie moved to her studio and sat on the piano bench. Her mind pictured Seth sitting here. Maybe he'd play the piano and sing tonight. She touched the keys and imagined his long fingers making music. No, she wouldn't go there.

She picked up the guitar, determined to keep her focus on music. She sang and played show tunes for about an hour then got up and looked through the stack of music she'd picked out for tonight. There were many options and she wondered what Seth would bring. She'd have to practice seriously for the next month in order to be ready, but now the work seemed exciting. She could hardly wait to get started. She played for another hour then set the table for dinner. She couldn't concentrate very long today and knew it was because of her anticipation for the evening ahead.

By the time the light began to fade, the prime rib was in the oven, and everything was ready except to toss the salad. She decided to take a shower and change. Afterward, she put on loose slacks and a cozy green sweater. The phone rang.

"Hello, this is Katie."

"Hi, Katie, it's me. I'll be leaving in about ten minutes and wondered if there's anything you'd like me to bring. It wouldn't be any trouble to stop on the way."

"No, I have everything. Just bring any music you think appropriate, and your appetite, and I'll provide the rest."

"Sounds great. See you in about half an hour."

"Perfect. Bye." She selected several CDs, including Mozart duos by Perlman and Zukerman, and turned on the sound system. She used the remote to start the fireplace and moved on to the dining room and glanced at the table. It didn't look like she'd forgotten anything. Her cane tapped lightly on the floor as she walked to the oven and opened the door to check the prime rib. She inserted the meat thermometer. It needed another half hour. The timing would be perfect because the potatoes would be done then too.

The doorbell rang, and Katie felt her heart skip a beat. Her cheeks were warm, and she told herself to settle down. She opened the door. Seth stood there with a briefcase in one hand and flowers in the other.

She smiled and moved out of the way so he could come in. She closed the door and turned around to find him watching her.

He held out the flowers, which were wrapped in tissue and tied with burlap string.

"Tulips in February. Oh, Seth, how fun! Look at all the colors. They're perfect."

"I'm glad. Spring is a time for new beginnings, and even though it's February, getting to know you is like a touch of spring to me."

Katie blinked and lifted the flowers to her face for a moment. She didn't know what to say so turned and gestured toward the entryway closet with the flowers. The cane was in her left hand and she couldn't open the door. "Do you mind hanging up your own jacket?"

"Of course not. He hung it up and followed her to the living room. Katie pointed to a chair by the fireplace. "Please, make yourself comfortable while I go put these beautiful treasures in water."

* * *

He watched her walk away with her cane in one hand and the flowers in the other. If he had judged her reaction correctly, he'd pleased her with the flowers. Good. He moved to the chair she'd indicated and sat. Heat from the fireplace warmed the air and the rich reds and blues in the Oriental carpet gave the room a warm atmosphere. It welcomed him, and he relaxed.

She certainly was a homemaker. This should be making him nervous and he felt just the opposite.

He heard her hum as she found a vase and filled it with water. She walked carefully into the living room without her cane because she carried the flowers with both hands.

He jumped up. "I'm sorry, I didn't think. Here, let me take those from you."

"No, I'm fine if I walk carefully." She continued on and put them on the coffee table. "Perfect! They're beautiful." She turned toward the sideboard where multiple bottles and several glasses sat alongside an ice bucket. "I don't have wine to offer, but I do have a variety of sparkling waters and juices. Go ahead and help yourself. I need to get my cane."

Seth added ice to a glass, selected fruit-flavored water, and served himself. Then he added ice to another glass and poured the same for Katie. She came back into the room carrying the cane and not using it. He raised his eyebrows, and she shrugged.

"I like to practice. If I walk carefully and pay attention, I do rather well. You might have to pick me up however, if my leg gives way." She giggled.

Seth handed her the full glass. "That would have its advantages." He immediately wished he had kept his mouth shut, but she didn't seem to take offense.

"No, it's embarrassing. I've actually had it happen." She lifted her glass and smelled it. "That's exactly the one I'd have chosen. Thanks." She sat in the chair on the other side of the fireplace.

They chatted quietly about daily stuff and when the timer went off for the oven, Katie got up. "Stay put. This won't take long."

Seth shook his head. "I can find my way around a kitchen if given detailed instructions. Let me help."

"Okay, follow me." She swiveled quickly to head for the kitchen and her leg buckled. She gasped and would have fallen but Seth caught her from behind with his hands on her upper arms.

He steadied her for a moment "Are you okay?"

"Yes. I know better than to move quickly. It makes me an accident ready to happen."

He let her go reluctantly and followed her into the kitchen. Except for the wonderful smell emanating from the oven, Katie's kitchen didn't look like dinner was in the process of being prepared. A baking dish holding what looked like some kind of turnovers sat on the counter. He walked over and leaned down to smell it.

"This is what I smelled when I walked in the door. Are they apple? I hope there's vanilla ice cream to go with them. Can we start with this?" He turned, crossed his arms and leaned against the counter.

Katie laughed. "If you're going to snitch your turnover before dinner, just remember you won't get any of mine later. And you'll be sorry because I only baked those two."

"Are you telling me there might be more somewhere ready for baking?"

"Well, yes, but I expected you to eat dinner first and then you'd be too stuffed with real food to have much room for dessert. I guess I should have had a clue last night when you tried to steal my half of the brownie."

Seth looked longingly at the turnover, shrugged resignedly, and said he'd wait and eat his when she had hers. "Can I help?"

She handed him the potholders. "You can take the meat from the oven. Just set it on top of the stove because it needs to sit for a few minutes. I hope you like your prime rib medium rare."

"Yup. Perfect." He bent down and took out the meat. "It looks to me like there are potatoes in here too. Do you want me to take them out?"

"Yes, thanks. Set them on the trivet by the stove."

He removed them then turned around and watched as she deftly tossed the salad. "Can I do anything else?

She handed him the salad bowl. "You can put this on the table, and I'll plate everything else."

He came back and took the plates from her when they were served. He set them down and came around to pull out her chair. The scent of her hair filled his nostrils as he leaned down to push her chair in. He stifled an impulse to kiss her hair, touched her shoulder, and seated himself.

Katie said a simple prayer of thanksgiving.

As they ate and talked, Seth realized how much they had in common. She was comfortable to be with and knowledgeable on a wide variety of subjects. They both enjoyed reading thrillers. They agreed on many things, including politics. She wasn't as enthusiastic about opera as he was. He'd try to change her mind on that one.

Seth placed his silver on his plate and patted his stomach. "What a great meal."

Katie pleated the napkin in her lap. "I'm glad you came. Do you want your apple turnover and coffee now? Or, we can wait until we've looked at the music."

"Let's look at the music, and then I'll be ready for dessert." He stood and pulled out her chair. When he reached for their plates she told him to leave them till later.

Katie turned and headed to her studio. Seth followed her and saw that she already had music on a stand.

He set his briefcase on her desk, pulled out the music he'd brought, and set it on the piano. "Where do we start? Your music or mine?"

She picked up her guitar, sat down on a chair close to the piano and ran her fingers lightly over the strings. "Whichever."

"Let's do yours."

She nodded. "Okay. I think two numbers are plenty. What about you?"

"I agree. You're providing entertainment to pull the crowd together after eating. A bridge between dinner and the speech, which is the main event. I think a classical guitar number without accompaniment would be appropriate. The vocal number should be one everyone knows. How about something patriotic?" Seth took her music off the stand and leafed through it. He set them back down with one by Bach on top. "Let's hear a little of this one." He sat on the piano bench with his back to the keys. He waited as she got comfortable.

Katie adjusted the stand and spread the sheets. She looked it over for a minute then leaned down against the neck and whispered something he couldn't hear. She started to play while still leaning slightly into her instrument. It added a touch of intimacy to her performance, as if she was listening for its answer to her whisper. She played for several minutes, only glancing at the music now and then. When she stopped, she looked at him with eyebrows raised.

Seth hadn't realized he'd been holding his breath and let it out now in a sigh. "Wow. Anne said you were good, but I had no idea. Doesn't matter which piece you pick, it'll be amazing."

She narrowed her eyes. "Were you testing me? It's the most difficult piece I had sitting there. It also happens to be one of my all time favorites. Once upon a time I could play it from memory."

He rubbed his hand behind his neck. Had he made her angry? "It was just a little test. I already knew you were good." He turned on the bench, quickly grabbed the music on the piano, and pulled out "God Bless America". Hopefully he hadn't messed things up with his stupid experiment. He turned the music so she could see his choice. "If you could lower this a bit it would be more comfortable if everyone wanted to sing along at the end."

* * *

Katie felt her heart speed up. Was this it? Would he sing? "What a great idea." She picked out the melody line in the key of F. After playing it through once she stopped and got more comfy. "Is that a good range for most people?"

"I think so."

Was that all he was going to say? Now what? She played it again and added embellishments. Still nothing from him except an absorbed look on his face. Oh boy. This wasn't going to be easy. She stopped and held out her hand. "May I have the words, please?"

He handed them to her.

She set them on her stand and started over.

He turned again to the piano and lightly picked out the melody with his right hand. Soon he included his left hand.

Katie played on and started to hum. When she heard Seth's voice join hers with the words, she forced herself to keep playing and not stare at him.

His beautifully trained, rich baritone wended its way to her heart. The slight rasp on certain notes added enchantment to his voice. She harmonized and didn't know whether to laugh or cry as she listened to how well their voices blended. They sang the song all the way through and after they stopped, Katie continued to play several more measures. "Seth?"

"Yes?" He lifted his right hand to the piano keys and played several chords then turned to her.

She gripped the neck of the guitar tightly. "Should we do it together on the eighteenth?"

"What?" He turned back to the piano and this time added his left hand and played a few more chords. He spoke toward the keyboard. "We're working on finding something for you to perform. I don't sing any more." Minor chords flowed forcefully from his fingers. "I don't know what possessed me to sing tonight." He stopped playing, bowed his head and rubbed his hands against his thighs.

She slid forward on her chair and touched his arm. "Seth, you know we sounded wonderful together. You also have to know your voice is exceptional."

He turned sharply toward her and took her hand off his arm and held it. "I know no such thing. It used to be my life, but since surgery took away my dream, I only sing in the shower."

She didn't think he knew how tightly he squeezed her hand. He let it go and hunched his shoulders with a shake of his head. He looked so sad she felt like crying. "I know you're no longer able to have a classical music career, but there's no reason for you to not sing in public. Your voice is beautiful. It surpasses almost any artist singing today. Our voices together almost took my breath away and I'm not one to pay myself compliments. Didn't you feel it too?" Katie wanted to make him admit he still had his talent. "You can still sing, only in a different venue."

His teeth clenched, and he looked at her with haunted, pain filled eyes. "I've never considered singing in public since my surgery. I let that dream go. I try not to think about the 'what if's'. It's been harder to do than it sounds." He turned back to the piano and played part of Gershwin's "They Can't Take That Away From Me". "I know I can still—well, it isn't all gone. It's just not good enough." He played several more forceful cords then moved back into "God Bless America".

She joined him with her guitar at the refrain. She looked down to hide the tears that came to her eyes. He was so talented. His piano playing was exceptional. Surely God meant for these gifts to be used. When the song ended, she set her guitar on the floor. "Seth?"

He turned. "Yes?"

"Can we do some stuff, just for fun? I mean, will you sing with me now? Tonight? Maybe you'll even like it."

Seth stood up and took a few steps toward her desk. He didn't turn around and his back was straight. "Ha. Like it? You've raised an old demon's head. It used to be my life—the rehearsals and performances. My singing would not only be painful for people who've heard me before, but painful for me too. I've worked hard to make a new life without it." He turned and faced her. "Oh, what the heck. You want to sing? What do you want to sing?" He moved back to the piano and sat down.

His voice had sounded so strained. Now what had she done? Was he angry? Oh well. She'd pushed this far, and wasn't giving up now. Her fingers fumbled through a stack of music by her chair and she pulled out a book of Gershwin numbers. He'd just played Gershwin so maybe he liked it as much as she did. "How about this?"

"I know most of Gershwin's music. It's fun stuff. Which one?" His fingers rippled down the keys as he waited for her to choose.

"How about "Nice Work If You Can Get It"?"

"Fine. What key?"

Was he humoring her? That was a rather curt answer. She'd ignore it. "G." She handed him the music. "Move down and I'll sit there with you so I can see the words."

He moved and they spent the next forty-five minutes playing and singing music they both knew.

Katie set her guitar down and rubbed her fingers. She spoke with her back to him. "We really should sing together at the fundraiser. Will you at least think about it?"

He put both hands on her shoulders and forcefully turned her around. "Is this the same person who struggled to decide if she'd help Anne out by taking part in the evening?"

Katie shrugged and gave him a timid smile. "I guess we're both coming from a similar situation. I never found it hard to play for a crowd and was often willing to sing too. I know I'm rusty, but somehow it seems as if I'm supposed to do this. I think you are too. Well, maybe I'm wrong about you, but I'd like to have you up there with me." She clasped her hands as if in prayer. "Think about it. Okay?" She lifted her guitar and hugged it. "Should I do the Bach?"

Seth nodded. "Yes. It's well known and won't take much longer for you to be totally comfortable with it. In fact, I've seldom heard it done as well as you did it tonight."

"I can certainly have it ready by the eighteenth of March. What about "God Bless America"? Do you think it would be appropriate, or should we choose another patriotic number?"

Seth picked up her stack of music, quickly went through it and set it back with a shake of his head. "I think "God Bless America" would be great. More than likely everyone will want to sing along toward the end and most people know the words. They could also be printed in the program." He touched the paper with his finger. "Let's try it together again. I'm not saying I'll do it with you, but something inside me says it might be fun to try. Let's give it a whirl. Here at least."

Katie nodded and started her accompaniment. As Seth started to sing, her heart lifted and she added her voice to his. They sang it all the way through and repeated the ending. After they finished, they smiled at each other.

He stood, put his hand on her shoulder, and leaned down to kiss her forehead. "Thanks, Katie. I've enjoyed singing tonight. I never thought I'd be doing this again. It's one of life's nicer surprises. So are you." He turned away and gathered up his music.

Katie's heart pounded and she wished she could think of just the right thing to say. She wanted to tell him he was a nice surprise too, but couldn't open her mouth to say it. She set her guitar on its case, picked up her cane, and stood.

"Maybe if you sing with me you could hold my hand when I go out on stage and I wouldn't have to use my cane." She held it up. "I'd feel a lot more confident and look nicer too."

"You don't need to worry about how you look. Even with the cane you're very beautiful and one hardly notices it."

"I don't think that was your reaction when we first met. I bet you thought it was a pity I had to use a cane. It isn't as noticeable now you know me."

Seth gave her a surprised look. "Well of course I noticed the cane, but I still thought you were very elegant. I can see your point about finding it easier to walk on stage with an arm to cling to. Needing me by your side seems a little like blackmail to me."

Her mouth dropped open and she snapped it shut. He laughed.

"Blackmail?" Katie shrugged. "I'm not beyond a little blackmail if I can get my way." She flounced out of the room and heard him laugh again. She walked to the kitchen. She'd set the timer on the coffee so it was done. She raised her voice. "Seth, do you still want ice cream on your apple turnover?"

"Yes." His voice came from right behind her.

She jumped. "Oh. You move so silently I didn't know you'd followed me. Good, now you can carry the tray into the living room." She placed the carafe of coffee on the tray already loaded with cups, napkins, silverware and turnovers. "Wait a minute. I need to add the ice cream." When she finished, he picked it up, headed to the living room, and set it on the coffee table. "Is this okay?"

"Yes, thanks." She touched a finger to the petal of a tulip. "I love them, Seth. Thanks so much." She handed him a plate and poured coffee for both of them. They moved to the chairs they'd occupied before dinner.

Seth took a bite of his turnover. "This is delicious and worth waiting for. Worth singing for." He had a mischievous look on his face, and his eyes looked very blue against his tan skin. How did he get that tan in a Minnesota winter?

"Do you take a winter vacation to warm up? It looks as if you've been in the sun lately and you don't seem the type to get an artificial tan."

"I've been to St. Thomas."

"Lucky you. Where do you stay?"

He settled back in his chair and took a sip of coffee. "Our family has a villa there. Occasionally I can get away to spend a few days in the sun. This time it was only my parents and me."

Katie remembered going there for a medical conference with John. "Is the water always that wonderful aqua color?"

"Yes, most of the time. Storms turn it dark of course, but I haven't been there during many of those." He glanced at his watch, uncrossed his legs and set his cup and plate down on the tray in front of him. "This has been a great evening." He stood and held out his hand for her plate and cup. She handed them to him and stood too.

He picked up the tray and carried it to the kitchen while she stayed by her chair.

"Thanks. I'll leave everything else until morning." It had been a long time since someone made thoughtful gestures like this for her. John would have carried their things to the kitchen too. Her stomach clenched at the thought of John and she looked away.

Seth came back and picked up his briefcase. Together they walked to the front door. She opened the closet to take out his coat, but he reached over her and took it off the hanger himself. He shrugged into it, then reached for the scarf. Katie turned to face him. He flipped the scarf over her head and started pulling her forward, but she ducked and slipped it off.

He wound it around his own neck. "Oops, wrong neck."

She chuckled and touched his arm. "I enjoyed making music with you. Thanks for coming and thanks for your help."

"I've had a wonderful evening. Dinner was delicious and the music, well, I guess I'd call it beautiful."

She opened the door and watched him push the elevator button. The door opened and he stepped in.

"Good night, Seth. And thanks again for coming." Katie raised her hand in a slight wave as the doors closed. As she shut her door, she did a little dance step with her cane. From deep inside, music bubbled up and she softly sang the first tune that came to mind. "I could have danced all night."

Chapter 14

Katie practically jumped out of bed Thursday morning. She grabbed her robe off the loveseat and would have danced to the bathroom if her leg had let her. This would be a great day. Lunch with Anne, the exhibition at the art museum, and then the concert in the evening. Wow. Today held promises of being a ten on the scale of one to ten.

She tied her robe tightly around her waist and examined her face in the mirror. Did her eyes sparkle more than they had yesterday? Last night with Seth had been fun. More than fun. When he'd flipped his scarf over her neck, she'd been tempted to move into his arms. She wasn't sure about those feelings. What did they mean? Why was she so drawn to a person she'd only known a few days? Fortunately, hashing over the evening hadn't kept her awake last night. She was ready to tackle the day with joy.

She walked through the living room and smiled at the tulips Seth had brought. What a thoughtful thing to do. Obviously he'd chosen them himself. These weren't a generic arrangement from 1-800-Flowers. He'd chosen them with her in mind. There were many things she liked about Seth Prentice. She continued to the kitchen and put the coffee on. While it brewed, she started her clean up. Nothing got done quickly because she needed to move carefully. She couldn't use her cane with her hands full.

By the time the coffee finished brewing, she had loaded the dishwasher. She tossed the linens into the laundry basket and gave a final swipe to the white granite counter tops. Her kitchen had a light, airy feeling. She'd added a touch of yellow by hanging a large painting of yellow daisies in a yellow frame. Her red teakettle and a whimsical red rooster sitting on the counter gave the room a smile. A bookcase graced the north wall. She loved to have books in every room. She toasted a bagel, then sat at the table and reached for her devotional book. Today's reading was about peace. "God will keep him in perfect peace whose mind is stayed on Him".

Katie bowed her head after reading and prayed for peace and direction in her life. She didn't want to miss the voice of God because she concentrated so hard on daily living, instead of heavenly listening.

She finished breakfast, cleaned up, and headed to her bedroom to get ready for the day. More than likely she wouldn't be coming back to her house before the evening concert so needed to choose an outfit appropriate for the whole day. She took a black cashmere pantsuit from her closet and laid it on the bed, then tucked a silk scarf into her handbag to dress it up for the evening. The scarf resembled an Impressionist's painting—a landscape of pink, purple, blue, and red wild flowers. After she applied makeup and finished dressing, she examined herself in the full-length mirror. Her dark hair gleamed in the morning sun. She turned one direction, then the other. Not bad. She laughed at herself.

She checked her purse to make sure she had the tickets, then called The Oak Grill and made a reservation for lunch. That done, there still was time before Anne arrived to do a little research on the senator and his re-election campaign. After reading several editorials on the computer about both him and his opponent, she switched to a news website, read the day's news and checked the stock report. She preferred reading news on the Internet or newspaper instead of watching it on television. That way she didn't hear the same thing over and over. Nothing earth shattering had happened and she shut down her computer just as Anne called to say she'd be there in five minutes.

Katie grabbed her cane, coat, and everything she'd need for the day and locked the house. Katie slid into the car and gave her friend a hug.

Anne spoke as she drove onto the avenue. "It's such a treat to take a day off in the middle of the week. I should do it more often. This day will be well worth staying late tomorrow to catch up."

Katie agreed and told her she'd made reservations at The Oak Grill. "The food's good and we'll be able to talk because it's never noisy. Just classical music playing. Is that okay with you?" She straightened her coat under the seat belt.

Anne nodded. "Great. We can leave the car in their ramp because the skyway goes to the museum."

They parked and took the elevator to the restaurant. After the waitress took their order and walked away, Anne turned to Katie. "Well?"

"Well what?" Katie tried to look innocent.

"You know well what. Tell me all about last night."

"You mean Seth?"

"Katie, I'll strangle you. Yes I mean Seth."

Katie took a long drink of water. "Don't you love the flower arrangements in here?"

"Cut it out. I'll make a scene if you don't start talking." Anne picked up her napkin, gave it a shake and placed it in her lap. "Hurry up."

"Okay, okay. First of all, he brought a huge bouquet of multi-colored tulips. He said they reminded him of spring and that getting to know me is like a touch of spring." Anne set her glass down with a thump. Water spilled onto the table and Katie laughed. "Hey. You're making a mess."

Anne dabbed at it with her napkin. "Oh, bother. Katie, Seth doesn't say things like that. Then what happened?"

"Well, we ate and talked. You know, the usual stuff."

"What did you talk about?" Anne leaned forward as if she didn't want to miss a word.

"A little of everything. Our families, travel, you know—dinner chitchat. Oh, and we had coffee on Tuesday night too." Katie casually tossed in that tidbit of information.

"Wait just a minute. You didn't tell me you were going to see him on Tuesday." Anne sat back and crossed her arms.

Katie waited to answer while their food was served. "Oh don't look all stern. I wasn't hiding anything. Tuesday night wasn't planned. I bumped into him in a bookstore." She stopped and took a bite of her Asian chicken salad.

Anne spread butter on her warm popover and motioned for her friend to go on.

"We were both surprised. He was looking at travel books." Katie took a drink of water.

"Where is he going? I don't think he gets away all that much. I know work keeps him really busy."

"He bought a book on Spain. He's interested in going there because although he speaks Spanish, he hasn't traveled to Spain. He enjoys reading the history of a country before traveling to it like I do."

Anne's phone buzzed and she picked it up and frowned. "Sorry. I have to take this call. It will only take a minute."

While Anne talked, Katie ate her salad and looked around the restaurant. Pachelbel's Canon was playing softly in the background. It was one of her favorites. She realized she had lots of favorites and smiled at the thought.

Anne ended her call and picked up her fork. "So what else have you learned about Seth?"

"He likes chocolate."

Anne laughed. "So do you. It's a good omen."

"Oh really? Enough about Seth." Katie speared a piece of lettuce on her fork and paused. "I'm going to ask my mother if she wants to come to town for the fundraiser. Can you get a ticket for her?"

"No problem. I'll make sure she's at our table." Anne put both elbows on the table and leaned forward. "Now for the big question. Did he sing or didn't he sing last night?"

"Who?"

Anne narrowed her eyes. "You're going to be in trouble girl. Don't mess with me."

"Oh, you mean Seth. I thought I said enough about him already." Katie covered her mouth with her napkin to hide her smile.

Anne threw her napkin down and started to rise. "That's it. I've had it. I'm coming to strangle you."

Katie giggled and waved her back. "Okay, okay. I give up. He asked me to play a Bach piece, the hardest one on my music stand. Devious guy. Fortunately I'd been practicing it, and I think I surprised him. My skills have come back faster than I thought they would, but I'll have to work very hard these next few weeks!"

"If I know you, the piece is probably good enough already. You're such a perfectionist."

"True, but I'd be foolish not to have it up to my own standards before performing in front of a crowd of people."

"You haven't answered my question yet. Did he or did he not sing?"

"Yup, he sang." Katie didn't say any more.

"Well?"

She looked at Anne, took a deep breath and let it out slowly. "He has one of the most beautiful voices I've ever heard. It's a rich baritone. Occasionally you can hear a rasp. I don't know why he doesn't still sing, because the slight rasp does nothing to detract from his voice. In fact, it might enhance the romantic sound, which would be very appealing to a large audience." She poked at her salad rather forcefully. "What a shame he stopped because of it. We actually sang together. And, if you want my opinion, we sounded great."

Anne opened her eyes wide and leaned forward. "Do you think he'd sing with you on the eighteenth?"

"He said he'd think about it. We'll see."

Anne nodded.

Katie reached across the table to touch her hand. "I do believe in miracles my friend. You started the first one."

"Yup. You're making music, thinking about travel, and entertaining a man in your home." Anne smiled smugly at her and glanced at her watch. "We need to leave."

They paid the bill. As they left, several people greeted Anne, and one gentleman actually got up and walked over to say hello. Katie picked up their coats while Anne had a brief conversation. After they left, Katie asked about him.

"He's one of the lawyers we've brought in for the upcoming malpractice suit. I've been spending a lot of time on this, and we're getting someone from outside the firm to help with it."

"Wow, this is obviously an important case."

"Yes. Dr. Browne is, in our opinion, an ethical man and a superb doctor. We're sure he's not culpable in this situation. We think it's totally a case of greed on the part of the family, and I'll do everything in my power to prove them wrong." Anne's stride got longer as she talked.

Katie had trouble keeping up. "Hey. Slow down. My legs aren't as long as yours."

"Sorry. My blood boils when people are forced to defend themselves from greedy predators." She adjusted her pace.

"Can you talk about it yet? How much do you know about him personally? I mean, how is this affecting his wife and children or extended family?"

Anne adjusted the shoulder strap on her purse and gave Katie a lopsided smile. "I can only tell you as much about the case as has been printed in the newspapers. He's been divorced for some years and has one daughter. This is all public knowledge."

"You must know more that that."

"Well . . ." She cleared her throat and shrugged.

They'd come to the elevator, and Anne didn't say more as they got on. It was full, and they took it to the skyway level. As they walked off, Katie touched her arm. "Well what?"

"I don't remember what I was going to say."

"Oh, yes you do. You grilled me all during lunch and it's my turn now. Come on. Give."

Anne's voice softened. "Really, Katie. He seems like a nice person. He's a client. That's all."

"Do you wish you'd met him somewhere other than work?"

Anne pulled Katie to the side of the skyway so their slow progress wouldn't hold up anyone in a hurry. "I don't know. Really. I don't know."

Downtown bustled with noontime traffic and lots of people took advantage of the heated skyways. They walked on in silence.

They were in front of a display of jewelry in one of the shops along the way. Katie put her hand on Anne's arm. "I love diamonds. I inherited my grandmother's jewelry and I think I'll have some of the pieces re-set." She pointed to a pendant. "That's stunning."

"Is it ever. What pieces did you get?"

"I got her original engagement and wedding ring. Grandpa had given her a diamond cocktail ring which she thought way overboard but wore because it came from him. Actually, I like it and will probably have it reset into platinum. I love the way diamonds look in platinum. A diamond pendant might be fun to have made of the other rings. The diamonds aren't large, but it would be special to wear them, instead of just having them sit in a safe deposit box." They walked on and finally came to the museum where they again checked their coats.

"We should have left these in the car since we're both dressed in pantsuits and the skyways are warm. You look very nice, Katie."

"Thanks. I brought a silk scarf to dress it up a little for tonight because I thought we might not go back home." Katie chuckled and indicated Anne's pantsuit. "Look at us. We're dressed so much alike one would think we called each other and agreed on what we'd wear—like teenagers."

Anne laughed and pulled a bright fabric from her purse. "I don't believe it. I did the same thing." They reached the museum, purchased their tickets and received a brochure to guide them through the exhibit, which consisted of works by Renoir, Monet, Berthe Morisot, Degas and others.

Their leisurely pace suited Katie. She could stand and gaze as long as she liked. A little voiced reminded her that she could have been here with Seth. She sat on one of the benches placed in strategic spots for viewing pleasure. Thoughts of Seth kept intruding into her mind. She forced herself to shut him out. She got up and walked into the next room to find Anne.

It was fun having a friend along so they could compare notes. They didn't always agree on what they liked and didn't like, but that made it more interesting. Katie didn't enjoy Degas as much as Anne, but both thought Camille Pissarro's *Garden of Les Mathurins* truly wonderful. They had his series of *Boulevard Montmartre,* which she hadn't seen before. Both of them agreed that Renoir's paintings had instant appeal and he communicated the joy he took in his subjects. Today several art students worked on copying various paintings. One student in particular stood out and they stopped and watched him for awhile. He chatted with them and admitted to being an instructor at one of the universities in the city. He thought copying the masters a great way to learn.

"Some would probably call this heresy, but I call it a great experience and an excellent learning tool."

They asked if he had his work in any of the galleries around town and he told them where he regularly showed. Katie had several spots where she'd like to hang new artwork in her home. "My I have your card? I might be in the market for something new soon."

He handed her one and they wandered on.

Katie put his card in her purse. "I bet he's a great teacher. He's interesting and not at all stuffy or self important."

Anne agreed. "I'd love to have that much talent. There aren't many people who can make a living at it. I think it's a lonely existence when you're starting out. Not many have the tenacity to keep at it until they can make a living. I suppose if you're truly talented, believe in yourself, and have financial support, you can eventually make it. I wonder what his story is."

"We can go look at his work together and you can get all lawyerly and grill him. Maybe he'll ask you out. He could be your next heartthrob."

Anne punched Katie lightly on the arm. "Cut it out. I'm not in the market for a guy."

"Oh, that's right. You have Dr. Browne on the waiting list."

Anne stopped and shook her head. "You need help girl. Has Seth twisted your brain?" They laughed and walked on.

Finally Katie said she needed to sit down and have a cup of coffee. "I need to absorb what I've seen or I'll go into overload." They found a table in the little coffee shop connected to the museum and Anne bought coffee for both of them.

"Thanks. Remember when we went to the Louvre? Talk about reaching a saturation point!"

Anne sipped her coffee and sighed in contentment. "We were so disappointed when we found out Claude Monet's paintings were on tour. I loved the time we spent together in France."

They drank their coffee and studied the brochure to decide what they had time for before they had to leave.

Anne tapped the information on the sculpture displays. "I'd like to go through some of these rooms. It would be a nice change of pace. I'm not very knowledgeable about sculpture but it interests me. What about you?"

Katie nodded. "I think it's a great idea. Then how about Edouard Manet's display before we leave." She smiled and wriggled in her chair. "What a great day this is. Thanks for playing hooky."

"Don't thank me. I'm loving today. It's about time we did stuff like this. When I told my dad about today's plans he looked a little jealous. I wish he'd start to cut back on his workload. Mother's been using the word 'retire' lately. Maybe if she talks about it enough, he'll think it's his idea and actually do it. At least he could be semi-retired."

"My dad didn't get to retire. Life certainly is unpredictable isn't it?" Katie walked toward a display of pottery she'd been eyeing. One piece was as tall as her. "Look at this. How in the world could a normal-sized person work with this on a potter's wheel?" She circled it. "Look at all these shades of blue. I think I've fallen in love."

"Oh, dear. Seth will be jealous." Anne had her back to Katie as she spoke.

Katie reached out with her cane and lightly poked her in the back. "Be quiet. I'm concentrating on art, not man."

Anne turned with upraised hands. "Don't shoot. Oh, that wasn't a gun." They both giggled.

Katie turned to walk away as a group came into the room. Would Seth have enjoyed the displays as much as she had? Would he have wanted to talk or view in silence? Why couldn't she stop thinking about that man? She walked faster and forced her mind to concentrate on what she saw.

Eventually closing time approached, so they picked up their coats and went back to the car.

Katie buckled her seat belt and turned to Anne. "What should we do for dinner?"

"How about going to my house? I'll throw together some sandwiches or salads. Then we can put our feet up for a little while before going to Orchestra Hall. Is that a good plan?"

"It's a great idea. I wouldn't mind relaxing. Do you have an extra toothbrush? I didn't put one into my purse." Katie ran her tongue across her teeth and grimaced.

"Yes and I'll have us home in a jiffy."

Katie and Anne had a light supper. After they cleaned the kitchen, Anne said she should check her messages so Katie went into the living room and turned on the news. Nothing newsworthy had happened during the day so she turned it off, leaned back, and closed her eyes for a few minutes. Thoughts and scenes of the previous evening with Seth floated through her mind. Would he be at the concert tonight? They hadn't talked about it.

Her thoughts were interrupted when she heard Anne come in. She opened her eyes. "I wasn't sleeping, just resting." She sat up. "I'll get ready."

Katie came out of the bathroom as Anne came downstairs. She reached for her coat. "I'm ready if you are."

The lobby at Orchestra Hall was packed with people of all ages, and they were dressed in everything from blue jeans to black tie. The mood was festive and the line for pre-concert drinks was long. Anne introduced Katie to several lawyers and a judge, but they didn't linger and soon found their seats.

Katie removed her coat and sat down. "Sean Sweeny told me the truth when he said we had great seats." She settled back to read her program and watch the people while waiting for the concert to begin. Katie gasped softly.

Anne glanced up. "What?"

Katie motioned with her program. "Look to our left. Several rows up."

Anne turned. Seth sat beside a woman with red hair. "Is she the woman you saw downtown on Saturday?"

"Yes. The one called Sylvia. Isn't it a small world? I saw her Saturday and wondered if the Seth she talked about could possibly be our Seth Prentice." A cold feeling of disappointment settled in her stomach. Was this jealousy? How could she be jealous? He meant nothing to her. He had every right to be here with this Sylvia.

Anne touched Katie's hand. "He probably asked her a long time ago. Before he met you."

"Right. Sure. Of course." She couldn't seem to keep her eyes from glancing their way. As if he felt her presence, he turned his head and spotted her. He smiled and nodded, then turned back to Sylvia.

Katie squirmed in her seat. She couldn't get comfortable. Her feet didn't touch the floor all the way and there wasn't room to cross her legs comfortably. Why was the velvet chair itchy? "Anne?"

"Yes?"

"Remember what I told you about the conversation I overheard? They were talking about a man named Seth and Sylvia admitted she'd like to 'catch' him." She kept her voice low so no one around would hear. "She wanted to catch him not only for his good looks, but all his wonderful money would be nice too."

Anne nodded her head. "Um hm. That sounds just like Sylvia."

"What do you know about her? Is she a nice person? She seems quite a bit younger than him."

Before Anne could answer, the concertmaster came on stage and everyone started clapping. She leaned close to Katie's ear. "I'll tell you more later. Forget about her."

Katie gave her friend a wan smile and turned toward the stage.

* * *

After seeing Katie, Seth remained outwardly attentive to Sylvia, but his mind constantly wandered to the woman sitting to his right and slightly back. Sylvia frequently touched him while she chatted, and he was glad Katie couldn't see it.

Why did he care? He didn't have a commitment to Katie Nelson. Still, it would have been more fun to be at the concert with her instead of Sylvia.

The thought surprised Seth so much he felt sweat break out on his forehead. He casually ran his hand up through his hair to unobtrusively wipe it away. Finally the concert started. He breathed a sigh of relief and smelled Sylvia's perfume. It seemed harsh compared to Katie's delicate scent. What was he thinking?

Soon he was able to erase everything from his mind except the wonderful music. They played one of his favorites, the Bach Double Concerto. In his opinion, no one could play it better than these two, Zukerman and Perlman.

What a great night. He wondered what Katie was thinking about it. Good grief. He had to get that lady out of his mind!

At intermission they stood. "Would you like a drink?"

Sylvia was waving to someone. She grabbed Seth's arm. "Just a second. Here's Mary. You remember Mary don't you?"

Seth nodded and greeted Sylvia's friend and her mother. They stood and chatted until the concert resumed. Seth couldn't keep his eyes from wandering back to Katie. She didn't look his way. He kept his face from showing his frustration as he helped Sylvia take her seat.

Although he tried to get his head and heart into the music, he couldn't stop thinking about Katie. He crossed and uncrossed his legs, tapped the program against his thigh and couldn't stop fidgeting. Finally Sylvia reached out, touched his hand, and gave him a questioning look. He mouthed an apology and forced his mind back to the concert. Soon he became completely absorbed and forgot everything except the music.

Seth smiled at Sylvia while he helped her with her fur coat. "This must be nice and warm."

She rubbed her cheek against the collar. "Yes. It's perfect for Minnesota winters."

When they got into the aisle, he took Sylvia's elbow and escorted her through the throng of people into the foyer. As they walked, he searched the crowd for a glimpse of Katie's shining dark hair or the bright scarf she had been wearing. What was he doing—feeling disappointment over not seeing one woman while out with another? Good grief. This wasn't right.

He pulled his attention back to Sylvia. "Do you want to wait here while I go get the car?"

She shook her head. "No, I'll go with you. It feels good to walk after sitting so long." They took the stairs to the skyway and walked across to the parking ramp. As he started the car, Seth reluctantly asked if she'd like to stop somewhere for coffee on their way home.

"No, as much as I'd like to, I really need to get home and finish a report I'm presenting tomorrow. I'll take a rain check though."

He heard the eagerness in her voice, but at that moment he pulled up to the cashier's window and didn't respond. He knew he was acting like a jerk, but wasn't going to commit himself to any more time with her.

When they arrived at Sylvia's house, he helped her out of the car and walked her to the door.

She turned to him. "I could put the coffeepot on, Seth. Do you have time to come in?"

He reached for her key and unlocked the door. As he pushed it open, he looked at her. "I thought you had work to do tonight before you went to bed."

"Well, I do, but a few minutes more or less won't make much difference."

"No, Sylvia, let's call it a night. Thank you for inviting me. I didn't want to miss it. It was everything I hoped it would be." She walked into the house and he stayed on the front porch. He smiled, lifted his hand as he said good night and quickly walked down the stairs. She called after him.

"Thanks for dinner, Seth. And thanks for your company. I enjoyed both a lot."

He stopped and looked back with a nod and another wave, but didn't speak.

As he drove away, he turned on his CD player. He laughed at himself. Chet Atkins? Was he becoming obsessed with guitar music?

Chapter 15

Seth was relieved that he'd managed to get out of staying for coffee with Sylvia. Making small talk would have tried his patience.

He quirked his lips in a wry smile. Sylvia would have been upset if she had known where his thoughts had wandered so often during the evening. After meeting Katie, he saw Sylvia in a different light. Her ambition bothered him. He knew he wouldn't have let a serious relationship develop. Now he didn't want any type of connection with her.

As he slowed for a stoplight, Chet Atkins' guitar music still played. He checked the display. Track two. This was all he could take of the guitar. He reached over and pressed the button to change to another CD. Josh Groban's music swirled around the car. When he heard the beautiful voice, his insides twisted into a knot. The timbre filled his whole being. He breathed deeply to release the pressure in his chest.

Where would he be now, if he hadn't had vocal cord troubles and surgery? Singing on world stages, confident and fulfilled? Making hearts melt with the power of his voice? This train of thought had to stop. He wouldn't let himself go there. It was too painful.

When he realized he was speeding, he eased up on the accelerator. Getting a ticket wouldn't be a nice way to cap the night. He put his hand on the passenger headrest and wished Katie's head rested there.

Thoughts of Katie wouldn't go away, and he gave in to the temptation. He tried to analyze the look he'd seen on her face when he'd turned around before the concert. Had it been hurt? Was it surprise? His glance had been quick and those beautiful green eyes had been in shadow. He was almost home. Should he call her?

Seth drove into his garage, got out of the car, and hurried to the elevator. Once inside, he leaned against the wall and shook his head. What was the matter with him? He was acting like a lovesick schoolboy.

Besides, Katie and Anne were probably still hanging out, analyzing the concert. He shouldn't interrupt.

He'd like to be part of their discussion. He'd love to hear Katie's view. She'd have understood the nuances—how the personalities of the musicians gave the performance its energy and joy.

Lovesick? Had he really called himself lovesick?

Seth walked out of the elevator and unlocked his door. He checked the time. Could he call her? He pulled out his cell phone and looked at it a moment. If she didn't answer, he'd leave a message. If she did, he'd admit that he would have loved to have attended the concert with her. He dialed her number, shocked when he realized he had it memorized.

* * *

Katie checked the caller ID, and her pulse quickened. She put her hand over her rapidly beating heart. "Hi, Seth."

"Hi, yourself. Are you just getting home?"

Warmth rushed through her at the sound of his velvety, rich voice. "Yes. I walked in the door this minute. Hold on. I need to take my coat off." She set down the phone, took off her coat, and tossed it on the couch. She didn't pick up the phone immediately. He'd brought back all those jangled emotions she'd fought so hard to suppress during the concert. How could he call her after spending the evening with Sylvia? She'd better find out what was going on. "Okay. I'm back. Did something happen? Why the late call?"

"I didn't want to wait until tomorrow to hear your thoughts on the concert, so I took a chance and called tonight. All evening I wished we'd been at the concert together."

Katie's heart picked up speed again, and she took a calming breath. Why did he say that? "Well, Anne and I thought it was wonderful. Both Perlman and Zuckerman were magnificent. Their music has so much life." She refused to make a comment on his "together" statement.

"I thought the same thing. After so many years of practice and performances, it's still fresh every time I hear them."

Katie sat on the arm of the couch. "There were times I was so moved my eyes filled with tears. The next minute I'd laugh. Don't you love it when they're willing to sit down at the end and do impromptu encores?"

Seth agreed. "It's generous of them. I'm sure they're exhausted by then."

Katie arched her back and sighed. The day had filled her visual and emotional senses to overflowing. She needed her space back. "I'm really tired myself, Seth. I've had a long day."

His voice got deeper. "I understand. Good night, Katie. How about dinner one night soon? We can do some more work on the benefit music."

"Call in a few days, okay? Bye." Katie put down the phone and rubbed her hands, as if wiping away the conversation. She grabbed her cane and limped down the dark hall to her bedroom without bothering to turn on a light. The moon shone brightly, and she sank onto her window seat. This was happening way to fast. He was much too appealing. That voice. Those eyes. He made her laugh. And she'd rarely found anyone who could talk about the nuances of music the way he could. Anxiety gripped her. She wasn't ready to be attracted to anyone.

She breathed deeply and got up to turn on the lamp. After the light came on, she saw the tulips from him. She'd moved them from the living room to her bedroom. Her finger traced the delicate petal of one of the red ones. Did tulips have a special meaning?

A flicker of anger coursed through her. What was he playing at? He gave her flowers, but was dating Sylvia. He claimed he wished he'd been at the concert with her. Well, he could have asked her. How many times had she looked over at him and Sylvia and wondered about their relationship? Or what his thoughts were about the concert? She looked toward the ceiling.

Was God in on this conundrum? She'd have a talk with Him about it. Yes she would. Soon.

Katie turned toward the bathroom to get ready for bed. Did he shower at night or in the morning? When she looked at herself in the mirror, her cheeks were flushed. What was she thinking? She shook her head and reached for her cleansing cream to start her nightly ritual. She'd shut him out of her mind and think about the day. What a day.

When she crawled into bed, her body was weary, but her eyes wouldn't stay closed. Her mind wouldn't calm down. Sleep wasn't anywhere near. A cup of something hot would do the trick.

She turned the light back on and got out of bed. With her cane, she walked toward the kitchen, turning on several lights as she went. Her book was on an end table. Maybe reading a few chapters would bring on sleep. Hot chocolate sounded good. One of the perks of living in the north on a cold winter's night included hot chocolate. The coziness of curling up with a book and something warm to drink was one of her pleasures. She picked up the tray, then looked at her cane, shrugged and left it there. After walking carefully back to her bedroom, she set the tray on the table in front of the loveseat.

She'd better go pick up her cane and turn off the lights, otherwise she'd be looking for it in the morning. What a nuisance. She hated the thought of more surgery, but it would be worth it to get rid of this blasted cane.

Back in her bedroom, she got comfortable, and became immersed in the heroics of the main character. She yawned and looked at the clock. More than an hour had passed. No wonder she was cold. She stretched, turned out the light and slipped into bed. As she snuggled in, the words from the Psalm she'd read during her morning devotional came to mind. She spoke them out loud.

"'I will praise You, O Lord, with my whole heart; I will show forth all Your marvelous works and wonderful deeds! I will rejoice in You and be in high spirits: I will sing praise to your name, O Most High.' Thank you, Lord, for a memorable day. I'll talk to You tomorrow." She rolled over and drifted off to sleep.

Chapter 16

As Katie got ready for church Sunday morning, she hummed along to a CD of hymns by Debbie Boone. Saturday had been quiet and now she looked forward to church. Worship would get her mind off Seth. She'd had to push thoughts of him away while she practiced yesterday. He'd even flitted in and out of her dreams. No more of that. She grabbed her cell phone and turned it to vibrate as she walked out the door.

She loved living close enough to walk to church. The sun shone and she lifted her face to feel the warmth. Feeble though it was, it felt great. Her boot caught on an uneven rise in the sidewalk and she almost fell. She gripped her cane tighter and breathed a thank you.

The organist was playing a classical prelude when she walked in. She found a place to sit halfway down the aisle on the right side. As she settled in she heard a voice on her left.

"Move in a little farther, Katie."

Seth? Surprise robbed her of words. She scooted over to make room then turned with raised eyebrows.

He set his coat beside him on the pew, leaned toward her and whispered close to her ear. "I wanted to check out the music for myself. You're right. It's wonderful and we haven't even heard the choir yet." He settled back and folded his arms, looking perfectly at home.

She realized he'd taken his coat off earlier. He must have waited somewhere in the back for her to get there. She unbuttoned her coat and started to take it off.

He immediately reached over to help. "Do you want it over your shoulders?"

She nodded. He placed it on her shoulders and brushed his hand over the fabric in a lingering touch.

Her heart did a funny little jump, and she inched slightly away. Did anyone notice? As the service got under way, she told herself to settle down.

Katie enjoyed sharing the songbook and lifting her voice with his during the worship time. He didn't know the contemporary choruses, but listened and hummed along when he realized he could follow the tune's pattern.

She fought to ignore Seth and keep her mind on the pastor's sermon. Today Pastor Schumann talked about not being able to give away what you don't have. One of his points stressed accepting mercy from God, because we need to be merciful to those around us.

The service ended. Katie picked up her cane, and they walked out together. The pastor stood at the back of the sanctuary and greeted Katie by name. She thanked him for another sermon that touched her mind and heart. "Pastor, I'd like you to meet a friend of mind, Seth Prentice. Seth, this is our pastor, Mike Schumann."

Seth reached out and shook the pastor's hand. "I'm happy to meet you. Katie wasn't exaggerating when she told me about the music. I enjoyed your sermon too." He took Katie's elbow.

"Thanks, Seth. I hope to see you again."

They didn't linger because many people waited to greet the pastor. They walked out, and Katie turned to Seth.

"I think he's a great pastor and teacher. I hope you enjoyed it as much as I did. Are you glad you came?"

"Yes. Now will you have mercy on me? And go to lunch or brunch or breakfast? I decided at the last minute to dash over here and haven't even had a cup of coffee."

He looked so much like a little boy it made Katie laugh. "All right, where should we go?"

"You mean it?" He grabbed her hand and started pulling her toward the side parking lot. "I don't have to get down on my knees to convince you?"

"Nope, I'm full of mercy and want to give some away." Did the sun shine brighter? She shielded her eyes with her hand.

Seth opened the car door for her, then went around and got in.

She buckled her seatbelt. "Do you have a restaurant in mind? Did you make reservations?"

He laughed. "I didn't dare. But there's a new place that's supposed to have great pancakes not far from here. What do you think?"

She leaned against the headrest and turned her face toward him. She bit her lower lip to keep from laughing. "I love pancakes and waffles and French toast. Do you mean the one on Grand?"

He nodded. "Yes. We might be early enough to beat the crowd." After checking for traffic, he drove out of the parking lot. They arrived at the restaurant within five minutes. He was out of the car and around to her door before she had her seatbelt off.

"Be careful, there's a patch of ice here." He reached for her hand and helped her out. She smiled and didn't say anything while he closed the door, then turned and took her hand again to walk to the restaurant. His prediction proved true. They didn't have to wait. Seth helped her with her coat and she sat down with a sigh.

"Are you tired?"

"No, contented. This is pleasant. She waved a hand taking in the garden theme with hanging lamps in the shapes of a variety of flowers, then settled deeper into the leather upholstered booth.

The waitress came, handed them menus, and asked if they wanted coffee. Both said yes.

They read their menus in silence. Katie turned hers directly to the pancake/waffle/French toast page and studied it for a moment. After taking a good look at the gentleman's plate on the table next to them, she closed her menu. The server had left a carafe of coffee so Katie poured and sat back to enjoy the aroma and sip while she waited. He looked up.

"What are you having?"

She answered quickly. "Eggs, over easy, bacon and French toast. I love syrup and have a hard time deciding what I want to eat with it, pancakes, waffles or French toast." She leaned forward and lowered her voice. "Take a look at the couple next to us." She indicated the couple to their right. "He's having French toast and the bread looks homemade." The waitress arrived and Seth ordered for both of them, then he too sat back looking relaxed and content.

"Well, Katie, I think I have a better understanding of why you enjoy going to church."

"Oh? Why?"

"Extraordinary music, and an above average sermon. What they called the worship time was interesting."

"You know, the worship time is when I clear my mind as much as possible and think on God. Eventually my mind doesn't wander, and I communicate through song with Him." She pointed up and smiled. "Some Sundays I'm more successful than others, but I always come away feeling as if I've been in the presence of God." She put both hands around her coffee cup. "I love to look around and check out who's there. It's a feeling of community. I'm always touched when they invite people forward for prayer at the end of the service. It's an awesome thing to go to the Creator with our needs."

"Have you ever done that? I mean, gone up to the front for prayer? I'd think a person would feel conspicuous."

"Yes, I've been prayed for, and yes, it's a little intimidating."

Seth paused for a moment, then looked directly into her eyes. "What about your leg? Do you wonder why it hasn't been healed? Have you had it prayed for?" He dropped his gaze and ran his hand behind his neck. "Is that a bad question?"

"No, it's okay." She crossed her ankles and shifted on the bench. How should she answer? Her eyebrows puckered, and she hesitated a moment. "No one has asked me that before." Her voice became more quiet and vulnerable. "And yes, I've had my leg prayed for. I honestly think it's a miracle that I can walk as well as I do. At first the doctors thought I might lose it. Then, even though they saved it, they thought I'd never walk again. It's a miracle I'm alive and I'm thankful every day." She squirmed on the seat to get more comfortable. "My surgeon has talked to me about having another surgery. It's one of the things I'm praying about. Having more surgery doesn't rate high on my favorite things to do, but if I could walk without this cane, I'd love it." She looked at the cane and back at Seth.

"Is this a recent development?" He frowned. "Would it be soon?"

"I don't know how soon. Last Wednesday I had a CT scan. There's a new surgical technique, and it might be a possibility for me. I'm tempted, but there's always a risk. I need to be sure it's what I want to do."

The server brought their food. Katie leaned over and smelled her plate. "Yum. This smells great and looks even better." She gave him a sheepish grin. "I didn't eat this morning either."

Seth chuckled and reached across the table. He took her hand lightly in his. "Do you want to pray?"

"I'd love to." A warm glow filled her heart and she bowed her head. "Father, thank you for this good food and a friend to share it with. Bless our meal and our conversation. Amen."

"I like your prayers." He let go of her hand and picked up his fork. "Who's your surgeon? Is he with a private group?"

"His name is Dr. Hanson. He's with the Mayo Clinic but does quite a bit of consulting here. My first miracle was that he was actually in the emergency room the night of our accident. He'd been in town for a teaching seminar. When the doctors in the ER recognized the severity of my injuries, they asked if he'd be willing to scrub and consult. I've been told that he insisted my leg could be saved." She shivered. "One of the surgeons who was there during surgery visited me afterward and told me his call would have been to remove the leg. Needless to say, I'll be eternally grateful to Dr. Hanson for saving it."

"I can imagine."

"Please, let's not talk about my leg any more. How's your food?" Katie reached for the maple syrup as she spoke and poured more over her French toast before taking another bite.

Seth laughed out loud. "I see what you mean, you like a little French toast with your syrup."

"Yes, and this is real maple syrup! Oh, my. I'll definitely come back here." She took a big bite and syrup stuck to her lip. She licked it off.

They continued eating, and the conversation flowed easily. When they finished, Katie noticed people waiting by the door. "We should leave so someone else can have our booth."

As they left, a hand reached out and touched Seth's arm. "Hi, Seth."

He quickly caught Katie's arm and she stopped and turned. Sylvia was there with her friend Mary. Katie felt her face start to flush. She forced herself to be calm.

Seth introduced Katie to both of the women sitting in the booth. "Hello Sylvia, Mary."

Sylvia looked her up and down, and looked pointedly at her cane. "I think I've seen you before. One tends to remember someone with a handicap."

Katie felt Seth's hand tighten on her arm. She squeezed it against her side, silently telling him not to make a comment. She shifted the cane to her other hand, then slipped her hand into his. She smiled sweetly. "It was nice meeting you. Enjoy your breakfast." She looked at Seth. "Shall we go?" They turned and walked away.

Chapter 17

Neither one spoke as Seth drove the few blocks to Katie's home. She wished she hadn't created a scene in the restaurant. After he stopped in the driveway, she reached over and touched his arm. "I'm sorry if I made things difficult for you with Sylvia. I don't know what came over me, reaching for your hand like that."

He tapped his fingers on the steering wheel. "Well, don't be sorry. I've been trying to think of a way to let Sylvia know I'm not interested. Nothing had come to mind and her seeing us together should tell its own story."

She frowned and hunched her shoulders. "Why did you take her to the concert Thursday night if you were trying to break it off? That doesn't make sense to me. It would have made me feel horrible."

He turned sideways, put his arm along the back of the seat and looked at her. "*She* invited *me* to the concert. I picked her up, but she had the tickets." He touched her hair. "Katie, we met such a short time ago but something is happening between us. I know this sounds crazy, but it's the truth."

Katie took a deep breath and blew it out slowly. Tears were near the surface and she wanted to get out of the car before they fell. Without speaking, she reached for the door handle.

He quickly took hold of her arm. "Please. You can't just leave without saying anything. I know this is too soon, but I'd like to be given a chance to get to know you, and for you to get to know me. There's no one else in my life, and from what Anne says, there isn't anyone in yours. Can we take this a step at a time?" He moved his hand from her arm to the back of the seat again and sighed. "I feel like a bumbling teenager." He touched her shoulder. "Katie, tell me your thoughts."

She looked up and his face was blurry through the moisture in her eyes. He touched her cheek and her lips quirked up in a half smile. "I don't know what's going on. I admit you've been on my mind, and I know we have lots in common, but I'm frightened and confused. Please give me time. Too much has happened. I need to sort this all out."

"Can I call you? Do you want space for a few days? A few weeks? Please don't say a few weeks." He again touched her cheek and she turned her face into his hand as she looked at him.

"Give me a few days. Why don't you call on Wednesday. I need to catch my breath."

He came around to open her door with a big smile on his face. As she stepped out he took her hand and continued holding it while he shut the car door, then walked with her onto the porch. He leaned down and placed a light kiss on her brow. "Thanks for the best Sunday I've had in years. I have lots to think about, including this morning's sermon. Are you going to write to your mother?"

"Yes, even though I've talked to her several times this week."

"Have you mentioned me to her yet?" He looked like a little boy needing approval. Without waiting for her answer, he laughed and turned away. When he reached the car, he turned around and spoke loudly enough for her to hear. "I didn't hear your answer. Have you told her about me?"

"No. I didn't know there was anything to tell." She waved and went inside.

* * *

He backed out of the driveway, and turned toward the church instead of home. The service that morning had triggered something.

Exposed a hunger he didn't know he had. He wasn't sure if he liked that feeling, so he'd tackle it the way he tackled any business problem. Confront it head on. There were several cars in the lot so it looked like people were still there. Maybe it wasn't locked. He got out of the car, walked to the door and grabbed the handle. Good. Still open.

He made his way to the same pew he and Katie had sat in earlier, took off his coat, and sat down. Dust motes floated in the sun canting through the stained glass window. He breathed in the smell of cleaner and candle wax. Leaning back with closed eyes, he absorbed the peace, and could almost hear the echo of organ music.

Would it be okay for him to pray? Would God listen to someone who hadn't prayed in years? Was he being presumptuous? He searched for answers and wondered how to pray. He bent forward, put his elbows on his knees and his head in his hands.

"How do I do this God? I need help, but I'm not sure about asking You for it. Do You talk to people? Do I just stumble along and hope for the best? I guess you know Katie Nelson. I'm getting to know her and the better I know her, the more I like her. It's all a bit confusing and . . ."

A hand touched Seth's shoulder. "Sir, is there something I can help you with?"

He sat up and turned. Mike Schumann, the pastor he'd been introduced to after the morning service, was at his shoulder. Seth stood and moved into the aisle. "Hi, Pastor. I'm Seth Prentice. We met earlier. I took a chance the church doors would still be open. I came in to think about some things." He looked at his watch. "I'm sorry. It's gotten late. I can come back another time. It looks as if you haven't been home since the end of services."

"No, I haven't, but my wife is out of town this weekend and I'm not in a hurry. I wanted to get several things done before I head over to the parsonage next door. You're welcome to come along and I'll put the coffee on. Please, call me Mike." He smiled as he made the invitation and looked directly into Seth's eyes.

"What about lunch?" Seth asked. "I don't imagine you've eaten yet have you?" He pulled his coat on.

"No, but I'll make sandwiches for us if you're hungry too."

"I'm not, thanks. Katie and I went for breakfast, but coffee would be good. I'll take you up on your offer if you're sure you don't have something else you need to be doing." Maybe he could talk to Mike about Katie.

Seth followed as Mike moved toward the back of the sanctuary. "I'll lock the front door. I'm surprised the custodian hasn't done it." He opened the sanctuary doors and motioned for Seth to pass through them ahead of him. "We have some beautiful artwork and don't want vandals coming in and destroying things. Maybe he got tied up with something and hasn't left yet."

After locking the doors, they walked together through the halls to the side door. Mike pulled it closed and made sure it locked after them. "I wonder if I need to come back later and check all the doors."

Seth raised his face to the sun and breathed in the cold air as they crossed the parking lot to the parsonage, a beautiful manor house made of the same stone as the church. He looked up at the house, then over at the church. "How old is this complex?"

"It was built at the turn of the last century. For some time the congregation struggled, but we've had a steady increase in members. Now we're wondering if we'll need to build another campus. We've added another service on Sunday and also a Saturday evening service."

"You wouldn't leave this facility completely would you?"

"No, we'd build another church in the suburbs. We have a large number of people who drive in from the north. They'd be able to participate more easily in the weeknight activities if they didn't have so far to drive. This is all on the church council's agenda for future considerations."

They stopped and looked back at the church before entering the back door of the parsonage. "I thank God every day for this wonderful place to work." Mike took Seth's coat and hung it, along with his own, on a coat tree by the door.

The area was large enough to accommodate a bench to sit on while putting on shoes, but books and papers covered the bench, adding to the lived in look. Obviously this was the catchall area and led right into the large, welcoming kitchen.

Mike headed for the coffee maker. "Find a chair by the table." When he had the coffee going, he opened the refrigerator and looked over his shoulder. "Are you sure you won't have a sandwich? I'm pretty handy with the toaster and make a mean sandwich."

Seth laughed and patted his stomach. "No thanks."

When the coffee was done, Mike poured and carried the mugs to the table then opened the cookie jar on the counter and filled a plate with homemade, oatmeal-raisin cookies. These he set on the table and smiled. "If you can resist Emily's cookies, you're much more disciplined than I am." He put his napkin in his lap and asked Seth if he'd mind if he said a short prayer.

"No, of course not, go ahead." Seth closed his eyes and bowed his head. Another prayer. This was becoming a habit. He smiled to himself.

"For provisions which are always so bountiful Lord, I give you praise and thanks. For the opportunity to help one of your children Lord, I also give you praise and thanks. Guide my mind and tongue today to hear and say what you would have me hear and say. Amen."

He reached for his sandwich and took a bite. After he swallowed, he looked at Seth and grinned. "I was hungrier than I realized. Go ahead and tell me what's on your mind." He took another big bite.

"This starts and ends with Katie Nelson. I've only known her a week and two days, and she's on my mind constantly. I've never met a woman like her."

The pastor nodded in acknowledgement. "How did you meet?"

"We have a mutual friend, Anne Dunbar. Do you know her?"

"Anne comes to church sometimes with Katie. I know who she is, but don't know her personally."

"Well, I went with Anne to Katie's home uninvited a little over a week ago. She was gracious over an uninvited guest and that impressed me. As the evening progressed, I became even more impressed. Anne convinced her to play her guitar and sing for us."

Mike lifted his head in surprise. He wiped his mouth on his napkin. "As far as I know, Katie hasn't done any performing since the accident. I understood she hasn't even had her guitar out of its case since then."

"You're right, she hadn't. Friday was the first time she'd practiced in over three years. Have you ever heard her play?"

"No, but my wife has. Katie used to do volunteer workshops at our son's school."

Sandwich finished, he took a cookie. His cup was empty so he got up and poured for both of them before continuing. "Emily said she also sang at some of these workshops. Before the accident, Katie and John went to a different church. She only started coming here after she moved into the neighborhood. We've slowly been getting to know her. I was surprised this morning when I saw you together."

Seth chuckled ruefully. "She hadn't invited me. I just showed up, sat by her, and then took her to brunch. She didn't have a choice, unless she was willing to be rude. And of course, rude isn't Katie's style. We've seen quite a bit of each other this week. The more I see of her, the more I'm interested."

Mike sat back and folded his arms. "What kind of reaction are you getting from her? Is she happy to see you?"

"At first, especially last Sunday, she seemed apprehensive." He laughed and admitted irritation might have been a better word than apprehension.

"Katie is a believer. God is an important part of her life. How about you Seth?"

Seth shrugged to ease the tension in his shoulders. That was the question he'd been dreading. "I haven't spent much time thinking about God. In the service this morning, my emotions and mind were touched. The music moved me, both the organ prelude and what Katie called worship." He drank the last of his coffee and set the cup down. "She had told me about your sermons and now I understand what she meant."

Mike raised his eyebrows in question.

Seth moved his cup in a circle on the table and spoke more slowly. "She said that often your sermons are about what she's struggling with.

I mean, they address what she needs to hear. Today it seemed as if you spoke just to me." He looked up from his cup.

Mike spoke. "I'm always humbled when I hear that. I ask God to put His words into my mouth so each person will hear what God wants them to hear. We all have different needs. Somehow God manages to direct those words to each heart. At least for the ones who are listening." He crossed his ankle over his knee. "I know many people just come to church because they feel they should. I think the ones who come with honest hearts, hoping to hear from God, usually go away with their desire fulfilled."

Seth rested his elbows on the table and leaned forward. "I know nothing about worship. I know almost nothing about prayer and the Bible. I remember praying years ago when I had surgery on my vocal cords." He cleared his throat. "I wanted to be a professional musician, and after surgery my dream was gone. That's probably the last big thing I prayed for." He put his chin in his hands and went on. "I haven't been carrying a grudge you know. I figured since I hadn't prayed before, God didn't hear me."

Mike's voice was filled with compassion. "Oh, I think God heard you, Seth. But it's impossible for me to tell you why your prayer went unanswered. You might understand some day and then again, you might never know while here on earth. Do you have a Bible?"

"I think I have one around somewhere."

"I wonder what version you have. I suppose it's a KJV. Have you had it since you were a little boy?"

Seth nodded. "Yes. What's a KJV?"

Mike laughed and explained that KJV stood for the King James Version of the Bible. "There are many more modern translations, and they'd be much easier to read." He got up from the table, told Seth he'd be right back, and walked out of the room. He came back carrying a book in his hand and laid it on the table.

"This version is called *The Message,* and it's easy to understand because it's written in contemporary language. It's not broken up in verses so the reading isn't interrupted. It's more like reading a book.

It's not an easy read though." He laid his hand on top of it as he spoke. "This book will help you to be 'at home' in God's world and His Word." He refilled his mug and asked Seth if he'd like more.

"Yes, thanks." Seth turned the book over in his hands while Mike poured coffee. Did he really want to do this? It would be embarrassing if he found it boring. He flipped it open and riffled through the pages. "This will take some time to read. I'm curious, but isn't religious reading sort of tedious?" He closed it. "Well, I'm willing to give it a try. Where do I buy one of these?" He set it on the table.

Mike touched the Bible. "This copy's for you. I always have several on hand so I can give them away. It's fine for you to start at the beginning, but you might want to start with the book of John. In Genesis, the first book of the Bible, God is presented as speaking creation into being. In the book of John, Jesus is presented as speaking salvation into being. John is so clear about who Jesus is. Personally, I think it's a good place to start. The table of contents will tell you what page the book of John starts on."

"Thanks. I'll do my best to read it. I don't know how long it'll take me, but I'll start on it today when I get home."

"This isn't a book to plow through. It's a book to savor and read over and over. If you don't understand something, read it again and ask God to help you understand it."

Seth glanced at his watch and stood. He chuckled and pointed at the empty cookie plate. "Something sweet went well with our conversation."

The pastor walked him to the door and handed him his coat. Seth reached out to shake hands. "Thanks, Mike. Today has been an incredible experience. I have a lot to think about, and I'll read this." He held up *The Message* and reached for the door handle.

Mike patted his shoulder. "I enjoyed our time together. Please don't hesitate to call. You'll find my phone number and email address on a label in the front of the book. I'll be more than happy to talk to you about what you've read. I'll be praying for you too."

Being told he'd be prayed for made Seth start to sweat. He couldn't remember anyone saying that to him before. It couldn't hurt could it? He lifted his hand in farewell.

He sat in his car for a moment and looked at the church with unseeing eyes. What a day this had been. Should he stop at Katie's house and tell her about it? No, he needed time to process everything before talking to her. Two weeks ago he wouldn't have dreamed he'd be interested in going to church, let alone having a meeting with a pastor. He started the car and drove off.

Chapter 18

Glaring at the phone wouldn't make it ring. She hadn't heard from Seth since he dropped her off after brunch on Sunday. Well, this is what she'd asked for. Why had she told him not to call until Wednesday? It was already after seven thirty and he hadn't called, so he probably wouldn't. They had talked so often the week before and now three days without hearing a word felt like forever.

Her practice had gone well and she'd taken time to do some reading, but the evening stretched ahead of her, and all of a sudden she felt lonely. Anne hadn't called this week either. Maybe talking to her would stop her thinking about Seth. Katie picked up the phone and dialed.

"Hello."

"Hi, Anne. It's Katie. I've been thinking about you. Have you met with your new client yet? I'm talking about Dr. Browne."

"Yes, we had our first face to face meeting this morning. Why?"

"Well? Is he a grandfather?" Katie sat down on her bedroom loveseat and put her feet on the coffee table.

"No, as a matter of fact he's about the same age as Seth. Remember, I told you he's divorced and has a daughter?"

"Yes."

"She must be fairly young because I asked for an early appointment and he said he needed to take his daughter to school, so couldn't be here until after eight."

"What's he like? I mean, tall or short, thin or heavy, dark hair or light?" Katie heard Anne sigh and papers rustle. "Are you busy? Is this a bad time to call?"

"No, I'm not busy. I was just picking up the newspaper. And, what does it matter? What he looks like has nothing to do with whether or not I take him as a client."

Katie chuckled. "I know. Crazy isn't it, but I got a feeling when you mentioned his name the first time. Maybe he's someone you should get to know on a personal level. I can't tell you why the thought crossed my mind. So, indulge me, what does he look like?"

Anne moaned. "All right. He's a little taller than me. Weight? Average. His hair is medium brown. He wears glasses and is quiet but seems friendly. He's articulate and somewhat reserved. End of critique."

"Oh, come on. Tell me more. Did he dress nicely? Were his shoes polished?" She snuggled farther into the pillows on the loveseat and grinned.

"Oh brother! Yes, he dressed nicely. He wore a conservative suit, and his shoes were so shiny you could see yourself in them. At least I'm sure that would have been the case if I had looked. You are so funny! Just because you've found someone interesting, don't think I need someone new in my life."

"Are you talking about Seth?" She sat up straighter. "Don't be making something out of nothing, girlfriend."

"Nothing? Speaking of Seth, have you seen him this week?"

Katie settled in again. "Not since Sunday. I haven't told you about that have I?"

"No, what happened?"

"I had just sat down in the pew at church on Sunday morning and felt a tap on my shoulder. There stood Seth. After the service he took me to that new restaurant on Grand."

"Did you have pancakes with your syrup?"

Katie chuckled at her friend's question. "No, I had French toast with my syrup. We had a nice time. He's easy to talk to." Her voice became animated. "When we left, you'll never believe who we ran into. Sylvia and her friend, Mary."

"Oh, my. Did feathers fly?"

Katie made an inelegant noise. "No. She looked me up and down. *Then* told me she thought she'd seen me before. The cane made me memorable." She remembered the feeling of hurt that had stabbed her and pulled a pillow to her stomach to hug.

"I'm sure that didn't impress Seth."

"Well, you won't believe this, but I got a little hot under the collar. I switched my cane to the other hand and then took Seth's hand to walk out of the restaurant. I'm usually not sensitive, but she didn't intend to be nice, and I felt it. She actually used the word handicapped. Now I can see the humor in it."

"Did Seth say anything?"

"Not much. I guess she had invited him to the concert on Thursday, not the other way around. He didn't seem concerned that I'd ruined anything."

Katie didn't tell Anne about their whole conversation. She needed time to digest it and evaluate her own feelings. Everything was happening too fast. She changed the subject. "Ah—your meeting with Dr. Browne. What's his first name anyway?"

"His name is Joseph. I, of course, call him Dr. Browne."

"Well, did he impress you? Will this case take a long time? Will you need to spend a lot of time with him?" She tossed the pillow aside and sat straighter.

"As of right now, I only know he's a remarkable person, our meeting went well and depending on what happens as the case goes forward, I might need to see him often. Now listen to me, Katie. Are you listening? I do not get involved with my clients."

"All right. I hear you. Just keep me informed. Have you seen Kent this week?"

"No, we haven't seen each other, nor have we talked. I wonder if he's feeling some of the same things I am."

Katie could hear the quandary in Anne's voice and pressed on. "You need to talk to him. If he feels the same way you do, then you don't need to have guilty feelings about wanting to move on. How will you know if you avoid the issue?"

"You're right, but I need to think about it a bit more."

"I'll pray for you, Anne. That you do the right thing if this relationship isn't in God's plan for you."

"Are you sure God wants to be bothered with something as little as this?"

"What do you mean, little? This is your life we're talking about and, of course God wants to be bothered! Every part of our lives is important to Him"

"Now about . . ." They both spoke at once then Anne hopped in first. "Yes, about Seth."

Katie grinned and shook her head. "No, I was going to say, 'Now about Dr. Joseph Brown.' What's wrong with getting interested in one of your clients?"

"Katie, read my lips. Well, you can't over the phone, so listen up. He's a client. It's unethical, and I've just met him. He could have had five wives for all I know. I'm not interested. What has gotten into you anyway? You're worrying this like a dog with a bone. Cut it out!"

By the sound of Anne's voice, Katie could tell she'd reached her exasperation point, so chose to be prudent and back off. "You're right. I don't know what's gotten into me either. For some reason, when you first told me about him I had a feeling he might be the man who will be more interesting to you than your work. Forgive me?"

"Of course. Isn't life funny? I've known Seth for a long time and never even thought about introducing him to you. Now he's trying to get to know you and develop a relationship. Who would have thought this would happen?"

"Certainly not me, or I, or whatever." Katie paused then went on. "I haven't talked to him since he dropped me off on Sunday."

"Oh my, three whole days. He's slipping."

"Actually, I told him he shouldn't call till today. I needed time. I'm surprised how often I think about things we've talked about. He's well read and current on world, national, and state issues. I like it that he takes time to be informed. It'll please my mother." Katie glanced over at a picture of her parents on one of the bookshelves and smiled at it.

"Speaking of your mother, have you told her about Seth?"

Katie sighed and reached up to twist her earring. "No. He asked me the same thing. I'll tell my mother when there's something to tell."

"I think you should tell her now. She'll be hurt if you don't. Besides, she's wise and might have answers to some of your questions."

"I know you're right, but I feel everything is still so new and fragile. What do I tell her? I've only just met him." Uncertainty gripped her.

"At least tell her you have a new friend you met through me. Tell her he's working with you on music for the benefit. She does know you're playing for it doesn't she?"

"Yes, I've told her. I might have mentioned Seth's name too. I'll think about it and try to find a way to talk about him without getting her hopes up. She worries about me and I know someone new in my life would make her very happy. Oh, Anne. Verbalizing it makes my heart jump. I wish I knew my own feelings better."

"Let your heart take you where it will. We know how short life is, don't we?"

Katie got a lump in her throat and she had to swallow before she said any more. "Do you sometimes wonder if the extra special people are taken when they're still young?" Katie heard Anne start to speak and went right on. "No, I won't go there. I'm not going to get caught up in the 'whys' again. I've done plenty of asking to last me a lifetime."

They talked a little longer then said their good-byes. Katie pulled a pillow back into her arms and rested her chin on it in thought. Life was getting more exciting. Was she ready for exciting? A change maybe, but not such a fast one. Her phone rang. Was this Seth? She tossed aside the pillow and grabbed it.

"Hello, this is Katie."

"Hi, honey." It was her mother's gentle voice she heard, not Seth's baritone. Her heart slowed to its normal beat. "Is anything new happening in the big city?"

"Hi, Mom. Anne and I were just talking about you."

"Oh? How is she? Still as busy as ever?"

She shoved aside her disappointment at not hearing Seth's voice and leaned back. "You know my friend. She's driven. Her father's turning more and more of the firm over to her. She's got a heavy caseload too. Speaking of her caseload, she has a new client and I have a feeling about him."

"What do you mean by a feeling?"

Katie pulled a cozy throw over her legs, tucked her feet in and got comfortable. If Seth called, she'd hear the beep of call waiting. "I suppose I shouldn't mention him to you, because she's been rather emphatic about it, but Mom, I think she was destined to meet him."

"Oh, no. Poor Anne. Once you get your teeth into something you don't let it go."

Katie laughed. "I say the same thing about Anne all the time."

"What makes you think they were destined to meet, dear?"

"That's the weird part. I know nothing about him and yet this feeling won't go away. Maybe it's because I've been praying she'll meet someone special. I'll have to wait and see. What's up with you?"

Her mother chuckled. "I suppose you could say I had a feeling about you too. Is something going on I that should know about?"

Katie gasped, then hoped her mother hadn't heard it. "Did I mention a man named Seth to you?"

"Yes, the musician Anne brought over one evening. Is there more? He's not just a friend of Anne's?"

"Yes, he's her friend, but I've seen him several times since then." Her words came in a rush. "He's called, we've been out to brunch the last two Sundays, and I ran into him at Barnes & Noble last week. I think that's about it. Oh yes, he came to church on Sunday and sat by me." Her breath came out in a whoosh.

"Hold it right there. Do you mean to tell me all this has been going on, and I'm just finding out about it? And furthermore, I had to call you to hear it? Should I be excited or offended?"

Katie wished she could see her mother's face. "I didn't have anything to tell you. I don't know my own feelings. Of course I was going to talk to you about him. Soon." Her throat tightened up and she swallowed. "I haven't even noticed other men or wanted to. Now all of a sudden this good-looking, dynamic man is making *sure* I notice him. I'm confused, scared, and overwhelmed."

Her mother's voice softened with compassion. "Oh, my dear, I wish I were there with you. Does he go to your church? You said he sat with you on Sunday."

"No, he doesn't go to my church. The week before he waited for me to come out. This week he came in and sat with me. Last Wednesday I invited him for dinner because he'd agreed to help me choose music for the benefit."

"And? Tell me more. How old is he?"

"How old? I don't know. Mid-forties. And to answer your unspoken question, he's never been married, and I don't know why. You can ask him when the two of you meet if you like." Katie could imagine the look of surprise on her mother's face when she heard they'd be meeting.

"I'm meeting him? When?"

"I thought you might like to come to town for the benefit. I can get you a ticket." Her mother's presence would give her courage. "I'd love for you to be there. I could use your support. Then I'd know there'd be one person in the audience who thought I was good." She giggled.

Katie heard the smile in her mother's voice as she agreed to come and she assured Katie everyone would love her. They chatted a few more minutes and said goodnight.

Katie spent the rest of the evening feeling restless and couldn't settle to anything. She tried reading and couldn't concentrate. Didn't want to practice and television held no appeal. She glanced at the clock for the sixth time. Why didn't he call? Didn't she say he could call on

Wednesday? She sighed, turned on the news and got ready for bed while she watched it. No waiting by the phone like a teenager for her.

The weather for the rest of the week didn't look good. It had started snowing and the forecaster predicted six to eight inches. She grabbed her robe and came out of her closet to watch.

"If the snow continues throughout the night, our morning commute will be slow and go. Flights have already been delayed at the airport and we predict cancellations so keep tuned to our station for further updates." The rest repeated the six o'clock news and she tuned it out while she finished getting ready for bed.

At ten forty she turned off the television and lights. Seth wouldn't call this late. She kicked off her slippers and sat on the edge of the bed in the darkness. Had she discouraged him too much and now he'd lost interest? Disappointment overwhelmed her as she lay down and pulled up the duvet.

Her mind wouldn't settle down. She turned on the light again and reached for her Bible. It would have a calming effect. Before she even opened it, the phone rang. Her heart jumped and she grabbed it. "Hello?"

"Hi, Katie. I hope this isn't too late."

Seth! She placed her hand over her heart. "No. I've just gone to bed."

"Good. I've wanted to call all day. I've been in L.A. since Monday and our meetings today went on and on. I barely got to the airport on time and our flight arrived here late. I wanted to call yesterday, but you asked me to wait until today. I was so frustrated when it got later and later. I even rode to the airport with a colleague so couldn't call from the cab."

Katie smiled to herself. Was he babbling? Was he nervous? "Seth, it's fine. Is it crazy at the airport? The news said we're getting six to eight inches of snow."

"I'd say we have several inches already and it's not letting up. How has your week been?" His voice slowed and lowered. "You've gotten under my skin, Katie."

"I've thought about you."

"And?"

She took a calming breath. "I'm not ready to rush into anything, but I'm willing to spend more time with you. I mentioned you to my mother."

"What did she say? Did you tell her I'm Farm Boy or Prince Humperdinck?"

Katie burst into laughter. "You've read *The Princess Bride* too?"

"I didn't read the book, I saw the movie. More than once too. Obviously you read the book."

"Yes, and I said I'd never see the movie. No way could it be as good as the book. I didn't compare you to Farm Boy, but Mother might have gotten the idea I think you're special." Oh, no. She'd told him more than she intended.

"Okay, I can live with that. Can I see you soon? Are you busy tomorrow night?"

"Hmm . . . Thursday. How about Friday instead? I haven't done anything fun on a Friday night for a long time. If it's okay with you, I'd enjoy doing something simple like going to a movie. Going to movies hasn't been a big item on my agenda. Going alone isn't much fun. What do you think?"

"Friday's good. Tomorrow is sooner, but I'll manage to wait until Friday. How does pizza before the movie sound?

"Pizza? Perfect. But just remember, I won't eat much because I love popcorn at the movies. I'm going to be an expensive date. Can you afford it, or do we need to go Dutch?"

"I can always get a second job. You'd be worth it." He laughed as they said their good-byes and hung up.

Katie turned her light out. He'd called. She snuggled under the covers and her heart finally slowed. So much for NOT acting like a lovesick teenager.

Chapter 19

The snow still fell on Thursday morning when Katie pulled up her shades. She sat on the window seat and peered at the winter wonderland. It was a good thing Seth had flown home last night. It would be crazy at the airport today.

Katie didn't leave home all day. In the morning, she sorted clothes in her closet to give away and did several other little odd jobs she'd wanted to get done. After lunch, she settled down to several hours of practicing. While working on some finger drills, she wove a tune into the arpeggios and scales. She played it again and watched her fingers pick out the melody. She liked what she heard and stopped to get staff paper to write it down. This was the first time she'd created her own music since John and J. J. died. So many firsts, and no one to share them with.

She set her guitar down and bent her head into her hands. She gave herself up to grief and sobbed. John and J. J. were gone forever. Did she have a right to happiness with someone else? Were her tears a mixture of sorrow and guilt? Slowly her sobs subsided. She cleaned her face with a tissue and raised her face toward Heaven.

God? It's me again. I'm thankful to be alive. Really. I am. Please give me wisdom to make good choices. You know what's in store for me and what I need.

For several minutes she sat listening to the quiet. The loneliness lifted and a gentle peace filled her heart. She picked up her pencil and finished transcribing the notes onto paper. Words would come in time.

Sometimes she'd set a poem to music or a scripture verse would cry out for music.

The room was cool, and she shivered. A pot of tea would warm her up. She picked up her cane and headed for the kitchen. She turned on the stove and then the television. A news bar ran across the bottom of a late afternoon program saying five more inches of snow had fallen, and the roads and highways were backed up with rush hour traffic. They advised everyone who could to stay home. The snow emergency crews were out but travel was difficult. Thank goodness she didn't need to go out.

The five o'clock news had just started when the doorbell rang. She picked up her cane. Who could possibly be at her door? She hurried down the hall. It must be her downstairs neighbor. She opened the door and there stood Seth, leaning with his hand resting on the doorjamb.

Katie's heart raced into overtime, and she covered it with her hand. "What in the world are you doing here? You're covered with snow. Did you have and accident? What happened?"

He straightened and laughed. "No, no. Everything's fine. I had a meeting not far from here and when it finished, I thought I'd see if you'd take pity on a lonesome guy. I'm hungry. What do you say? Get your coat and let's go. My car tracks well in snow."

"Seth, are you nuts? I've been watching the news. There are cars stuck in drifts and in the ditch everywhere. There's a travel advisory and it's a mess out there." She couldn't help laughing as she shook her head and backed up. "Oh, come on in."

He brushed off his coat before entering. "Don't you want to have an adventure? It's pretty crazy." He smiled down at her.

The teakettle started whistling and Katie turned quickly. Even though she had her cane, her leg buckled. He reached out, grabbed her and pulled her close.

She wanted to stay in the circle of his arms but smiled and pulled gently away. "Thanks. I know better than to turn swiftly, but the whistle's so loud I always rush to get it. Take your coat off so it'll dry and come into the kitchen when you're ready." She walked away.

When he came into the kitchen, she looked up from preparing tea. "Where was your meeting?"

"I met with your pastor this afternoon."

She raised her eyebrows. "I didn't know you knew him. In fact, I got the impression you hadn't met him before I introduced you to each other last Sunday." She turned around and reached for mugs.

He took a big breath. "You're right. I hadn't. After I dropped you off last Sunday, I went back to the church. I thought I'd just sit there and think for awhile. Sort things out. Pastor Mike was still there."

"So you talked?"

He nodded. "His wife was out of town, and he invited me over to the parsonage. I took him up on his offer. We talked for quite awhile."

Katie leaned against the counter with crossed arms as she looked at him. His hair glistened from the melting snow and a drop of water ran down his cheek. He wiped it away. She'd almost reached up and done it. To cover her confusion, she spoke quickly. "I'd choose church as a place to think, but I'm kind of surprised you did." She winced. "Sorry. I didn't mean that to sound negative."

He smiled crookedly. "It's okay. Church is so important to you, I thought it would be a good place to start." He shrugged. "I don't know, it seemed a good idea at the time, and it turned out I was right."

This sounded genuine. "You mean, meeting Pastor Mike and having a talk with him answered some of your questions? Why'd you meet with him again today?"

"He gave me a Bible last Sunday so I took it along to Los Angeles. I've been trying to read it. I had some questions and he'd told me to call if I wanted to talk. So I did."

Katie turned and placed everything on a tray. As she started to lift it, he came to her side, took it out of her hands and carried it to the table. They sat across from each other and Seth pointed to the shortbread. "Do you think cookies are a good idea before dinner?"

She reached for one and smiled. "We need something to sustain us while we have this discussion. I have chicken tortellini soup in the refrigerator. You can have some later." She sat back and met the intent look in his blue eyes. "Did Pastor Mike answer your questions?"

"Yes, and we talked a little about you." He looked down and shifted in his chair. "I told him I'm interested in getting to know you better."

Katie gasped and touched her chest. If her heart didn't quit jumping around, she'd soon have a heart attack. "And?"

"He gripped his mug in both hands and looked into her eyes again. "He said you wouldn't be interested in a relationship with someone who didn't know God intimately."

She reached out and touched his arm. "Knowing God intimately takes time and desire. It doesn't happen just because you think I'd like it."

"I know. But each of us needs a starting point, don't we? I've never known anyone like you. I find it—the God part—appealing."

Katie struggled to swallow a bite of shortbread around the lump in her throat. His vulnerability touched her heart. "I'm glad. I don't know what I'd do without God in my life." She pushed her chair back. "Let's move to more comfortable chairs."

They walked to the wing-backed chairs and Katie asked him to start the fire. "I think the remote is on the mantle." She sat down and watched him look at the pictures of John and J. J. before picking up the remote. She'd always display them somewhere in her home. They wouldn't take anything away from a new relationship would they?

She shook herself free of her thoughts. "Tell me what you read in the Bible."

"Mike told me it might be a good idea to start with the book of John. So I did. I need to read it again though." He leaned his head back and watched the flames.

They talked about what he had understood and what didn't make sense. The conversation slowed and they sat in silence for several minutes. Katie couldn't believe how comfortable she was sitting here with him. Finally she asked if he'd like some soup. When he started to get up, she told him to relax. She picked up her cane and touched his shoulder.

"This won't take long. There's the paper if you want to read it." She pointed to the end table and walked to the kitchen.

* * *

He grabbed the paper and returned to his chair. How many women of his acquaintance would be this comfortable with someone just dropping in? She sure was easy to be with. Did she feel the same about him?

When they stood close he could hardly restrain himself from taking her into his arms. Did she have any idea how much her casual touches affected him? When she put her hand on his arm he'd feel the warmth left from her touch after she removed it.

She came in from the kitchen. He started to rise but she motioned for him to remain seated. "The soup's on. It's cozy in here but sure looks terrible outside." She glanced toward the windows. "This makes me nervous, Seth. Are you sure you should stay and eat?"

"Don't worry. I've driven in every weather condition you can imagine, including a hurricane on St. Thomas. I love a driving challenge. I won't stay long after we eat, unless you invite me to stay over." Oh, no. He cringed inside. Why had he said that?

Katie looked at him without smiling.

He held up both hands. "It was a joke. A really stupid one. I'm sorry."

She smiled lopsidedly. "It's okay. It's forgotten." She went back to the kitchen and he picked up the paper again. He couldn't concentrate so folded it and watched the fire.

"Seth?" Her voice came from the kitchen.

"Yes?"

"We're going to eat in here."

"Coming." Seth smiled, set the paper aside and went to the kitchen. Candles were lit and steaming bowls of soup, along with hot rolls and butter sat waiting for them. The domestic scene welcomed him. What was happening? He used to flee from this type of situation. Now he felt comfortable and wanted to be here.

Katie finished pouring water and set the pitcher down. "This is simple but I have more in the kettle. I love comfort food on a cold evening. It's fun to be sharing it with you tonight."

He pulled out her chair. When he leaned down to push it in, the smell of her hair filled his nostrils. Longing coursed through him, but he resisted touching her and sat at the place set for him.

She put the napkin in her lap and reached across the table for his hand. He took hers, and she bowed her head and prayed. His mind was on the feel of her hand, and he didn't realize she'd said amen until she tugged her hand out of his. He looked up. "Nice."

She smiled, picked up her spoon and started eating, so he did the same.

After several bites he stopped. "Did you make this?"

She nodded.

"I can see why you enjoy soup. This is wonderful. Did you make the rolls? They taste homemade too."

She shook her head and swallowed. "No, but I'm glad you like them."

Like them? Yes, he liked them. He liked everything about this woman. The evening was going by way too fast.

It seemed as if only a few minutes had passed when she looked at the clock.

"Your car will be buried under a foot of snow if you don't leave now. I've enjoyed this so much, but humor me. Knowing a friend is driving in bad weather makes me nervous. Please, I don't want you to have an accident."

Seth stood and reached for their plates. Helping her clean up would give him a few more minutes with her.

She put her hand on his arm. "No, Seth. I'll do this after you leave."

He gave up and followed her down the hall. At the coat closet she took his scarf and topcoat down while he slipped his shoes on. She held his coat and he turned and put his arms into the sleeves. She pulled it up and smoothed the fabric across his shoulders with her hands.

He shuddered at her touch and turned around. His hands framed her face, and he bent down and kissed her. Her lips were warm and soft against his. The kiss lasted only a moment, and he straightened. He moved his hands to her shoulders.

Katie looked bewildered, and she bit her bottom lip. Tears sprang to her eyes, and he gathered her into his arms. She put her head on his chest and held on while the tears flowed.

His soothing hand moved up and down her back while she cried. "Katie, I'm sorry. So sorry."

She shook her head and didn't say anything, just continued to cry. Eventually she pulled back.

He looked at her tear-stained face, then turned around. "Just a minute." He walked quickly to the bathroom and came back carrying tissues.

She took them with a watery smile. "Thanks. I don't know what came over me." She took a big breath and let it out slowly.

"I'm sorry. The kiss—it just happened." He pulled her into his arms again and laid his cheek against her hair. "I've wanted to kiss you almost from the first night we met. There's something in the air whenever I'm near you. I can't explain it."

She moved slightly away and looked up. "I'm not ready for that something yet. Everything's happening at once, and I'm on overload."

Seth nodded and cupped her cheek with his hand. "I understand. Really I do. I'll try to be patient." He opened the front door and walked to the elevator. He turned and smiled. The elevator door opened and he stepped in without saying more. Oh, he had lots more to say but now wasn't the right time.

Framed in the doorway, Katie raised her hand in a slight wave. "I'm glad you came. Drive safely and please call when you get home or I'll worry."

He nodded while the door slid shut.

* * *

She closed her door, walked to the studio windows, and looked down at the driveway. Snow flew every which way as he brushed it off his car. After he finished, he tossed the brush into the back seat and looked up. When he saw her standing there, he smiled and raised his hand in a wave. She waved back. He slid in and drove away.

Katie stood at the window long after his taillights disappeared. She put her fingers to her lips. At the thought of his kiss, a warmth coursed through her. Where was this going? The fire was still burning in the living room, so she walked down the hall and sat in the chair he'd occupied earlier. She leaned back and took a deep breath. His scent lingered in the fabric of the chair. Good grief. She was becoming obsessed with him.

She jumped up. Cleaning the kitchen would bring her down to earth. She loaded the dishwasher and squirted a generous amount of dish soap into the sink. The soup pot got a good scrubbing.

The phone rang as she finished wiping down the counters. She looked at the caller I.D. and smiled. "Hi."

"Hi, yourself. I'm checking in just as you asked. Boy is it crazy out there! I think every nutty driver is out tonight."

She heard a smile in his voice. "I'm glad you're home. Now I can relax and enjoy the fire."

"Thanks for a special evening. I'll see you tomorrow."

The husky tone of his voice sent a sensation of warmth through her. "I enjoyed our evening too. Goodnight, Seth."

"Night, Katie."

She turned out the kitchen light. Her leg ached and she limped slowly into the living room. Before sitting, she checked the CDs in the sound system. Oh, good. James Galway fit her mood to perfection. She pressed the play button and curled up in the chair.

What an amazing evening. She'd seen a whole new side of him. Seth had actually spent an afternoon with her pastor. If this was for real, he wasn't the same man-about-town who'd been dating Sylvia. Music surrounded her, the fire warmed her, and God's peace settled into her heart as the snow continued to fall outside. She watched the flames. She'd see him tomorrow.

Chapter 20

When Katie opened her eyes Friday morning, she looked toward the window. She hadn't pulled the shades last night and could see the snow piled high on the outside ledge. She put on her robe and knelt on the window seat to peer into the backyard. White drifts covered the ground, and snow clung to the evergreens and oak branches. All was quiet except for the distant hum of snowplows. Standing, she picked up her cane and headed to the kitchen where she put on the coffee and television.

Schools were closed. Over the last two days, they'd gotten a total of fourteen inches, the biggest snowfall of the season. The forecasters said it wouldn't last long. Warmer weather was headed their way.

J. J. would have been ecstatic to get a snow day. He'd have pestered her until she gave him permission to get his cross-country skis out. John would have tried to find time to go with him too.

They'd lived next to a nature preserve and loved the walking paths. Those same paths were groomed into ski trails during the winter. Katie had gone with John and J. J. occasionally, but when they'd wanted to ski seriously, they hadn't invited her because she had trouble keeping up.

Now she couldn't ski even if she wanted to. She wondered if Seth skied. She shook her head in exasperation. He never seemed very far from her thoughts.

While the coffee brewed, she made breakfast. Her street hadn't been plowed yet so she couldn't go anywhere and that suited her just fine. She'd start the fire and get cozy with a book as soon as she'd practiced.

After breakfast she moved to her studio. The score she'd written the day before sat on her music stand. She played it through and thought about Psalm 92, which she'd read for her morning devotional. She hummed the melody, then put her translation of the Psalm to the music.

> "I love to say 'Thank You' to you Lord,
> I love to sing praises to Your name.
> You have done so much for me,
> I sing to You for joy.
> Thank you for Your kindness in the morning,
> Thank you for Your faithfulness in the evening.
> I love to say 'Thank You' to you Lord,
> I love to sing praises to Your name."

The words fit the melody perfectly and she sang it several times, then picked up the page and penciled in the words. She sang it once more and wanted to share it with someone, so called her mother.

"Hello." Katie could picture her mother reading the paper while curled up in her oversized chair.

"Mother, I have a song I want you to hear. Just listen." Before her mother could say anything, Katie put her phone on speaker, set it on her desk and started to sing.

"Well, what do you think?" Katie smiled while she waited for her mother's answer.

"I think it's beautiful, Dear. Where did you hear it?"

"Yesterday, while I practiced, the melody came to me, so I wrote it down. This morning I played it and remembered the words from Psalms 92. With a little editing, the words fit the melody perfectly." Her fingers picked out the melody while she talked. "I'm so happy that I had to call and sing it to you. I know this is just a little worship chorus, but, Mom, I haven't lost everything." Her eyes filled with happy tears and she blinked them away.

"Oh, Katie. I'm delighted. Remember to play it again when I come in two weeks."

"You remind *me,* Mom. I'm glad you'll be here." She took the phone off speaker and put it to her ear.

"I wouldn't miss it for the world. Has Seth said he'll sing with you for sure?"

"I think he's committed. Our voices blended so nicely it gave me goose bumps. I hope he felt the same way. Well, maybe not the goose bumps, but our blend seemed to surprise and please him. I think he's been starved for singing."

"What do you mean?"

"Well, as far as I can tell, he hasn't done much with his voice. Not being able to sing has wounded him. He's very talented."

"Is he also kind and good looking?"

Katie heard a smile in her mother's voice and chuckled. "Trust you to ask if he's kind. Remember what you said to me each morning when I left for school?"

"Yes. Be kind. I couldn't stand it when someone hurt you and I wanted you to be kind to your friends. You know, I think my mother used to say that too. Well, does he seem kind?"

Katie wrinkled her brow and shrugged. "I don't know." An image of him comforting her last night flashed through her mind. He'd seemed genuinely sorry to have caused her pain. That hadn't been manipulative had it? "I haven't heard him speak harshly about anyone. I've only known him for two weeks so it's a little early to say, but my guess is he's kind. He sounds warm and gentle when speaking about his family, which is important."

"What about the good looking part?"

Katie smiled. "You might say that. I love the way he dresses. He wears Gucci shoes and they always have a high polish. He also has very short fingernails." She heard her mother's quiet laughter. "Are you remembering one of my high school boyfriends and his extra long little fingernail?"

"Oh, my. That's exactly what I thought of when you said short nails."

Katie ran a hand through her hair. How much should she say? She threw caution to the wind. "I think Seth would pass all of your tests." She held her breath while waiting for her mother's reply.

"Oh?"

That's all? She wasn't going to say any more? This was her mother for goodness sake.

Her mother interrupted Katie's thoughts. "Oops, I need to run. It's my day to deliver Meals on Wheels. It's a good thing we didn't get the huge amount of snow you got or we'd have some hungry people today. Have a good day. I love you."

"I love you too, Mom. We'll talk soon." Katie sat thinking about the conversation with her mother after they hung up. Were things moving too fast with Seth? He dominated her thoughts and conversations. She needed to get her emotions under control and watch his character in action before getting too entangled. Her fingers plucked at the strings of the guitar, and she watched them as they picked out the melody she'd just played for her mother. She bit her lip and wished she didn't feel so unsure of herself.

The phone rang and she flicked her fingers across the strings and picked it up. "Hello?"

Seth's voice brought a rush of happiness. "I'm calling to find out what movie you'd like to see. Here, let me read them." He read several descriptions. "Do any of these sound good to you?"

"I saw an ad for the action one on TV. It sounds entertaining. What time does it start?"

"Seven forty, so we have time to go out for dinner. What do you want to eat?"

She frowned. "Weren't we going to have pizza?"

"Yes, but you could have changed your mind."

"Not likely. I love pizza." Was she really going on a date? Pizza no less?

"There is a little bistro which serves wonderful pizza not far from the theater. Should we go there?"

Katie heard someone say Seth's name in the background, and he asked if she'd hold a moment. He didn't put her on hold so she could hear part of the conversation. A woman spoke rapidly, and then Katie heard him tell her to wait just a moment.

"Katie, my brother's on the phone and I need to talk to him. I'll pick you up at a little after five."

"Okay. See you then." What was that all about? She'd find out when she saw him tonight.

Katie practiced another hour and then wandered into the living room. The travel book she'd purchased at Barnes & Noble sat on the coffee table. She turned on the fireplace and curled up on the couch. She opened her book to the table of contents. Maybe going to a spa in Germany would be a fun thing to do with her mother. Lots of old convents there had been turned into spas and retreat centers. Katie knew Germany fairly well and would be delighted to go back.

The phone rang again. She'd brought it with her into the living room and she absentmindedly reached for it.

"Hello."

"Katie, it's Seth. I'm on my way to the airport. My father is being flown to Miami from St. Thomas because he has suffered some kind of heart distress. I don't know all the details. I'll call you when I get to Miami and know more. I'm sorry about tonight, but don't find someone to take my place!"

"As if I could. Oh, Seth. I'm sorry about your father. Please let me know what has happened. I'll be praying for him and all of you."

"Thanks, Katie. I knew you'd say that. Dad has been so healthy. I can't imagine how this is affecting my mother. He has always seemed indestructible."

"What about your brother and sister? Will they be there too?"

"As far as I know, we're all on the same flight. When Peter called me, he'd already talked to Sarah so she could arrange for an after-school sitter. Fortunately it's Friday and her husband, Chris, will be available for the children over the weekend. If Dad gets stable and everything looks good, I'll be home the first part of next week. Can we save the movie and pizza for next weekend?"

"Of course. Travel safely." She heard him tell the driver to stop at door four.

"I'm at the airport. I'll talk to you tomorrow. Do you have my cell phone number?"

"Yes, it's on the caller I.D. and I have it written here somewhere."

"Okay. Mm—Katie?"

"Yes?"

"I'll miss you."

"Bye, Seth." She hung up and closed her eyes. She hadn't told him she'd miss him too, but she would. Painful disappointment washed over her at the thought of their cancelled date. She opened her eyes and put her fingers to her lips. How could she be thinking like this when his father's life may be in danger? She prayed. "Please God. May his father be okay. Be with his mother and give her strength."

She stood, picked up her cane, and walked to the windows. The rest of her day seemed kind of bleak. Maybe she'd go out and rent a move and buy a pizza. She needed several things at the grocery store too. Grocery shopping didn't compare with pizza and a movie with Seth, but at least she wouldn't be staying inside and alone all day.

She changed her shoes for non-skid boots, picked up her purse and cane, and grabbed her coat. The sun reflecting off the snow as she drove out of the garage almost blinded her. She slipped on her sunglasses and smiled. Sunshine. It always lifted her spirits.

The grocery store she frequented was located in a fairly large mall so many things could get done with one stop. She took her time and eventually headed toward home with only the pizza left on her list. A take-and-bake place was on her route home so she went there.

The evening was lonesome, and Katie had trouble concentrating on the movie she'd chosen. Seth and his family in Miami kept invading her mind. He hadn't called by the time she went to bed after midnight. Had something terrible happened? Her heart felt heavy.

Chapter 21

What was happening in Florida? Was Seth's father still alive? Should she call his cell phone? No, she'd wait for him to call. She busied herself by straightening her bedroom. Finally as she poured her second cup of coffee, the phone rang. She almost spilled her mug as she grabbed the phone. "Hello?"

"I'm sorry I didn't call last night, Katie. It was too late by the time Dad got out of surgery."

Oh, good. His dad was still alive. Relief at hearing Seth's voice filled her and she sat down by the table. "Tell me what happened and what's been done." She gripped her coffee mug.

"Mother said Dad was at the beach and she decided to bring him an afternoon snack. She walked down the path and called his name. He looked up, smiled and waved, and then collapsed. She dropped everything and ran. When she got to him he was in pain, but he told her to go for help. Fortunately the caretaker and his son were at the house."

He sounded so weary and far away. "Oh, Seth."

"By the time they got Dad up to the house, the paramedics had arrived. Dad remained conscious the whole time. They took him to the hospital and the doctor there recommended they charter a plane and fly him to Miami as soon as possible."

"Didn't that take a lot of time?"

"There's an airfield just minutes from the hospital, and a plane was ready for immediate takeoff. The hospital takes care of emergencies like this all the time because of all the tourists. Anyway, two paramedics went along, plus my mother. She held up until she saw us."

"Oh, dear. She must have been so frightened." Katie wanted to reach out and touch him.

"I know how I felt on the flight down here. I'm sure it was much worse for her. They did tests immediately when he got here, and he needed bypass surgery so he went right into the O.R. Thankfully, it doesn't look like there's much damage to the heart."

"What do the doctors say now?"

"He came through surgery very well. I don't know how long he'll be in the hospital. I walked outside to call you because I can't use my cell phone in this area of the hospital."

"I've been praying for your father and all of you. I remember the anxiety we went through when my dad got sick." She stood and went to the kitchen window. The white world beyond the glass looked bleak and cold, like she'd felt at her father's diagnosis. His voice brought her back to the present.

"What did your dad die from, Katie? I don't think you ever said."

Why had she brought up her father? This was about Seth's dad, not hers. "He had a fast-growing type of cancer, and by the time they found it, nothing could be done. He only lived for four months after diagnosis. I'm glad you don't have such horrible news." The expression on her mother's face when she was told the news flashed through Katie's mind. Sadness couldn't describe the heartbreak in that look. He wouldn't have to go through that.

"So am I. We're so thankful the doctor on the island chose to send him here. Miami has a wonderful heart hospital, and his surgeon is one of their best." He paused and she could hear the wind whistling into the phone.

"We're going to check into a hotel near here. By then we should know more. The doctor told us Dad wouldn't be awake for several hours. Mother wants to stay with him, so we'll come back after we've had a short rest."

"I'd want to do the same. This is such good news. Thanks for calling."

His voice softened and became intimate. "I counted on your prayers, Katie. I'll call later. Bye."

He disconnected before she'd had a chance to say goodbye. Maybe that was a good thing. She might have said more to him than she intended. How could she miss him when they'd only known each other for two weeks? Florida seemed far away. She set the phone back in its cradle. Why did she feel like crying? She told herself to get over it.

She was too restless to practice. A walk would give her some energy and the fresh air would help clear the cobwebs from her mind. Snuggly boots and a down jacket would keep her warm.

As Katie walked out the door, Anne's car pulled into the driveway and she rolled down the window. "Where are you off to?"

Her spirits lifted as she walked toward the car. "I'm going for a walk. I need sunshine and I'm headed to the shops on Grand. Want to come along?" She smiled. "What are you doing here anyway?"

"I had some books to return to the library so I thought I'd drop in and see if you wanted to go for coffee or something. Hop in and we'll find a place that isn't too busy."

Katie put her hands in her jacket pockets and shook her head. "Why don't you leave your car right there and walk with me? I need a little exercise. Are you dressed for a walk in the cold?"

Anne grabbed her purse and got out of the car. Her outfit was almost identical to Katie's. Jeans, boots, and a down jacket. "I'd love to walk. Especially in this neighborhood. Let's go."

They walked south to Grand and looked in the windows till they got to one of their favorite stores. Anne found a red cashmere scarf on sale she couldn't resist. Katie replaced a pair of black leather gloves she'd lost. They wandered in and out of several more stores. Katie stopped at the window of a pottery shop. "Look at the glaze on this pitcher. It's the same yellow that I have in my kitchen."

"Should we go in? Do you want to buy it?" Anne stomped her feet. "I'm getting kind of cold. We can go in and warm up and look around."

Katie had begun to feel the strain in her leg and needed to sit down. "No, let's go to the French Café in the middle of the next block. I love their coffee and the pastries are to die for." They walked into the café and warm air, filled with the aroma of fresh-baked bread, surrounded them. Katie breathed deeply. "What's better than the smell of bread baking?"

Anne agreed as they followed the hostess to their booth. After giving their orders she turned to Katie. "How has your week been?"

Katie gave a dramatic sigh. "I had a date last night, but he stood me up."

Anne's eyes opened wide. "No. Come on. You're kidding, right?"

"Really, I had a date, but he called and cancelled. I'm not kidding!" She worked hard to keep her face serious.

"Are we talking about Seth? No way would he cancel a date with you and besides, I didn't think you dated." She leaned forward with her hands clasped on the tabletop and looked Katie in the eyes. "Tell Mama all about it."

Katie giggled, then sobered quickly.

"Seth planned to pick me up after work to take me out for pizza and a movie. It sounded so fun. He called from a cab on his way to the airport. His father had a heart attack."

"Oh, Katie. How awful!"

"His brother and sister met him at the airport and they flew to Miami. Their dad was flown from St. Thomas to the Miami Heart Hospital."

Katie told Anne everything Seth had told her as they sat over coffee. "He'll call later to give me an update."

Anne leaned back and tilted her head to the side as she looked at her friend. "Do you want to talk about your feelings for Seth yet?"

"I don't know how I feel." Her stomach tightened at Anne's question. What should she say? That he made her happy, frightened, alive, and unsettled? "I guess confused says it best."

They chatted awhile over their coffee and pastries. The café had filled up so they decided to leave. Anne looked around for the waitress so she could ask for the bill and turned quickly back to her friend.

"Do you see the man standing by the door with his hand on the shoulder of a little girl?"

Katie nodded. "Yes. Do you know him?"

"Um, hm. It's Dr. Browne, and I suppose the girl is his daughter. She looks about eight years old, don't you think?"

"I'd say that's a good guess. Isn't she cute?"

Just then the child looked up and smiled at her father and lifted her shoulder to rub her cheek against his hand resting there. He smiled back and said something to her, then the hostess came and took them to their booth. Katie felt a lump form in her throat while watching the tender by-play between father and daughter. She swallowed to relieve the pain.

"It still hurts doesn't it?" Anne's voice was tender.

"I suppose it always will. J. J. would have been a teenager now and probably giving us fits. But I'll only remember him as being an active boy, full of life and mischief. Sometimes I feel such anger at the waste." She bit her lip.

Anne reached across the table and squeezed Katie's hand. She opened her mouth to speak but Katie spoke first.

"Don't worry, I'll be okay. Each time I think about what could have been, I'm reminded of how much I have and how faithful God is. I'm fine, really." She signaled to the waitress for their bill.

They gathered up their packages and put on their coats. As they walked toward the door, Dr. Browne stood and moved toward them. He greeted Anne and shook her hand.

Anne smiled and touched Katie's arm. "Katie, I'd like you to meet Dr. Joseph Browne. Doctor, this is my dearest friend, Katie Nelson."

"Hello, Dr. Browne." Katie held out her hand and he clasped it in his. She liked the feel of his firm grip.

"Hi, Katie. I'm pleased to meet you, and call me Joseph." He pointed to his booth. "My daughter would like to meet you, Anne. Would you mind? We were talking about you when I saw you leaving."

As they walked toward Dr. Browne's booth together, his daughter slid out. She looked up at Anne, held out her small hand and smiled. Anne reached out and shook it.

"Hi, I'm Annie. My daddy says you're a really good lawyer and I wanted to meet you. Isn't it great you're here? I think it's nice we have the same name, 'cept I'm called Annie. Now I get to ask you to take good care of him. We've been talking about this trial stuff and he says I don't have to worry 'cause you're the best. Is he right?" Annie took a deep breath and let it out on a big sigh.

Anne didn't glance away from Annie and looked very serious as she told her she'd work very hard for her father. "I think I'm a pretty good lawyer, and I'll have some of the best help I can find. I know your father is a wonderful doctor, and I'll do my best to take care of him, just as you asked."

"Good." Annie nodded and turned around to scoot back into the booth.

The scene tugged at Katie's heart. Dr. Browne looked at his daughter with so much love. What a nice man. She turned back to her friend.

Dr. Browne smiled at both of them, told Katie he was happy to have met her, and thanked them for their time.

Katie and Anne walked home at a leisurely pace, stopping to look in shop windows. Smells of coffee and food wafted out through opening restaurant doors and were quickly swept away on the slight breeze. Anne was quiet and seemed preoccupied. Katie wanted to know what she was thinking. Oh well, she'd leave her to her thoughts for now.

More people walked the sidewalks now and Katie tried to dodge a young child who ran from his mother. When he bumped into her, she laughed and held him so this mother could catch up. The mother apologized and they walked on.

They got to Katie's driveway. "Can you come in for awhile?"

Anne stopped at her car. "No. I have several more errands to run and things to catch up on at home. This was great. Just what I needed. Call me when you hear from Seth. Okay?"

"Of course. Take care. Love ya." She lifted her hand in a small wave as Anne got into her car and drove away.

Later, while Katie practiced, she thought about Dr. Joseph Browne and his daughter. Why hadn't Anne talked about them on the way home? Was she more worried about the lawsuit than she let on? Was Anne interested personally? Dr. Browne seemed like a nice person and obviously loved his daughter.

Katie hugged her guitar. Had that been a look of interest she'd seen on the doctor's face when he'd looked at Anne? She smiled at herself. Maybe.

Chapter 22

Vivaldi's "Gloria" poured from the organ pipes and swirled through the church on Sunday morning. Katie leaned back against the pew and smiled. Seth would have loved the flawless phrasing of the organist. It seemed impossible it had only been a week since they'd sat together in church. She bowed her head to pray for him and his family. A touch on her shoulder interrupted her prayer. Seth? A quick turn of the head revealed Anne. She smiled and slid over to make room for her friend. "What are you doing here?"

Anne leaned close and whispered, "I woke early and felt restless so thought I'd join you this morning. Am I ever glad. Listen to the music!" She smiled and said no more.

After the service they waited in line to shake hands with Pastor Mike and Katie told him about Seth's father. He said if she talked to Seth to tell him he'd be praying.

They left the church and Anne offered Katie a ride home.

"No thanks. I think I'll walk." She squinted up at the sky. "The sidewalks are clear so no slipping on ice today." They stopped beside Anne's car. "What are your plans for the rest of the day?"

Anne slipped on her sunglasses. "I have some briefs to read and then the usual. You know, Sunday paper and stuff."

"Me too. Well not the briefs, but the rest." She pulled up her collar and snuggled her chin into it. "Thanks for coming today. I loved sharing the service with you." She hadn't felt lonesome with Anne there. Why had Anne really come?

Anne opened her car door and slid in. "It was great. Your pastor could have had me in mind when he prepared today's sermon."

Katie laughed. "You know what? I feel that way almost every Sunday. He's anointed."

"What do you mean anointed?"

"Well—it feels as if God puts His words into the pastor's mind and then he speaks them. I can't think of any other way to explain what happens. Seth said he felt the same way. Granted, it's not as strong every Sunday, but at least some part of the sermon touches my heart every week." What had touched her friend's heart today? Was Kent part of Anne's struggle? Katie stepped back as Anne closed the door. She'd have to wait until Anne was ready to talk.

Anne started the engine and rolled down the window. "Are you sure you don't want a ride? It's not out of my way."

"Thanks, but the walk will feel good. Have a great day. I'll let you know when I hear from Seth."

Anne nodded and rolled up her window as she smiled and drove away.

Katie watched as Anne drove out of the parking lot. Something was going on. How much had she missed while in her cocoon? If she'd have been a more involved friend the past few years, she'd be better able to help Anne with her struggles. Well, things would be different from now on.

Even though winter still reigned, the sun and melting snow brought a promise of spring. She walked toward home. The sun reflected back at her from the windows of the homes lining the street where she lived. Her father used to say twinkling windows meant the house was smiling. Memories of him were bittersweet. Bitter because he'd died too young, and sweet because he'd been such a wonderful father. What would he say about Seth? Would he like him?

The afternoon loomed before her when she opened the front door. She chided herself for feeling lonely. It was all Seth's fault. The last two

Sundays he'd shown up unexpectedly and made her day special. She gave herself a stern talking to as she took off her coat and hung it up. Having him around could become a nice habit and she wouldn't fall into that trap. She kicked off her boots and wanted to slam the closet door but didn't. To calm herself, she made a pot of tea and carried it to her room where she curled up on the love seat to read the paper and think.

After a few minutes she remembered she hadn't checked her voice mail. She played her messages. The first one was from Seth.

"Hi, Katie. Oh, I guess you're in church. Sorry I missed you. I'll call back later so we can talk in person. I just want you to know Dad's doing well. Have a good day. I'm missing you. Bye." His voice brought a picture of him to her mind. She could just see his half smile and touched her own lips with a finger. She played the next message without deleting his.

Her mother had left the next one, also mentioning that Katie would be in church. She'd call back later too. After deleting her mother's message she concentrated on the paper.

Eventually her stomach rumbled with hunger and she went to the kitchen. The last two Sundays she hadn't cooked because she'd been with Seth. Oh, how irritated she'd been that first Sunday. She grinned to herself and admitted she'd enjoyed their time together. Had she really only known him for a few weeks? What if he had to stay in Florida and couldn't be at the benefit. Her stomach did a flip at the thought. Oh, dear. Maybe she'd better practice a few extra hours today.

Katie made a sandwich, poured a glass of milk and found fresh veggies to round out her meal. She set the table and turned the sound system on. The first CD to play was Horowitz in Moscow. Today his magic fingers on the piano keys couldn't capture her imagination. Her mind wandered and played scenes of long ago Sundays. John coming home tired after being gone all night on call. J. J. lying on the floor, reading the Sunday comics or watching some sport on TV.

Did they know in Heaven how much she missed them? Their lives hadn't been perfect, but awfully close to it. Did they know she'd been playing music again? She'd love them to know. Would God tell them? Their deaths were so senseless. She placed her elbows on the table and put her face in her open hands and cried quietly.

Her sorrow wasn't only for what she'd lost, but also for what she was leaving behind. Sometimes when she thought about John, Seth came to mind and it made her feel disloyal. Those moments broke her heart. Time was helping her heal, both mentally and physically, but it didn't make things easier when the feelings washed over her.

She dried her eyes and blew her nose on her napkin, then stood and picked up her cane and walked to her bedroom.

She looked at her bed and longed for sleep. Staying awake and working through her grief might be what a counselor would tell her to do, but she felt physically drained. Today, napping wouldn't be avoidance but strengthening. She sought rejuvenation, not escapism. She flipped back the duvet and snuggled into bed. Dreamless sleep came almost instantly.

When she awoke, several hours had passed. As she sat up her phone rang. She reached for it, looked at the caller ID and leaned back against the pillows. "Hi, Mother. I got your call. Didn't you go to church this morning?"

"I went to church, but just a little late. As you know, it's only two minutes from the house so I can leave at the last minute. What are you up to?"

"I took a nap."

"You took a nap? Is something wrong?"

Katie pulled the duvet back over her feet. "After lunch I had an emotional breakdown and needed a nap." She heard her mother catch her breath. "Don't worry, I'm fine. Crying and a nap have made me feel better. What's up?"

"Well, dear, I know the fundraiser isn't quite two weeks away so it might not be possible, but I wondered if you'd be able to get another ticket."

"I'll ask Anne. Why? Who wants to come?"

Her mother cleared her throat. "Do you remember Samuel Bowen?"

Katie sat up straighter. "The guy who lives in the red brick Tudor several blocks from you?"

"Yes. I mentioned you'd be involved in the event and I'd be there. He said he'd be interested in coming too if we could get another ticket."

Now she was interested. "Mother, are you seeing him? I mean, are you dating him?" Her voice rose.

"Now, Katie. I'm not dating anyone. We just get together every once and awhile. He's been a widower for some years and enjoys having someone to squire around."

"Squire around is a quaint way to say date, Mother. How often does this squiring happen?" She grinned at the phone.

"See, I knew you'd grill me. That's why I haven't mentioned him before."

"Come on, Mom. This is great. I'm not grilling you. I'm just having a little fun at your expense. Do you see him often? Every week?"

"We ah—probably see each other at least once a week. He golfs at the Country Club so we sometimes have lunch or dinner there. I have other friends who belong so we often get together as a group."

"How long has this been going on?" This was fantastic. Her mother had a friend.

"Oh, I don't know, a couple of years now I suppose."

Katie gasped. "Mother! You've been *squired* around by Samuel Bowen for two years and haven't said a word about it to me? Didn't you think I'd be interested?"

Her mother's voice was gentle and caring. "Of course, dear, but you've had so much to deal with and I didn't want to add anything more. Not that there's anything to deal with, but you know what I mean."

Katie sat up and swung her legs over the side of the bed. "So. You're telling me this is just a friendship and nothing more serious? He wants to come to the city with you. Earth to Mother! I think this means he wants me to finally know about your relationship, don't you think?"

"Well, he's not actually coming to the city with me you know. I'm not asking him to stay at your house or anything. I'm just going to ride with him. It's a whole lot nicer than driving myself, and if the weather turns nasty, I'll feel safer riding than driving."

"Of course, Mother. I understand." Was there any thing else her mother hadn't told her? "I'm sorry if I've seemed so fragile you couldn't tell me about him. I'm glad we'll get to meet." She frowned at herself for being oblivious to what was going on with her mother. "Is he quite a bit older than you? I seem to remember he had a daughter at least ten years older than me."

She heard her mother laugh quietly. "I'm sixty-four and he just turned sixty-nine so he's not a lot older. Yes, he does have a daughter but I think you're eight years apart. She lives out east and doesn't come home very often. Her husband is some high-powered executive and she's always busy with social events and doesn't like small town life much."

"A town of one hundred thousand isn't so small, but I get your meaning. So, you both have one child. Does he have any grandchildren?" As long as her mother was willing to answer questions, she'd keep asking them.

"Yes, a granddaughter of twenty and a grandson who's seventeen."

"Is the oldest one in college?"

"Yes. She's going to a university out east, and the boy is at a prep school. I don't think Bobby—her name is Roberta—enjoyed motherhood much and sent the children away to school."

"Poor kids." Why would a mother do that? She looked at J. J.'s picture. Sending him away to school would have broken her heart.

"Samuel has felt badly about it. He thinks she lives more for show than reality. I haven't met any of them, but it sounds as if they're coming out here sometime this summer, so maybe I'll meet them then."

Katie heard her mother's doorbell ring. "It sounds like someone's at your door."

"It's Leah from next door. We're going for a walk. The sidewalks are clear and she called to see if I wanted to get out. If you can get a ticket for Samuel, let me know. I love you, Katie. Bye."

"Bye, Mom. Love you too."

Had life been this interesting and she hadn't noticed? Her mother has dated for two years and hadn't told her. Should she laugh or cry? This won't happen any more. Katie was alive and paying attention.

She looked at the phone in her hand and called Anne. Might as well get that ticket while she was thinking about it.

"Hi Anne, it's Katie. I just talked to my mother and guess what she told me?"

"She has a boyfriend."

She flopped back on her bed. "What! Did you know and didn't tell me?"

"No, I made a wild guess. You told me to guess."

"I didn't mean it literally, for goodness sakes." She looked up at the ceiling from her position against the pillows.

"Come on Katie, hurry up and tell me everything."

Katie could hear the cheeky grin in Anne's voice. She rolled over and propped her chin on her hand. "Do you remember Samuel Bowen?"

"Yes, he had that daughter who thought highly of herself."

Katie gave a rueful laugh. "It doesn't sound as if she's changed. Anyway, it sounds like Samuel and my mother see each other quite often and he wants to come to the benefit. Personally, I think he wants their relationship out in the open—so to speak. Do you think you can scare up another ticket?"

"Of course. We'll put them at our table. I can juggle things around."

They chatted a few more minutes and Anne asked if she'd heard from Seth yet.

"I had a message from him when I got home from church. He said he'd call when he could. I'm not going out any more today so I won't miss his next call."

After they said goodbye Katie spent some time playing her guitar. She chose a piece by Vivaldi to warm up before tackling the Bach again. It soon became more intricate and she dug deep into her skills. Her eyes were fixed on the music and her fingers flew over the strings. The melody wove itself around her and enclosed her in its cocoon.

The phone jangled and interrupted the music, sending a pang of regret through her. She glanced at the clock. It could be Seth. Her spirits lifted when she saw his cell phone number on the caller I.D.

"Hi, Seth."

"Hi, yourself. Are you smiling?"

"Yes, how'd you know?" She set her guitar against its case.

"Your voice gives you away."

Oh, dear. Was she that transparent? "Ah, ha! Can you also tell when I'm crabby or sad?"

"I don't know. We'll have to talk more often."

She bit her lip. A change of subject was in order. "How's your father?"

"He seems to be doing well. I can hardly believe how quickly people are up and about after major surgery. He's already telling us he wants to go home. I don't think it will be long, but if he had his way, it would probably be tomorrow."

"Are they going to go back to St. Thomas?"

"No. My mother would never allow it and he'll need to have several check-ups. Flying back and forth isn't practical. Mother wouldn't be comfortable far from a specialist, which brings up another topic."

"Oh?"

"I'm going back to the island. They left in such a hurry Mom just grabbed a few things. I said I'd pack up what they need. This means I'll be gone several more days."

"You will be back by the eighteenth won't you?" Katie held her breath while waiting for his answer. Did he hesitate?

"Don't worry. I'll be there."

She let her breath out on a sigh and decided to push her luck. "What about being there to sing with me? That would be the best support possible, and I think it would be wonderful for everyone, including us." Had she gone too far?

He gave a bark of laughter. "You know, you're awfully persuasive. I guess most of those people wouldn't have heard me so won't be thinking that it's a shame my voice is no longer what it was."

She shook her head in wonder at his lack of vanity. "On the contrary, people will say it's a shame you're no longer performing. Your voice is wonderful. I can't tell you how much I loved it."

"I wish you had heard it before, then you'd understand what I'm talking about. Forgive me for whining. I take it all back."

"I do. And I don't think you're whining. This is now, not then. Your voice is beautiful and has tremendous appeal. I might even say it has captivating charm. How's that? Shall I go on with the accolades?"

"No more. I give up." He laughed. "I should be home in time for us get in some good practice time and you're right, doing this together could be fun. Unless something happens I can't control, I'll be there."

"Did you just commit to singing with me on March eighteenth? Is that what I heard you say?"

"By George, I think you're right."

"Do I hear a smile in your voice, Seth? It sounds like it to me."

"By George, I think you're right again. See, smiles can be heard, not only seen."

Katie pushed her hair off her forehead. "Now let's get this straight. I want to hear it spoken. Yes or no. Will you sing with me on March eighteenth?"

"Yes, Katie. I'll sing with you on March eighteenth. I'm committed. Now I need to get myself home. Peter is leaving tomorrow because there are some issues at work he needs to deal with in person. Sarah will stay here with Mother a few more days."

"I'm glad. Any idea when you'll be home?" She knew she shouldn't ask, but couldn't help herself.

"I'm not leaving till tomorrow night. Hopefully I'll be back in Miami on Wednesday morning. I should be home for sure by the end of the week. Sooner if possible." His voice softened. "I miss you."

Her stomach clenched. "Travel safely, Seth. Bye."

* * *

She hadn't said she missed him too. He looked at his phone and turned back toward the hospital. His mother sat on a bench several feet away.

She smiled and raised an eyebrow. "That didn't look like a business conversation."

He walked over and sat beside her. "What does a business conversation look like?"

She laughed and shrugged. "Oh, you know. You had a gentle look on your face. Sarah told me you've met someone. Was that her?"

Seth put the phone into his pocket and nodded. "Yes. Her name is Katie. I only met her a few weeks ago and it seems as if I've known her for years."

"Your dad's sleeping and Peter and Sarah are in the room with him. I can be gone for awhile. Want a cup of coffee?"

"Sure. Starbucks?" He pointed to their sign down the street.

She nodded and reached for his arm. Neither one spoke as they walked. The air was humid and a slight breeze carried the smell of the ocean. He took a deep breath and looked down at the top of his mother's head. A rush of protective tenderness filled him. She'd gone through so much these last few days and had exhibited such incredible strength. What would she think of Katie?

Chapter 23

Starbucks wasn't busy when Seth and his mother walked in. They chose comfortable chairs some distance from the counter so they could have privacy. Seth ordered their coffee and brownies. He remembered the brownie he'd shared with Katie. Hopefully they'd do that again.

Seth handed his mother her coffee and treat. He sank into the matching armchair, stretched his legs out and sighed. The air conditioning felt good, and he watched his mother over the rim of his cup as he drank. Her dark hair had sun streaks mingling with touches of grey. Why didn't she color her hair? He'd have to ask her some time. Her blue eyes reminded him of the ones he looked at each morning in the mirror. He smiled. She'd always been a restful person and he appreciated it. He braced himself for her questions.

She licked chocolate off her fingers. "Can we start at the beginning?"

He nodded.

"How did you meet Katie?"

He told her about their first meeting. It felt so good to be talking about her. He answered her questions willingly.

"What do you know about her first marriage?"

That one touched a raw nerve and he frowned. "From all she says, they were happy. I just can't understand how a man with such a talented wife wouldn't encourage her to rise to her full potential."

She had a thoughtful look on her face. "Maybe, as far as she's concerned, she did. Just because she's talented doesn't mean she needed more of a career than she had."

Seth leaned forward to rest his elbows on his knees and held his cup between both hands. "I don't mean she had to have a career, but she has so much to give. I don't know, Mom. It's hard to explain."

"I think I understand. You'd have encouraged her to do something you considered worthwhile with her talents. From what you've told me, she definitely did. Her story breaks my heart."

"I hope to give her story a new ending." Seth smiled at his mother and checked the time. "Do you want more coffee?"

He refilled their cups and as he walked back to their corner, he felt his mother's gaze studying him. In the years since his surgery he'd been a little distant. More private. Not drawing away from the family, just not as open and spontaneous. He'd sensed the hurt it caused her, but never knew how to bridge the gap. Maybe it was time to give a little ground.

His mother reached for her cup and smiled as he sat down.

"Are you through grilling me?" Seth smiled so she'd know he was teasing and not throwing up a warning barrier.

"Can I ask one more question?"

He shrugged. "I guess."

"Do you think she'd like to have more children? I know this is early in your relationship, but I've always thought you'd make a wonderful father." A flash of pain crossed her face. "It hurts to think you might be interested in someone who wouldn't consider children."

He hesitated and rubbed the back of his neck. "I'll tell you what I know." He told her about his conversation with Anne that first night. How Katie had a difficult pregnancy and their decision to be happy with one healthy child. "Obviously we haven't discussed any of this. I'm sure she'd be surprised I even know this much."

His mother nodded. "Thanks for telling me. I just want life to stop being so difficult for you. It seems like all the hard things miss your siblings and fall on you. And here I am leaning on you again." She reached into her handbag, pulled out a piece of paper, and handed it to him.

"What's this?" He opened it.

"I made a list of things to be taken care of on the island. I think it's all on there. Are you sure you can be away from work this long?"

Seth sank back in the chair with a relieved sigh. At last a shift from the awkward conversation about emotional issues to a concrete list of problems he could solve. "I'm happy to go. Dad's collapse seems like a bad dream doesn't it? I have friends whose parents have dealt with serious health issues and never realized how frightening it can be. I've taken you and Dad for granted. Nothing is supposed to happen to our parents." He reached over and touched her hand. "Promise me that both of you will get your annual check-ups."

She turned her hand up and twined her fingers with his. "Don't worry, Seth. I always go for mine and I'll be more of a nag with your father. It's been several years since he's been in. It's strange. He has had absolutely no signs of coronary blockage. I always assumed there would be physical indications." She frowned at their entwined fingers.

"I did too. And I know he didn't have high blood pressure."

"Oh? How do you know that?"

"Do you remember when Dad and I visited Uncle Phil in the hospital last year?" She nodded. "There was a blood pressure machine in his room. Dad and I both took ours for the fun of it. We had an identical reading and thought it must be broken. Right then the nurse came in so we asked her about it. She offered to take them for us again. Sure enough, one ten over seventy-one. Dad said he'd stick around until he reached one hundred. We all laughed, and I remember feeling pleased about his health."

His mother nodded. "I won't ever take your father's or my health for granted again. We've been given more years together and I'm so thankful."

Life without his parents would be horrible. Seth knew they wouldn't live forever but he certainly wasn't ready to lose them any time soon.

Did his mother look more fragile than he remembered? *Please keep them safe, God.* Was that a prayer? He nodded to himself.

She looked at her watch. "Should we go?"

Seth stood and pulled her to her feet. "Dad will be watching the door for your return."

She chuckled. "You're probably right."

They cleared their debris away and walked out into the sunshine. Seth smiled down at his mother and put his arm around her shoulders as they walked. She put hers around his waist and gave him a squeeze.

They entered the hospital and walked to the elevator. Seth cleared his throat as the doors closed. "Um, Mother?"

She looked up.

"I'll be singing with Katie on March eighteenth. She talked me into doing a duet with her."

The door opened on their floor, and Seth waited for her to walk out. He followed her down the corridor and as they reached his father's room she reached out and touched Seth's arm, stopping him before he opened the door.

"My dear son, this is almost as big a miracle as your father's life. I've prayed so many times you'd find joy in singing again." She swallowed hard and cleared her throat. "I can hardly wait to get back home and meet your Katie."

"She's not my Katie yet, Mother. But I'm working on it." They smiled at each other and he pushed open the door so his mother could enter.

His dad looked at them from the bed and asked what mischief the two of them had been up to.

Seth covered a yawn. "Mother will tell you all about it. Right now I'm going back to the hotel to take a nap. This Florida sunshine makes me think I'm on vacation. Peter, Sarah, are you coming with me?"

Sarah nodded. "Sure. Sounds great to me. Can we hit a mall on the way so I can send gifts for the children back with Peter tomorrow?"

The guys agreed to her plan. They gathered up their belongings and were soon out the door. Several steps toward the elevator, Seth realized he'd left his phone. "Hold the elevator for me. I'll be right back." He turned to go back into the room. He hadn't closed the door all the way and his mother and father were holding hands. He heard his father speak.

"Well Beth, did Seth tell you what's been going on?" His father looked weary but pleased.

She nodded and dropped her husband's hand and hopped up beside him on the bed. She picked it up again and held it to her cheek. "Oh, Charles, our middle child has been experiencing a miracle while we've been gone."

Seth hesitated then turned and walked back to Sarah and Peter without getting his phone.

Chapter 24

The week passed slowly for Katie. She hadn't heard from Seth since Sunday, and now it was Wednesday. Her level of disappointment surprised her. Anne had called to inquire after his father's health and Katie told her everything she knew. After their conversation she knew her feelings for Seth were obvious to anyone as perceptive as Anne. Fortunately Anne hadn't pushed or asked questions she honestly couldn't answer. Part of her wanted to talk about him, but what would she say? He makes her confused? Her emotions frighten her? She missed him but doesn't want to feel this way?

She sat in the bay window of her bedroom as daylight faded and watched a squirrel scamper across the snow. It dashed up the big oak to its nest. Why couldn't life be as simple? Then she remembered watching a squirrel hunt for acorns last fall. The job hadn't been easy for the little guy. She appreciated easy when it came her way, but knew easy wasn't always God's plan.

She sat for several more minutes, then looked at the clock. Time for the early evening news. She picked up her cane to get the remote and the doorbell rang. She changed directions and headed down the hall to the front door. Who'd be coming over this evening? Lately, only Anne dropped in unexpectedly. She didn't think to check her peephole and pulled the door open. Seth stood in the opening brushing show off his coat sleeves. A broad smile creased his cheeks that were flushed with the cold.

"Oh, my!" Her heart did crazy things and she could feel her cheeks blush. She held her hand out and he pulled her into his arms. She wrapped her arms around his waist and clung to him. He smelled so good she didn't want to let go, but she stepped back and took his hand to pull him inside. "When did you get home? I guess you can tell I'm happy to see you."

"Katie, your smile is worth every minute of my long day. I came directly here from the airport."

"I didn't think you'd even get back to Miami until this evening. How in the world did you manage to get home? What happened?" She reached up and smoothed his hair from his brow then pulled her hand away shyly when she realized what she'd done.

He reached for the hand she'd used and kissed her knuckles. "I got everything done on the island yesterday and managed to catch a very early flight to Miami today. While I was still at the airport, I changed my ticket for today's afternoon flight hoping no one needed anything more from me. I squared everything away with Mom, Dad, and Sarah and left." He unzipped his jacket.

She opened the closet door and he hung up his jacket and followed her to the living room. He looked drained, and she was glad the fireplace was burning. She pointed to the chair he'd sat in before, and she moved to the other one. She watched his eyes glance around the room. She had a huge vase of gerbera daisies on the dining room table. She noticed him looking at them and laughed.

"Whenever I can, I have tulips or gerbera daisies. I call them my promise flowers. They promise me spring. I don't dislike winter so much, but I love the thought of everything coming alive in the spring. Kind of like a new birth." She knew she was babbling. "Are you exhausted?"

"Not any more." He leaned his head against the back of the chair and smiled.

"Tell me about your father. All the details."

He told her about the surgery and what had actually happened on St. Thomas. He also told her about the talk with his mother on Sunday after he had talked to Katie. He looked down at his crossed ankles, and sighed.

Katie wanted to ask more questions about his conversation with his mother, but let it go. "I'm sorry, Seth. I know you're tired and I've been grilling you for over an hour. I made ham and split pea soup earlier today for my evening meal. Will you share it with me?"

"That sounds great. May I help?"

"No. Stay there. You have time to close your eyes for a few minutes if you'd like." She reached for her cane and stood up. As she passed his chair, he reached out and caught her hand. She stopped and he lifted it to his lips then smiled at her as he released it. She smiled back and walked into the kitchen, where she stopped for a moment and gently rubbed her fingers over the spot he'd kissed. He'd come directly from the airport. What did this mean? How could she be confused and happy at the same time?

After turning the burner on under the soup kettle, she quietly made a salad and oven toasted French bread to go with it. She glanced into the living room before she set the table in the kitchen. He had his eyes closed and looked relaxed, so she didn't hurry with her preparations.

When she finished, she walked over to his chair and touched his shoulder.

"Seth, dinner's ready."

He opened his eyes and got smoothly to his feet. She turned to walk back to the kitchen but he caught her upper arm and stopped her. She turned to look up at him, and he took a step that brought him close. He wrapped his arms around her. He said nothing, simply hugged her. She hugged him back, briefly laying her head against his chest.

She enjoyed the warm, solid feel of him. He released her and they walked to the table without speaking. He pulled out her chair. She loved the little courtesies that seemed a natural part of him.

Katie laid her right hand on the table toward Seth, palm up, and he reached out and laid his over it. She bowed her head. "Thank you, God, for Seth's safe return and that his father's recovering. Thank you for this food, and bless us I pray. Amen." When she opened her eyes, Seth was watching her. Smiling, she picked up her spoon. Having dinner with him could become a very nice habit.

Their conversation was relaxed and low key. Katie asked if he'd had time to read more of the book of John.

He put his spoon down and nodded. "I've read it several times. I've also read Matthew, Mark, Luke and the rest of the New Testament. I can't tell you much yet because I need to read it again. I have questions."

"Are you going to get together with Pastor Mike again?" She tore off a piece of bread and plopped it into her mouth. When had he had time to read the whole New Testament?

"I'd like to. I'll see if he has time in the next few days. Some of the stuff I've read, well, I know what I think it means, but I need some help."

"I've been reading it all my life and some things are still a mystery to me. You said Pastor gave you *The Message.* I think that's easier to read than most versions."

"I didn't know the Bible would be so interesting. Do you think parents should be influencing their children about God stuff into adulthood?"

"Well, if God has been an integral part of your life since childhood, I'd think He'd continue to be so when you're an adult. Parents have influence when you're young, but after you've left home, it's pretty much your decision." She took a drink of water and used her napkin. "You know, my mother always asks me what I'm studying or about church on Sunday, but I don't think she's a motivating factor for my spiritual life. I love talking to her about something new I've learned from my daily devotions or something special I'm reading. She does the same with me. I think we're equally inspirational to the other. What did your family do?"

"We went to church together when we were growing up. Going to church constituted doing our duty." Seth stifled a yawn, and Katie smiled.

"You need to go home and get some rest. Your long day is catching up with you." He scooted his chair back and stood, then reached over to help her up. He started to clear the table, but she laid a hand on his arm and told him to leave everything. She had lots of time to clean up, and it wouldn't be a bother.

They walked together to the front door, and she helped him on with his jacket. When he turned around, he cupped her cheek with his right hand and smiled down at her.

"Flying home today, I could hardly wait to see you. Every time we're together I enjoy it more." She reached up and covered his hand with hers, then drew them both down and stepped back. He looked at her, and she could feel her heartbeat quicken. Restraining herself from stepping into his embrace took willpower. She'd already hugged him twice tonight. Where was her control? She reached for the doorknob as he zipped his jacket.

"Thanks, Katie. For being here. For listening. For the food." He walked to the elevator and pushed the button. The door opened right away. He stepped in and held it so it wouldn't close immediately.

"I'll call you tomorrow. Will you be home?"

"Yes, I'll be home. Oh, and will you look at your calendar and let me know when you're available to practice?"

"Sure. I'll tell you tomorrow when we talk. Good night."

She smiled and lifted her hand in a brief wave as the elevator door closed, then turned back and shut the door softly. After turning off the hall light, she walked into the living room and sat in the chair Seth had occupied earlier by the fire. She closed her eyes and leaned back with a big sigh. He'd looked so dear standing there when she'd opened the door to him tonight. She had no doubt about the attraction they felt for each other. If she let him, he'd move their relationship along quickly. She needed to curb her spontaneous reactions when she saw him. Her heart wanted to encourage him, but her head said "careful." This was so hard. She liked him more each time they were together. After her husband's death, she'd never imagined anyone taking his place. She looked up at John's picture on the mantle. What now?

Chapter 25

Katie's pastor called on Thursday morning wondering if she'd heard from Seth, and about the status of his father's health.

"As a matter of fact, he came back from Florida last evening. His father is doing really well. Thanks for praying. He's been reading *The Message* you gave him and told me he has questions."

"Great. If you talk to him, tell him I'm looking forward to another visit. I'm sure he'll have some tough questions, but I love a challenge."

After their conversation, she did some serious practicing. She tried to avoid thinking about how many important people would be there. Her skills were returning, but would she truly be ready? When she finished, she moved behind her desk and booted up her computer. While her emails were downloading, the phone rang. "Hello?"

"Hi, Katie. I have a few minutes between meetings and thought I'd give you a call. Are you free for dinner tomorrow night?"

Seth. "Hi, yourself. I don't have plans for dinner and if you're asking me out the answer is yes." She laughed. "What time and where are we going?"

"How about six thirty? I should be able to leave work tomorrow by four thirty so we'll go somewhere casual if that's okay with you."

"Casual's great. Oh, by the way, Pastor Mike called this morning to see if I'd heard from you about your father. I gave him an update and told him you wanted to talk again."

"Thanks. I'll give him a call."

After they said goodbye, she bowed her head and prayed out loud. "Please give Pastor Mike wisdom when talking to Seth. Thank you that you are tugging at Seth's heart." What if God never became an integral part of Seth's life? Some of her sweetest, most meaningful times with John had been spiritually related. Having someone to pray with had given their relationship depth and security. Many times, when he had a difficult surgery scheduled, they'd prayed about it. They'd often knelt by J. J.'s bed to pray for him when he'd been sick. Even though John was a doctor, they'd relied on God for physical and mental healing. She couldn't imagine how anyone could live life without God's guiding hand directing it. Would Seth understand? Uncertainty gripped her.

She sighed and turned back to her computer. Anne had written asking if she had plans for Friday night. She quickly typed a reply saying Seth just called and they were going out to dinner.

What was going on with Anne? She was usually busy on Friday nights. Had something finally happened between her and Kent? Katie had never felt Kent was God's choice for Anne, but couldn't put her finger on the reason why. That didn't take away from Kent's worth, it just meant he wasn't perfect for Anne.

She sat idly looking into space. Doctor Browne came to mind and she remembered the sweet exchange she'd witnessed between him and his daughter. Was he the one God had for Anne? She chuckled when she realized she was acting like a matchmaker.

She turned back to her computer and found a note from her mother wondering if Katie had been able to get the extra ticket for the fundraiser. Instead of writing back, she picked up the phone.

"Hi, Mother. It's Katie."

"Hi, Love. You didn't have to tell me who was calling after you said 'Hi, Mother.' You're the only person in the world who can call me mother, you know."

Katie could hear a smile in her mother's voice and ran a hand through her hair. "Are you feeling a little sassy today?" Her mother laughed and Katie went on. "I got your email, Mom. There were still tickets, and Anne has seated you and Samuel at our table."

"Great. Are you ready for the evening?"

"Ready? No. Working? Well, I've been practicing daily and doing lots of vocal exercise, but Seth and I haven't had a chance to practice again. Hopefully this weekend."

"Has he come home from Florida? And how's his father?"

"He came home last night. His father's doing well and will be out of the hospital in the next day or so. They'll stay in Florida for a few more weeks. When he leaves, they'll send his files to a cardiologist at the Mayo Clinic. That's all I know right now."

"Did you talk to him today? How is his mother handling everything?"

Should she tell her mother she'd already seen him? Why not? "I talked to him last night. He came here directly from the airport." She thought she heard her mother speak to someone. "Did you say something, Mother? Do you have company? Am I interrupting anything?"

"No Katie, I don't have company and you're not interrupting anything. Tell Anne I'm pleased we'll be able to sit at your table. You'll be wonderful, Honey."

"You know something, Mom? I'm enjoying it more than I imagined I would. But, if I spend too much time thinking about it, I get butterflies in my stomach." Katie thought she heard a tapping sound over the phone.

"Mother? What's that noise?"

Her mother laughed. "The tapping?"

"Mm, hm."

"Oh, that's just a little happy dance I'm doing."

Katie joined her mother's laughter. "As J. J. used to say when he was little, 'You funny, Nana.' Bye, Mom."

Katie set the phone down and paused in thought. Was her mother doing her happy dance over her picking up her music again, or Seth? She told herself not to go there. She didn't need the pressure.

Chapter 26

On Thursday evening, Seth and Pastor Mike sat in comfortable leather chairs before a roaring fire in the pastor's office. Seth sighed and looked around the room with appreciation. The fire cast a warm glow over the rich dark wood of the walls and bookshelves. It was a beautiful room and obviously well used. Like the rest of the house, the furniture had been chosen for comfort. It served a dual purpose of both library and home office. Seth smiled and indicated the chess game in progress on the table between the two chairs. "Who's winning?"

Pastor Mike looked down. "Emily usually wins." He pondered the board for a moment and laughed. "It looks like she's going to do it again." The pastor smiled as she came into the room with a tray loaded with cups and a carafe of coffee.

Both men stood and she handed the tray to Mike. She glanced at the board, and quickly moved one of the pieces. "It's the one thing I can do better than him, and I love it."

Mike groaned. "See. She did it again."

Emily grinned and sashayed out of the room with a wave.

Seth was touched by the loving look on Mike's face as he watched his wife leave.

Mike turned to Seth. "You've been in my thoughts and prayers since Katie told me about your father. She said he's doing well."

Seth nodded. "We're thankful for all the prayers said for Dad. His recovery is truly a miracle." He took a drink and leaned forward with his elbows on his knees and the mug in both hands. "I've been reading the Bible you gave me. I'd like to talk to you about it."

Mike sat back and crossed his ankles. "I'm listening."

This wasn't going to be easy. Seth wasn't sure how to put his thoughts and feelings into words. "Okay. Here goes. I've analyzed my motives for this God search from all angles. I don't want Katie to be the reason I'm going down this path. Granted, she started it, but I'd like to think that even if she hadn't come into my life, I'd have done this. You know, had this quest. It might not have been this soon though."

Mike nodded. "Sometimes we need a nudge."

"You said the book of John would be a good place to start. I read it twice. After that, I went back and read the whole New Testament. In some ways it all seems very simple." He ran his hand through his hair and sighed. "But how does one live without error or sin? And then I read the part in Matthew about Jesus on the hillside teaching about being blessed. At first I was bothered by the premise that we're blessed when things weren't going well. And then I read on and it touched a chord in my heart. It personalized Jesus for me."

Mike grabbed his Bible, opened it and looked up. "The fifth chapter of Matthew is amazing isn't it?" He ran his finger down the page. "I love this." He started reading. "'I'm telling you to love your enemies. Let them bring out the best in you, not the worst. When someone gives you a hard time, respond with the energies of prayer, for then you are working out of your true selves, your God-created selves. This is what God does. He gives His best—the sun to warm and the rain to nourish—to everyone, regardless: the good and bad, the nice and nasty.'" He closed the book.

Seth looked into his empty mug without really seeing it. "I guess that sort of addresses about good things happening to bad people and bad to good people. But it still seems complicated." He looked at the pastor.

Mike nodded. "It is if you try to take it all in at once. Go slowly. You asked how anyone can live without error or sin. My friend, we all make mistakes. None of us are sin free. That's why Jesus came to earth."

Was Pastor Mike including himself? "You too? You're not sin free?" Seth knew he'd asked an important question when sorrow shadowed Pastor Mike's face.

"How I wish I could answer that I am. No, Seth. I too fail miserably. But that's where Jesus comes to the rescue." His expression softened as he talked about forgiveness.

The time flew by. Seth was inspired by Pastor Mike's knowledge of the Bible. He felt as if a whole new world was opening up in front of him. When he glanced at his watch, several hours had passed. Seth rolled his shoulders to loosen them. "I can't tell you how much this evening has meant to me."

"Me, too." Pastor Mike picked up his Bible. "Read the introduction to the book of John again. Here, let me read some of the last paragraph. 'Our words are more important than we ever supposed. Saying "I believe," for instance, marks the difference between life and death. Our words accrue dignity and gravity in conversations with Jesus. For Jesus doesn't impose salvation as a solution; he narrates salvation into being through leisurely conversation, intimate personal relationships, compassionate responses, passionate prayer, and—putting it all together—a sacrificial death.' That's what the book of John is all about and it'll become clearer each time you read it." He set down the Bible and stood.

Seth also stood. "Thanks, Pastor. I have lots to think about." He sighed. Life and death. Those were some powerful words. He was filled with anxiety, and he ran his hand through his hair. He really wanted to ask one more question and decided to go for it. "Is it too soon for me to become a follower of Christ? Do I know enough? Do I need to study and understand more before I make the commitment you've been talking about?"

Pastor Mike laid his hand on Seth's shoulder and gave it a gentle squeeze. "There's never a wrong time. Can I pray with you now?"

Seth nodded. "Yes. I guess."

"Do you want to repeat a prayer after me, or do you want to pray in your own words."

Seth cleared his throat nervously. Why did he suddenly feel like he was five years old and learning his first piano scales? "I think I need help. I'll follow the leader and repeat the prayer after you." He bowed his head and wished he were sitting down. His knees felt weak and his throat was tight. He took a big breath and repeated the pastor's simple prayer. "God, thank you for giving me life. Thank you for the gift of Your Son so I can also have eternal life. I believe in Him. Please forgive my sins and accept me into Your family. Amen."

Seth slowly opened his eyes and for a moment watched the glowing embers in the fireplace. Their warmth seemed to penetrate his being as a strange tingle blossomed in his chest. Was it really that simple? He turned toward the door as Pastor Mike gave his shoulder a squeeze. They walked side by side to the front door without speaking.

Seth took his jacket off the coat rack and slipped into it. He reached out to shake hands. "Thanks, Pastor. Tell Emily I'm sorry I took up your whole evening."

Pastor Mike smiled and shook his head. "No apologies necessary."

After the door closed, Seth stood a moment and raised his face to the stars. Were they brighter? He breathed deeply. Was the air purer? What would Katie say when he told her about tonight? He pushed back his sleeve to check the time. Disappointment rushed through him. Too late to call.

Chapter 27

Katie sat in her window seat soaking up the sun during her morning devotions on Friday. The snow was melting. It wouldn't be long before the crocuses, daffodils, and delicate primroses poked their heads through the soil. The gardener she shared with her downstairs neighbor had a wonderful variety of plantings beautifully laid out in beds around the yard. She especially loved the early bloomers. Those blossoms held a sign of promise for her every spring. They looked delicate, but were so hardy.

She spent several hours practicing. Concentration didn't come easily because her mind kept wandering to the upcoming evening with Seth. Fed up with doing bookwork and correspondence on her computer she decided to get out of the house. Looking at the clock every fifteen minutes wouldn't make the time go by any faster.

The air smelled of spring, and melting snow created rivers along the curbs. It felt great to be outside. She reached up and removed the hat she'd worn. A breeze lifted her hair and the sun bathed her face as she walked toward the bank.

Shop windows enticed and she stopped to gaze, but didn't go inside. The fresh air held more allure than merchandise in the shops. The thought of an evening with Seth made her heart skip a beat and she saw a smile on her reflected face in the window.

Katie started walking again and went into the bank a few doors down. Next she stopped to pick up a dessert at the French Café where

Anne had introduced her to Doctor Browne. Hopefully Seth would want to come in when he took her home. Maybe they'd practice. She pushed up her coat sleeve, then shook her head. No checking the time. She couldn't suppress a smile though.

Back home, she placed the dessert box on the countertop. Did Seth like raspberries? She glanced at the clock and rolled her eyes. Not long now. A bath seemed a good way to relax. As the tub filled, she moved to her sound system and selected several favorite CDs. During the renovations of her home, speakers had been hardwired into each room so she could listen to music or the radio from anywhere in the house. She especially enjoyed this feature while lying in the bathtub.

She sprinkled her favorite magnolia bath salts into the water, lit several magnolia-scented candles, and then lowered herself into the water with a sigh. As Karen Carpenter's rich voice poured out of the speakers she was reminded once again how short life could be. She looked at a picture of John and J. J. on her bathroom wall and saw their blurred faces through misty eyes. "I love you guys. I'm going out to dinner tonight. I'm opting for pizza. Your favorite, J. J." She splashed water toward their picture but not far enough to actually hit it. "Now look what you made me do. I'll have to clean the floor." She grinned over her silliness.

The warm water relaxed her. It wasn't long before her voice mingled with Karen's singing "Top of the World". The water cooled, so she opened the drain and rinsed under the shower. Wrapped in a fluffy terry robe, she walked into her closet. What to wear? She shuffled through her slacks and chose dark brown chinos and grabbed an oversized mango-colored sweater off the shelf. She dressed quickly and turned this way and that before her full-length mirror. She'd do.

The doorbell rang just as she finished cleaning the bathroom. Hmm. Six o'clock. Hadn't Seth said six thirty? It must be Dottie, her downstairs neighbor. She picked up her cane and headed toward the front door. Nope, there on the threshold stood Seth, with his hands in his pockets and a grin on his face.

Katie laughed. "At least tonight I'm dressed." She looked down at her bare feet and wiggled her toes. "Almost. Come on in. You're early, right?" She backed up to make room for him and closed the door.

He ran his hand through his hair, making it stand up a bit in front. "I could say I worked late and instead of going home, came right here hoping you wouldn't mind. I'll tell the truth instead. I watched the clock all day and finally left at four. I got home, cleaned up, changed, and couldn't wait any longer so came on over." He reached out and touched her hair, then ran his finger alongside her right cheek. She turned away so he wouldn't see the emotions coursing through her.

Seth reached out and gently turned her around. He put both hands on her shoulders. "Katie, what's wrong? Am I too impulsive?"

She shook her head and stepped back, fighting the impulse to move into his arms. She turned to walk down the hall. "I'll be right back. I'm going to put my shoes and socks on."

She came out of the bedroom carrying them and sat on the chair by the fireplace to put them on. He looked puzzled but she didn't want to tell him why she'd left so abruptly. She put her foot back down on the floor. "Where are we eating tonight? I was really looking forward to the pizza date we cancelled."

"Should we go to Mia's? The food's excellent, the tables and booths aren't too close to each other and it's never too noisy to talk. What do you think?"

She stood. "It's been years since I've been there. I'd forgotten about it, but it's a great choice."

Seth helped her into her jacket. She grabbed her purse and cane and turned off the lights. Why did she struggle with uncertainty when she was so happy to see him? She told herself to get over it.

Seth took Katie's hand as they walked down the driveway to the street where he'd parked.

She didn't pull away and looked up and smiled. "It's dry out here. I won't fall."

"Yes, I know, but do you remember the song you had playing when I came in the door?"

She shook her head and looked up expectantly.

He sang one line. "I Want To Hold Your Hand." He raised her hand and squeezed. "I thought it was a good idea. Are you a Beatles fan?"

She laughed. "I enjoy some of their music. I've been listening to CDs from the sixties and seventies today." She'd been so surprised to see him she hadn't remembered the song playing when she'd opened the door. She hadn't turned the sound system off either when they left. "Are you a Beatles fan?"

They'd reached the car and he didn't answer as he held her door. He grinned at her as he slid behind the wheel. When he turned the engine on, out of the sound system poured the song "Michelle".

Katie laid her head back against the headrest and laughed out loud. He lowered the volume. "The Beatles fit my mood. My mother's a fan so I know lots of their music. Isn't it uncanny? We both listened to music from the sixties and seventies today."

Katie nodded. What in the world was going on? He filled her thoughts all day and now even their moods were similar. She looked down at her tightly gripped hands and forced herself to calm down.

Seth reached over and touched the back of her neck through her hair. "Katie, tell me what you're thinking."

She turned to him. "I'd like to wait till we get to Mia's, if that's all right with you."

"Sure." He drove and neither one spoke.

The music played softly and the car was warm. What was that scent? She took a deep breath. Leather and soap. Why was she so aware of everything around her when Seth was near? She shifted restlessly. Good. Here was Mia's.

He entered the parking lot, quickly parked, and came around to open her door. She took the hand he held out and stood up.

"I wish I didn't always have to have this with me." She thumped her cane on the ground.

"You can leave it in the car if you want. I'll hold you up. In fact, I'd love to hang on to you." He made a comical face, took the cane and put it on the front seat. After locking the door, he turned and held out his arm.

They were seated and given menus. Katie didn't open hers. She folded her hands on top of it and gave him a cheeky grin. "Pizza. With everything."

He raised his eyebrows. "Anchovies? Chicken? The kitchen sink?"

They weren't sitting side by side or she would have punched him. "No, silly. Meat and veggies."

"Okay. Not everything. What do you want to drink?"

"Coke, thanks."

Their server came and he ordered for both of them then turned to her. "Should we practice after dinner?"

"I was hoping you'd say that. I think I'm about as ready for next Wednesday as I can be until we practice. I'd like to tell Anne what we're doing for sure so she can get the information to the printer."

Seth agreed. They sat for a moment looking at each other without speaking and finally he reached for her hand over the table. He rubbed his thumb over the calluses on the fingertips of her left hand. She started to pull her hand away, and he gripped it tighter.

"I saw Mike Schumann last night. I'm struggling to find a starting point. I want to tell you the important things, but not take all night while I do it."

She gave his hand an encouraging squeeze.

"He seems like a very wise person and his education is obviously extensive. The diplomas on the wall were impressive, especially the Ph.D. Oh yes, I also met his wife, Emily."

"Emily's great. I'd like to spend more time with her if her busy schedule would allow it." She smiled encouragingly so he'd continue.

"The pastor and I talked for several hours. I told you I'd been reading the Bible he gave me called *The Message*. There's so much in there I've never heard or read before." Seth told her about his long list of questions and Mike's more than satisfactory answers.

Their server came with the food. After she walked away he asked Katie if she'd like to pray. They both reached over the table to clasp hands.

She bowed her head. "Thanks, God, for great food and wonderful company to share it with. Amen." She grinned and reached for a piece of pizza. "I had to make it short. My mouth was watering."

Seth picked up his fork and started to eat.

She swallowed. "Excuse me, Seth. You can't stop now!" She picked up her fork and pointed it at him.

He raised his eyebrows. "How's the pizza? My pasta's great. I've always loved the food here. Everything's fresh and who in town has better bread?"

She set her fork down, glared, and leaned toward him. "You're not funny."

He laughed and continued with last night's details. She had questions and comments but kept them to a minimum. This was his story. Something wonderful had obviously happened last night. She could picture the pastor and Seth in the rectory library. There would have been a fire in the fireplace and Emily would have provided coffee. As he talked he confirmed these insights. When their food was gone, Seth signaled the server for the check. "Let's go to your house and I'll tell you the rest. Is that okay?"

Katie agreed. After getting settled in the car, he reached over and touched her hair. "You're an incredible lady, Katie Nelson."

She turned her head just enough so his hand touched her cheek instead of her hair. "Oh?"

He shifted into gear and drove out of the parking lot before answering. "I think it has something to do with how you make me feel when we're together. Maybe this discussion would be better held at your house too."

Chapter 28

They entered her house, and Katie turned on the fireplace. They settled into the chairs in front of the fire and she waited patiently while he gathered his thoughts.

When he started talking, the rest of the story flowed out of him. She loved how simply he was able to talk about a life changing experience. Katie had tears in her eyes when he finished. He stood and moved to stand beside her chair and put his hand on her shoulder. She reached up and grasped it then put her cheek on the back of his.

He hunkered down and smiled into her eyes. "My story made you cry?" She nodded and pulled a tissue out of her pocket. He took it from her and wiped the tears, then leaned in and kissed her softly. She wanted more but turned away. Her emotions were doing crazy things. She wasn't thinking straight.

He sat on the floor and leaned against her chair. They watched the fire, music playing softly in the background. His soft kiss still warmed her lips. She reached out and touched his hair. It was silky to her touch and curled around her fingers. When she realized what she was doing, she pulled her hand away. This had to stop. She uncurled her legs. "Do you have any energy left to practice?"

He nodded. "Absolutely. I'm looking forward to it. When I left the pastor's house last night, I desperately wanted to stop and talk to you."

"You could have stopped. You ought to know by now that I don't mind your unexpected visits."

His eyes crinkled as he smiled. "It was late, and I didn't want to rush through the telling. I also wanted to think about what I'd done." He stood and put out his hand. "Let's practice." He pulled her up and gave her a quick hug.

Katie took a minute to tune while Seth sat down on the piano bench and waited. When she finished he lifted the lid and ran his fingers lightly up the keyboard and glanced at her over his shoulder. "How about a little jamming first?"

She smiled and nodded. "Great."

He turned back to the keyboard and started to play Gershwin's "They Can't Take That Away From Me".

Katie loved Gershwin and immediately picked out the melody. She could hear a smile in his voice as he started to sing the words and wished she could record it. His voice was even better than she remembered.

They finished that song and continued to play for another twenty minutes or so. When he stopped, he turned and held out his hand. She stood up and walked over, still holding her guitar. He patted the bench and she sat down with her back to the keys so they faced each other.

He folded his arms and leaned back a bit so he could see her face. "What do you think? Are we a great team or what?"

She smiled. "You're so talented it makes me feel able to do almost anything."

"Making music with you is incredibly fun. In fact, everything I do with you is fun."

Katie nodded her head and looked at her intertwined fingers gripping the fingerboard. She was aware of their thighs touching and glad she held the guitar. It would have been so easy to move into his arms.

"You're nodding. Are you agreeing with me?"

"Yes. I've enjoyed each time we've been together. My head says, 'Careful, you've only known him for a short while.' My heart says, 'Forget it and enjoy being together.' Do you feel that way too?" She looked up and tilted her head to the side.

"Actually, my heart and head have surprised me. They both tell me I've found what I've been looking for, and I should pick it up and run with it." Katie bit her lip as she lowered her eyes.

"Don't worry, Katie. I'm not making a declaration. I do want you to know that my feelings are serious though. I'm not playing games. I won't rush you, but I'd like you to think about our relationship." He reached for her hand and moved it to his chest. She could feel the solid warmth of his body and his beating heart. "It's strange. I'm not normally aware of my heart beating, but when I'm with you, all my senses seem fine-tuned. I've felt more alive these last weeks than I have in years." She started to pull her hand away, but he held it there for another moment and then raised it to his lips, placed a kiss on her palm, and curled her fingers into a fist around it. "That's so you don't lose it." As he spoke, he laid her hand in her lap.

She stood and put her hand in her pocket, pulled it out and patted the outside. "There, now it'll be safe." She fought the urge to sit back on the bench beside him. He was like a magnet, drawing her heart toward him. She forced herself to smile and turned back to her chair. Three feet of space would lessen the pull. "Let's practice. Okay?"

She played the Bach number they'd chosen for her solo. Seth told her it sounded flawless. She knew she'd spend many more hours on it before Wednesday evening, but it gave her a great deal of confidence to know he thought she was ready.

Next they sang "God Bless America" together. Katie took the lead, and after a few bars she stopped. "Seth, this is in my range but I'm not comfortable with the lead."

"Okay, let's start from the beginning and see how it sounds with me singing it." They sang it through and made a few notations on the score.

After several more times, they decided to call it a night. Seth took the guitar from Katie and set it in the open case while she stood up and reached for her cane.

He motioned to her cane. "If I carry the guitar on stage, and you hold my hand, you won't need that. I think it would look completely natural. In my opinion the cane isn't an issue, but you've mentioned it several times, so don't use it."

"It's tempting. I felt comfortable tonight holding your arm without it. And such a nice arm it is." She patted his right arm. Goodness. Was she flirting?

At the door he reached out and cupped her face with both hands and slowly bent down. Katie didn't back away, and he covered her lips with his. Joy surged through her, and her arms involuntarily rose. She slid her fingers into his hair and pulled his head down to deepen the kiss. When she realized what she'd done, she loosened her hold and drew back.

He immediately let go and brought his hand back to her cheek. "I don't know if I've ever been happier than I am right now, Katie." She opened her mouth to speak and he put his finger on her lips. "Just sleep on that and I'll call you tomorrow."

Katie gently shut the front door and walked into her studio. Did his scent still linger in here or was she imagining it? She sat on the piano bench and lightly touched the keys. Had she encouraged him to kiss her? Yes, and she wasn't sorry.

Chapter 29

Katie pulled her new dress out of the closet on Saturday morning. She loved its subtle elegance. She twisted it this way and that in the morning light. Satisfied, she carefully hung it back. She couldn't settle to anything so called her mother. No answer. Where could she be? She tried phoning Anne. No answer there either, so she left a quick message. She stood at her studio window. The sunlight was so inviting she couldn't stay inside. She grabbed her jacket, cell phone, keys, and tossed a scarf around her neck, picked up her cane, and left the house.

Just as she had suspected, the day was beautiful. She raised her face to the sun as she crossed the front porch toward the steps. As she reached the edge, her cane and feet flew out from under her. Ice! Oh, no! She twisted to the right, trying to regain her balance, but her leg collapsed and she flew off the steps. She hit the ground with such force, the breath was knocked out of her. When she could finally breathe again, she felt pain knifing through her previously injured leg. She tried to move. Tears spurted from her eyes and a groan escaped her lips. The pain was excruciating. How would she make it back into the house? She wouldn't. Then she remembered her cell phone. She shifted to get it out of her pocket. Not only was the pain in her leg unbearable, but everything else ached too. She dialed 911.

By the time help arrived she was shivering with cold and shock. They appeared within minutes, but it felt like an hour. No sirens. Thank goodness. The paramedics were gentle and kind. During the ride to the hospital she couldn't stop the tears. This was so horrible. Before they lifted her out of the ambulance, she dried tear-wet cheeks on the scarf around her neck.

The first voice she heard when they wheeled her through the emergency doors was Dr. Hanson's.

"Katie Nelson, is that you?" He quickly took her hand and turned toward the paramedic wheeling her in. "What happened?" He walked beside the gurney as they moved toward an examining room.

"She slipped on ice and fell off her porch," the paramedic answered. "She had her cell phone so didn't lie there long." He stepped back while several nurses transferred her to an examining table. After they finished, the paramedic took the gurney and with a sympathetic look at Katie left the area. Dr. Hanson turned back to Katie. When she saw the look of compassion on his face, tears once again filled her eyes. She was so embarrassed and tried to stop them, but they continued to fall.

"I'm so sorry, Katie. We'll get an x-ray immediately and take a look at the damage."

Katie put her hand to her lips to stop their tremble. "I thought I was hallucinating when I heard your voice. What are you doing here on a Saturday morning?" How could Dr. Hanson be in the city from Rochester again just when she needed him? If God had this accident planned, it certainly wasn't fair.

"I came late yesterday to consult on a case and stayed overnight so I could check on the patient before leaving this morning. I was on my way out just as you were wheeled in. Let me make arrangements for that x-ray." Katie nodded and he left.

How long would this take? Her leg throbbed and she fought to keep from moaning. Eventually a nurse came and whisked her away. Fortunately, it didn't seem like a lengthy ordeal because she faded in and out of awareness from the pain medications.

Katie had been admitted into a hospital room before she saw Dr. Hanson again. When he arrived, the serious look on his face frightened her, and she put a hand to her throat.

He gazed somberly at her. "I think we should proceed with the surgery we talked about when you came to my office in Rochester. I'd prefer to do it there, but the team assisting me here is also very competent and I don't want you moved more than necessary. There's definitely damage from today's fall. As far as I can tell, surgery will correct that damage and still achieve the results we discussed before."

She sniffed and blew her nose. "Do I have a choice?" Her mind seemed foggy. Her fingers shredded the soggy tissue and her bottom lip trembled. "I'd made up my mind to go ahead with the surgery you recommended, but not until next month. Can you just give me a cast or something? Do I need to do this now? Today?"

"I've studied the x-rays and waiting would only compound your pain and delay your ultimate recovery. We'll do what you want, but my recommendation is surgery."

"Will I have to be in here long?" She indicated the hospital room.

He shook his head. "You're young. I wouldn't think more than a couple days. You'll be in a cast for awhile, but certainly will be mobile."

They talked for a few more minutes. She knew having surgery was the only possible decision, but oh how heartbreaking this all was. What about the benefit? She'd worked so hard. Was it all for nothing? She flexed her wrist. It didn't feel injured. Maybe she could still play at least. She swallowed the lump in her throat. "Okay. Let's just get it over with." She tried to smile but felt her chin quiver instead.

He patted her shoulder and left her to schedule an operating room and pull his team together.

Tears rolled down Katie's cheeks after he left. *Why did I have to fall God? Couldn't I have had the surgery next month without this added pain and grief? Are you listening? Do you care? What about Wednesday evening's performance? Now what do I do?*

She calmed down then rang for a nurse. When the nurse arrived, she asked for her cell phone and called her mother. Her mother answered on the first ring. Tears once again flooded Katie's eyes at the sound of her voice and she took a deep breath. "Hi, Mom. I'm calling from the hospital."

"Katie, what happened? Who's sick?" Anxiety laced her mother's voice. Katie told her what had happened. "If things go as planned, surgery should be under way before you get to the city, Mother." They talked for several minutes. Her mother prayed before saying goodbye, which made Katie feel better.

She tried calling Anne, but didn't get an answer. She left a message asking Anne to call her mother if she got this message within the next hour and gave her the number. She wanted Anne to hear about the accident from her mother instead of a voice message. After hanging up, she thought about Seth but was too weary to talk to anyone else. She knew Anne would tell him what had happened.

A nurse entered and told Katie she'd been assigned to her case and would be getting her ready for surgery. "Dr. Hanson is briefing the surgical team on the procedures he'll be performing. You're fortunate he's here and available. I'd trust him with my life."

Chapter 30

As if from far away Katie heard her mother's voice speaking softly. Then someone else spoke, and she felt a touch on her arm. "I think she's waking up. Mrs. Nelson. Can you hear me?" She didn't recognize the voice. She tried to open her eyes but the lids were too heavy. Everything ached.

The next voice she heard was her mother's. "Katie, dear. I'm here. I love you." She felt her mother's warm hand push the hair off her forehead and was comforted. Somehow the pain seemed less. She tried to smile, sighed, and drifted off to sleep again.

Was that Anne's voice? Yes, and she seemed to be having a conversation with someone but Katie couldn't make out the other voice.

Anne's here with my mother. Surgery must be over. I wish I didn't feel so tired or hurt so much.

Later when she finally opened her eyes, the sun shone through the windows of her room. Looking down the length of her body she could see her leg cradled in some kind of contraption that kept the bedding from touching it.

"Katie, you're awake." Anne came around the side of her bed. It was obvious she'd been there for awhile. Her hair was rumpled and she was yawning.

"Um, hm." She reached out and Anne clasped her hand. Another figure moved into her line of vision. Seth. She tried to tell him she was sorry she hadn't called him but couldn't form the words. Her eyes closed as sleep overtook her again.

The nurse came in and asked them to leave while she checked vital signs and took a look at the incision. Katie opened her eyes and watched them leave.

The nurse talked quietly while she worked. She said Dr. Hanson would be arriving soon and asked if she needed anything, then gave her a drink. Katie heard the doctor talking to someone in the hall, but he came into the room alone. After going over her chart he told her the surgery had gone well. "I'd like to tell you that your recovery will be complete, but until you're healed we just won't know."

She nodded and swallowed the lump in her throat. "But you think it was successful?"

He nodded. "Yes, Katie. I do." He put the chart back.

"But you can't guarantee it, can you?"

"You know I can't, but it really looks good, my dear." He smiled and touched her hand.

"How long have I been sleeping?"

"It's eight thirty Sunday morning. You've awakened several times but probably don't remember. You're mother's been here all night. I wanted you to remain lightly sedated so we could manage the pain for you."

"Do you have any idea how long I'll be in the hospital?"

"Since nothing else seems to be injured, I'd predict you can go home by Tuesday if everything goes well. Do you have any areas of pain other than your leg?"

"I don't think so. If I do, the pain medication's made me numb." She moved her head restlessly.

"We checked for bruising on your body and found none, which is remarkable considering your fall."

"It was so stupid." Her voice broke and she cleared her throat so she could go on. "I remember looking up and feeling blessed by such a beautiful day. The next thing I knew I was crumpled on the sidewalk. I still can't believe that you were here when they brought me in."

They talked for several minutes before he left. She was falling asleep when the door opened. Seth came into the room. He walked to the bed and reached for the hand without I.V.s.

Regret coursed through her. "I'm sorry about Wednesday. What's going to happen?"

"Katie, don't even think about it. New plans are made, and I'm taking your place."

Her chin quivered, and she opened her mouth to speak.

He touched his finger to her lips. "It's okay. I suggested it, and by Anne's reaction it makes her almost as happy as when you said yes."

She gave him a wan smile. "You'll be great." Weariness overcame her. She tried to keep her eyes open and couldn't. She felt him kiss her brow, and then he tucked her hand under the blanket. After she heard the door softly close, she drifted into a deep sleep.

Chapter 31

Katie sat on the side of her hospital bed and reached for the crutches. These were new. She'd thrown her old ones away hoping she'd never need them again. She sighed. This too would pass. Thankfully, the surgery on her lower leg and ankle had been successful. She wore a large removable boot instead of a cast. This gave the hospital staff easy access to the surgical site and meant she could remove it to shower when the incision healed. She stood as the door opened to admit her mother.

"Careful, Katie. Here, let me help you." Her mom moved quickly around the bed, but Katie had already positioned herself in front of the wheelchair.

She sat down with a sigh. "Hi, Mom. Did you have a decent night's sleep?"

"I was so tired when I got to your house last night I could have slept on the floor. Everything's lovely, and I slept like a baby." She kissed Katie's forehead.

"Look at you. They've already taken the I.V.s out. Are you really feeling well enough to be out of bed on your own? It's only Monday."

"I'm hoping to go home tomorrow, Mom, so I need to practice on these things." She indicated the crutches. "I'll admit I get tired easily and don't feel like taking a road trip."

"Oh, Katie, tomorrow's awfully soon. Don't get your hopes up."

They both looked toward the door as it opened again. Dr. Hanson walked in. He smiled at Katie's mother. "Your girl's not easy to keep down." He put his hands on his hips and observed Katie for a moment, then looked back at her mother. "She had me worried when I saw the original scans."

Katie's hands gripped the armrests of the wheelchair. Was he bringing bad news after all?

He went on. "However, that fall might have been a blessing in disguise." He smiled down at Katie. "My prediction is that you will have much less pain in the future and much better function in that leg."

Katie let out the breath she'd been holding. She cleared her throat and glanced from her mother to the doctor. "Oh, boy. For a minute there, I thought the news wasn't going to be good." She pushed the wheels on the chair back and forth several times and smiled at both of them. "I feel like dancing."

The doctor chuckled. "Well, the way things are going, I wouldn't rule it out." He turned and picked up her chart. "I need to make a note in here." Katie and her mother watched as he wrote. He put the chart down and turned. "I'll be back before I leave for the day." He touched Katie's shoulder. "I'm pleased with the results so far." He smiled and nodded farewell to both of them and walked out.

The door closed behind him, and Katie turned to her mother. "I have such conflicting feelings about this accident, Mom. Oh, how I wish it hadn't happened now when I worked so hard to be ready for Wednesday." She hesitated and then went on. "But now I'm through with the surgery and already in the healing process. I don't have to wait. It's over. And beside that, Seth's taking my place on Wednesday. That's another miracle."

"Yes, Anne and Seth told me." She sat down on the bed and faced Katie. "I like what I've seen of him. He was so concerned about you. Tell me about him."

Katie looked down at her hands and ran her finger over the bruises where the I.V.s had been. "I don't know what there is to tell, Mother. I find him attractive and, oh my, you should hear him sing." She looked up and smiled. "I guess you will on Wednesday night. I admit something about him touches my heart, but I've only known him a month." She shifted in the wheelchair to get more comfortable.

"Katie, dear, how long did you know John before you told me he was the one?"

Katie felt as if she'd been punched. She gasped and covered her mouth with her hands.

Her mother hopped off the bed and wrapped her arms around her shoulders. "Darling, I'm so sorry. Please forgive me. What a stupid thing to say."

Katie tried to find a tissue in the pocket of her robe. Her mother grabbed some off the bedside table and handed them to her.

After wiping her eyes and blowing her nose, Katie moved the wheelchair to the side of the bed. Seeing the worried look on her mother's face, she spoke. "I'm fine, Mom. Really. Maybe I should get back into bed."

"Here, let me help." Her mother picked up the crutches from where they'd fallen and helped her get back into bed. After Katie got settled, she patted the blanket. "Sit here." She gave her mother a watery smile. "I'm an emotional mess, but if you can take a few tears, I'd like to talk."

Her mother climbed up beside her and took her hand.

Katie looked at the flowers on her window ledge without really seeing them. "Mother, when did I tell you John was the one?"

"You don't remember?"

Katie shook her head and reached up to twist her earring, forgetting they'd been taken out and she hadn't put them back in.

Her mother drew her knees up and wrapped her arms around them. "You'd been on exactly three dates with him when you came home for Christmas. We were opening presents and you were surprised and delighted to get one from John. He had mailed it, and I didn't tell you, just put it under the tree. You burst into laughter when you opened it to find a monkey playing a guitar. Then you got all flustered because the monkey had diamond studs in its ears."

"Those are the diamonds I wear all the time. I just don't remember saying anything about him being the right one."

"Well you did, and your father and I were anxious to meet him. Young men hadn't played a big part in your life, so that was a new experience for us."

Katie absently pleated the blanket between her fingers. "I remember you liked him when I brought him home."

"He called your dad, 'Sir,' which I found endearing." She paused and smiled. "He called me Jane."

"Why does the thought of John calling you Jane make you smile?"

"I don't know. Just the way he said it was, oh, warm maybe? I felt as if he'd love us because we were part of the package. Love our daughter, love us. I've often thanked God your father lived until after your wedding."

Katie nodded in agreement and tried to stifle a yawn.

Her mother stood. "You're tired. Why don't you take a little nap while I go get a cup of coffee. Do you need anything? Want anything?"

Katie's lids sagged heavily. "It seems like all I've done since surgery is sleep." She lowered the head of the bed.

"Sleeping's the best thing you can do my dear. Hopefully the nurse won't come in and wake you up as soon as you fall asleep." She patted Katie's hand and quietly left the room.

Katie closed her eyes and her dad's face drifted behind her closed lids. She'd love to be able to ask her dad's opinion of Seth. Her mom liked him. That was good. Wasn't it? She'd think about this later. So tired.

* * *

Jane walked to the elevator, and when the doors opened, Seth emerged.

"Mrs. Eckstrom, are you leaving? How's Katie?"

"She's doing remarkably well and hopes to go home tomorrow. She looked so tired I left so she could sleep. Do you want to go with me to the cafeteria and get a cup of coffee?" She watched him look toward Katie's closed door. Was that disappointment reflected on his face? Maybe she should have told him to go on in. "Seth?"

He turned back to her. "Yes?"

Jane glanced at her watch. "You probably don't have much time. Why don't you go on in. I'll get a cup of coffee and be back in a little while. I know she'd love to see you and can sleep later."

"You're sure?"

She nodded and pressed the button for the elevator. "Go ahead. I've got several calls I want to make. I'll find a quiet corner in the cafeteria to have my coffee and make those calls." The doors opened and she waved him away.

Chapter 32

Katie opened her eyes and found Seth at her bedside. She smiled. "Hi. How long have you been here?"

"Not long. I came to check on you." He reached out and covered her hand resting on the sheet.

She turned it palm up, threaded her fingers through his and glanced at the clock. "Shouldn't you be at work?"

"I have to go back for a meeting soon. I needed a moment alone with you. I met your mom at the elevator, and she told me to come on in." He gave her a lopsided smile. "I like her."

"I'm glad. We talked about you this morning. She likes you too." She grinned. "At least what she knows about you."

Seth sat down on the side of the bed. "You talked about me, huh?" He squeezed her hand and looked down at their entwined fingers.

Katie thought he looked uncertain and a little shy. She found it endearing. A lump formed in her throat and she swallowed. Drat these emotions sitting so near the surface. She would not tear up.

"Your mother said you might be released tomorrow. Don't you think it's kind of soon?"

She shook her head. "No. Dr. Hanson said the surgery went fine, and besides, no one can recover well in a hospital. I miss my home." She pulled her fingers out of his hand so she could scoot up a little higher in the bed. "It's such a miracle that I didn't even bang my head. I wish I'd have looked down instead of up. I'd have noticed the ice."

He picked up her hand again. "Anne told me you had been considering another surgery."

She nodded. "Yes, but I wanted to wait until after Wednesday night to schedule it. I'm so sorry about the gala, Seth." Her voice was husky with regret.

"I'm looking forward to it. I only wish you could be there." He lifted her hand and brushed a kiss across the knuckles just as her mother opened the door and entered.

Seth stood and gently placed Katie's hand back on the bed. "I need to leave." He turned to her mom. "Will I see you on Wednesday evening? I'd be happy to pick you up."

"If Katie's doing well, I'll be there. I have a friend coming, and he'll take me. Thanks though."

They said their goodbyes, and when Seth turned at the door, Katie lifted her hand in farewell. He hesitated, then strode back to her bed, leaned over and kissed her. When he lifted his head, he cupped her cheek and brushed her lips with his thumb. "See ya." He left without glancing back.

Katie watched in shocked silence until the door closed.

Her mother broke the silence. "Well. I think he gave us a message, my dear. He doesn't seem the type to play 'show and tell' without meaning it."

Katie brought her hands to her flushed cheeks. "Oh, Mom. When I opened my eyes and saw him standing by the bed my heart jumped and happiness zinged through me. When he kissed me just now . . ." She sighed and reached for her earring, then remembered again she didn't have them in.

"Mom, will you please find my earrings? They should be in the plastic bag in the closet. I miss having them on." They were in a small plastic bag along with her watch and rings. Katie took them from her mother and twisted them in the sunlight before putting them in her ears.

"Thanks. Part of me is missing when I'm not wearing them."

"Let's get back to Seth. You said, 'when he kissed me just now' and then stopped. What you were going to say?"

Katie looked at her mother and frowned. "My feelings for him scare me. We've known each other for a month. I'm thirty-nine years old and not impulsive. I told God over the Christmas holidays how lonesome I felt for John and J. J., but I didn't ask for a replacement." She took a big breath. "Part of me is frightened. The other part looks forward to seeing him and hearing his voice."

Jane reached for the chair, pushed it closer to Katie's bed, and settled in. "If it's his relationship with the Lord you're worried about, I don't think it's an issue. He's independent and intelligent, not the type of man to make a commitment because of a woman. Give him time."

"Give him time? Don't you mean 'give me time?' I feel like a snowball which turned into a snowman because I accidentally rolled down an unseen hill. It's exciting and yet makes me dizzy."

Her mother laughed. "It's about time life made you dizzy."

The door opened and Dr. Hanson came in and looked over her chart. Katie couldn't tell by his face if he was pleased or not. He wrote a few notes and turned to her.

"Unless you fall out of bed today and injure something else, I'd say you can go home tomorrow."

Katie realized she'd been holding her breath and let it out slowly. She tugged at the side rail and grinned. "I'll sleep with this up just in case."

He laughed. "I'm pleased with your progress, Katie. Let's schedule an appointment for two weeks from today. I have the use of an office here at the hospital so you don't have to come to Rochester. My nurse there will call you with the details. I'll do your discharge paperwork today before I leave." He said goodbye to both of them and left with the promise of seeing Katie soon.

Katie looked at her mother after the door closed and saw weariness etched on her face. "Mother, you don't have to stay the rest of the day. Hanging around in a hospital room is exhausting."

"I'm happy to be here with you, my dear."

"I know, and I love having you. However, Anne called this morning to say she's coming by after work, and I'm going to take a nap before the dinner trays are delivered. Why don't you go back to the house and put your feet up."

Her mother stood and stretched. "If you're sure, I'll leave you to take your nap. How should we handle the morning?"

"I'll get the details and give you a call."

The head of the bed had been raised so Jane stretched up to kiss Katie. Although the years had added a few pounds to her frame, she still remained a beautiful woman. Katie kissed her back and smiled. "I love you, Mom. Life is always better when you're close."

"I love you too, Katie. You're sure you're well enough to come home tomorrow?"

"Don't worry. Dr. Hanson wouldn't let me go home if he had any qualms over it."

"Okay." Her mom gathered up her belongings and waved from the doorway as she left.

Quiet settled over the room and Katie relaxed into her pillows. Her leg had started to ache and she felt as weak as a kitten. If she asked for more medication would they think she wasn't ready to be discharged tomorrow? Now she was getting paranoid. She told herself to stop it. Taking medication relaxed the muscles and helped the healing process. She rang for the nurse.

Chapter 33

Katie opened her eyes to the light of a new day and snuggled her nose into the pillow. When she smelled the light cologne she habitually wore she smiled. *I'm home. It's Wednesday. Thank you, God!* A light tap on the door was followed by her mother's entrance.

"Morning, Katie. Look what just arrived." Her mother walked to the bed holding a crystal vase filled with a huge bouquet of multicolored roses and lowered them so Katie could breathe in their fragrance.

"Hmm, beautiful. Who sent them?"

Her mother made an inelegant sound as she placed them on Katie's bedside table. "As if you don't know. I was surprised he didn't send flowers to the hospital. Oh, here's the card." She reached into her sweater pocket and pulled out a small note card. Katie opened it, read it quickly, smiled, and put it back into the envelope.

"Katie, you little tease. What did he say?"

Katie laughed and handed it to her mother to read aloud.

"'Dear Katie, I didn't bring flowers to the hospital because they're always hard to get home. Hopefully my message is clear. S.' Ah. This is even more interesting than I thought."

Katie raised an eyebrow at her mother. "Oh? Why?"

"Don't you know what the different colors stand for?"

"I've always been told red ones mean 'I love you.'" Katie blushed when she looked at the bouquet. There were quite a few red ones mixed in.

Her mother touched the different colored blossoms as she spoke. "Yes, and pink communicates admiration and friendship. Lavender stands for enchantment and love at first sight. Peach conveys excitement and desire. Yellow is remembrance of a loved one and white and red together signify unity. Well, well. I see white positioned next to red here several times."

"Mother, how in the world do you know this stuff?"

"When I was young, every girl knew the language of flowers. It's something you don't forget. Your father spoke the language quite well." She glanced toward the window and Katie thought she looked wistful. She turned and smiled at her daughter.

"Are you ready for a late breakfast? I can help you with a bath after we eat."

"Food and a bath would be heavenly. I don't want to eat in bed. I'll come to the kitchen." She tossed the duvet aside. Her mother handed her a robe and held the crutches until Katie stood. When asked if she'd rather use the wheelchair, Katie refused, and together they moved toward the kitchen.

"It looks like you've been up for awhile Mom. Are those fresh muffins? Yum. I'm surprised the smell didn't wake me." The doorbell rang. Katie's hand flew to her hair and pushed it back.

"Sit down, and I'll see who it is. Don't worry. You look great even though you just got out of bed." Her mom chuckled and headed toward the front entrance.

The door swished open. "Hi, Anne. You're just in time for breakfast."

Katie heard their exchange and felt her heartbeat slowing. She'd been anticipating Seth's voice. She told herself to be thankful he took the time to send flowers. After all, tonight was the big night.

Anne walked into the kitchen and gazed down at her friend. "You look great. Why are you sloughing off tonight and not performing?"

Katie twisted around in her chair and brought her surgical boot into view without saying anything.

"Oh, yes. What some people will do to get out of the spotlight!" Anne bent down and hugged her. "Seriously, how do you feel? You do look great, but are you in pain?"

Katie shook her head. "Honestly, I don't feel bad. Oh, it's there, but I've been worse, believe me." She gave her friend a twisted smile. "I think the pain of not being able to perform tonight with Seth is greater than my physical pain. Until this happened, I didn't realize how much I wanted to play and sing." She paused. "I know God's plan isn't always our plan, but I admit I'm disappointed."

Anne went to the coffee maker and filled a mug, then came back to the table and sat facing Katie. "If we asked Seth's mother, I bet she'd tell us tonight's performance by her son is a miracle directly from God."

"But he'd already agreed to perform with me."

"You're right. Not as the star performer, though. More attention would have been on you than him. I never expected him to call and tell me he'd take your place." Anne moved her mug in a circle on the table as she talked. "Something's happened to Seth, and I think you're that something. He didn't want you to fret. Doing the complete program is his way of caring for you."

At that moment Katie's mother placed fresh muffins and fruit on the table, so Katie didn't have to say anything. Her mother sat down with them, and they bowed their heads while her mom thanked God for the food.

Katie broke off a piece of muffin. "What are you doing away from work on a Wednesday morning? Shouldn't you have your nose to the grindstone? Don't get me wrong. I'm more than happy to see you."

"I wanted to make sure you arrived home safely yesterday, and to check on your mother's ability to take care of you."

Katie smothered a laugh with her napkin and hung her head trying to look longsuffering. "It's difficult for her since she's such an old woman and all, but we're managing."

"Cut it out, you two." Her mom flicked her napkin at Katie and laughed. "If you're not nice to me I'll leave you on your own. Don't forget, you'll need help with a bath."

"I take it all back, Mother. You're the best." She reached over and touched her mother's hand. "You really are the best of mothers. I love you." Katie felt herself getting emotional again and took a sip of coffee.

Anne chimed in. "Katie, I actually stopped by to ask if you're considering attending tonight's event. Have you thought about it?"

Katie's mom frowned. "No. It's out of the question, Anne. She's just been released from the hospital."

Katie reached up, turned her earring contemplatively, and looked from one to the other. Her mother started to speak, and Katie interrupted her. "Just a minute, Mom. This idea has been running through my head ever since I realized I wouldn't be able to perform myself. I'd love to be there. I *have* to be there. If I went in the wheelchair, I think it'd be doable." She looked at the frown on her mother's face. "Seriously, if I arrived at the last possible moment and left right away, I could do it. I'll take a nap this afternoon." She grinned sheepishly at them. "Listen to me. It sounds like I'm an infant."

They discussed the pros and cons of Katie's attendance, and Katie and Anne overrode her mom's objections. Finally Anne said she had to be going.

Katie touched her arm. "I'd like this to be a surprise tonight. Please don't tell Seth I'll be there."

Anne agreed and said goodbye, then turned around again. "Good grief! We haven't discussed how you'll get there. I have to arrive early, so I can't pick you up."

Katie's mom spoke up. "Samuel and I will bring her if she insists on going. We'll see how she feels later today." Anne and Katie exchanged glances. Katie insisted she'd be fine, so Anne left with a brief wave.

Katie was weary and returned to her room to rest. The evening would be a drain on her strength, but she'd set her heart on going. She'd also get a chance to observe her mother and Samuel together. How serious was their relationship?

After crawling into bed with a stack of pillows propping up her shoulders, she picked up her Bible and read Psalm sixteen, one of

David's songs. *The Message* version brought a smile to her lips when she read verse seven.

"The wise counsel God gives when I'm awake
is confirmed by my sleeping heart.
Day and night I'll stick with God;
I've got a good thing going and I'm not letting go."

Yes, I do have a good thing going, and I'm hanging on tight! Thank you, God for a peaceful spirit. I'm trusting You. I know You have my interests close to your heart. Give Seth confidence tonight. I don't have to ask You to help him do well because that's a given. May he once again discover the satisfaction and joy of singing for other people's pleasure. May he also recognize Your place in tonight's event.

Katie set her Bible aside. She had intended to stay awake for awhile to think about the evening and savor her anticipation of the coming event. Instead, she slid under her duvet with a sigh and fell asleep almost immediately.

Chapter 34

The banquet room buzzed with the sounds of talking and laughter as constituents, politicos, and fundraisers milled around, greeting each other and waiting to get close enough to the senator to shake his hand. Huge chandeliers cast a warm glow over the formally dressed throng. Katie hated viewing the scene from a wheelchair. She couldn't see anyone except those close to her. She'd have been better off on crutches. The pain in her leg would have only allowed a few minutes of being upright, but she'd have had a better view.

Samuel and her mother guided her chair in the direction of their table. As people parted for them to pass, many recognized Katie and stopped her for greetings. She felt flushed and overwhelmed by all the people who appeared delighted to see her.

Katie and her party found their table and had just gotten settled when a hand touched her shoulder. She looked up. Seth. Lifting her shoulder she touched her cheek to his hand and smiled.

He spoke first. "Hi, Katie Nelson. Who let you out of the house tonight?"

"Hi, yourself, Seth Prentice." She tipped her head toward her mother. "My mother couldn't keep me home, even though she tried mighty hard." Katie grinned at him. "You see, I know the gentleman performing tonight, and I was determined to come. Even if I had to crawl."

"You would have, huh?" He squeezed her shoulder.

Anne arrived at that moment looking frazzled. She pointed to a place setting without a chair in front of it. "Seth, put Katie there so she doesn't have to transfer from the wheelchair. You sit next to her. They're going to start. I'm sitting across from you. I'll be right back." As he sat, a young man from the senator's retinue got everyone's attention from the podium. He introduced himself and asked them to bow their heads while he said a brief prayer to start the evening. Seth reached over and took Katie's hand. She curled her fingers around his and squeezed. Was she really holding hands under the table with Seth? Yup. Reluctantly, she withdrew her hand when the prayer was over.

Numerous servers swarmed around the room placing dinner before everyone. Seth leaned in close enough so she could hear him. "I'd like you to meet my brother and sister-in-law." He indicated the couple to his right and got their attention. "Katie Nelson, this is my brother Peter and his wife, Joanne." They were too far away to shake hands and no one could move easily.

Peter half rose out of his chair as he spoke. "I'm so happy to meet you. This is my wife Joanne." He sat back down and Joanne smiled at her. Joanne whispered something to Peter.

Katie wondered what Joanne had said. Did they approve? Did she care? Her stomach muscles tightened. She cared more than she'd realized and told herself to get a grip. She glanced from Peter to Seth. They had similar features. Both had beautiful blue eyes set under well-defined brows and lots of dark hair. Peter was going grey at the temples. Seth was better looking of course. Katie bit her lip to keep from smiling at the thought. She in turn introduced Peter and Joanne to her mother and Samuel.

Their meals were set before them. Katie wasn't very hungry. Her stomach was a little nervous for Seth, and her leg ached. She needed to eat to keep her mother from worrying, so she cut the chicken on her plate and took a small bite. Hmm. It didn't taste like sawdust after all.

Conversation swirled around the table to an accompaniment of utensils on china. Food disappeared from everyone's plate except Seth's. Katie noticed. "Aren't you hungry?"

He pushed his plate away. "I don't usually eat before singing." He leaned close to her ear. "We can go out afterward and indulge. What do you say?" He pulled back and scrutinized her face. "On the other hand, I'll take you home immediately when this gig is over. You're pale. Is all of this too much?" He laid his hand over hers on the table.

She shook her head. "I took pain medication right before leaving home. It makes me tired. I'm fine, really. I can sleep all day tomorrow, and I'm being careful. Don't worry, I know my limits and they haven't been reached yet." She gently pulled her hand from under his.

Looking up, Katie saw Anne and Joanne smile at each other. Now there'd be speculation. Did she care? Nope. Where did that answer come from? Katie took a sip of water and realized Joanne was asking her a question.

"Sorry. What did you say?"

Joanne smiled. "I thought Peter said something about you performing tonight too. Am I wrong?"

Katie felt Seth's arm go to the back of her wheelchair and she whispered that it was okay. She answered Joanne. "I had an accident on Saturday and ended up having surgery. That's what put me into this chair. Your brother came to my rescue. She felt his hand touch her shoulder, and warmth seeped into her heart.

At that moment the master of ceremonies came to the microphone and made several introductions. Financial business was briefly discussed, and finally Seth was invited to the platform. As he strode to the piano Katie watched with anticipation and some trepidation. Had she pushed him into something he wasn't ready for? Oh, dear. What if his voice gave out on him? She breathed a quick prayer.

The hearty round of applause his introduction produced intruded into Katie's thoughts. She realized that numerous people knew him and wondered how many knew about his musical talents. He looked straight at her as he pulled the mike toward himself. Her mouth went dry, and her heart beat a crazy rhythm. She touched her fingers to her lips and then touched her heart. He smiled.

The smile remained on his lips as he started to play. A hush settled over the crowd. He played an intricate medley of patriotic songs he had arranged in a classical style. Katie marveled at the complexity of the arrangement and his stunning finger dexterity. Her heart swelled with pride. What a wonderful man. What a wonderful gift God has given him.

The crowd erupted when he finished and he stood to accept their applause. Once again his eyes found Katie's. She wanted to shout, "bravo," but controlled the impulse and touched her heart again. He nodded and sat back down. After a brief piano introduction he began to sing "America the Beautiful." His rich baritone filled every corner of the room and the sincerity with which he sang brought tears to more than just Katie's eyes. After the first verse he raised his hand to indicate everyone should stand. "Join me if you know the words."

Katie couldn't stand, and no one noticed she didn't sing. She had a lump in her throat and couldn't force words or music around it. She knew this was a gift he was giving her. How courageous he was. It would be wonderful to be up there singing with him. Maybe someday.

Everyone surrounding her sang with enthusiasm. After the last verse the crowd clapped until Seth agreed to sing "God Bless America." After the last note died away, total silence filled the hall. Seth sat with his head bowed, and Katie realized the song had been sung as a prayer for the country. No one clapped, and after several moments he rose from the piano bench and made his way back to the table.

The young gentleman who had offered the opening prayer made his way to the mike and thanked Seth. He then introduced the senator and the room erupted with cheers, shouts, and applause.

As the senator started to speak, Katie reached for Seth's hand. She needed to touch him. His hand was warm and strong and reassuring. She knew he'd seen her wipe tears from her face while he walked toward their table, and she wasn't ashamed of crying. Her emotions were fragile because of surgery, but Katie would have cried anyway at hearing his beautiful rendition of that special song.

Throughout the senator's speech, pain throbbed through her leg with increasing volume. By the time he finished, her knuckles had turned white on the arms of the wheelchair. Seth glanced at Katie, noticed her hands, and turned to her mother. "My car is parked on this level of the parking ramp, right next to the elevator. Why don't I take Katie home, then she won't have to wait one more minute." He looked at Katie with a raised eyebrow, waiting for her approval.

Katie sighed with relief. "I'll admit I'd like to leave as soon as possible. The back door would be great then I won't have to talk to anyone."

They said goodnight to everyone at their table, and Seth whisked her out the door. When they got to the car, he lifted her out of the wheelchair and placed her gently into the front seat. As they pulled out of the ramp Katie leaned against the head rest and turned her head toward him as she spoke. "I'm feeling guilty for letting you leave so quickly. I know everyone would have wanted to talk to you. I can't say I'm sorry for getting out before the rush though."

He lifted his right hand from the steering wheel and touched her cheek. "You're so beautiful. I wanted to tell you earlier, but not with everyone listening. I'm glad to be out of there. I need time to sort out my feelings about tonight. I'm glad Peter and Joanne came and got to meet you."

Weak and weary, Katie closed her eyes as she spoke. "Seth, you're moving too fast for me."

"I'm sorry, Katie. I seem to have lost all sense of timing. Whenever I read my Bible I notice the verses speaking about God's gifts, and your face passes before my mind's eye. You're constantly in my thoughts."

Katie kept her eyes closed and stretched her hand toward him. He grasped it and squeezed gently without saying anything more until they were at the house. He got the key and went in to open the door then came back down. He once again lifted her and this time carried her into the house elevator and didn't set her down until he could place her on the edge of her bed.

"I'll bring the wheelchair up. It'll only take a minute." She nodded and twisted around until she could lie down as he walked out of the room.

* * *

When Seth returned he found her sleeping. He glanced at his watch. It had only taken him five minutes to get the wheelchair. She must have been exhausted. He pulled the duvet up and stood for a moment watching her sleep, then placed a light kiss on her forehead. "Good night, my darling."

Chapter 35

Seth was waiting in the living room with the fireplace burning when Katie's mother and Samuel arrived home. Her mother smiled as she removed her coat. "How is she? Was the evening too much for her?"

"Probably, but she wouldn't admit it. She looked exhausted."

Samuel came into the living room still in his coat. Jane raised her eyebrows. "Aren't you going to stay for a cup of coffee? It's ready to brew, and I made oatmeal cookies today in case you'd both stay."

Samuel immediately started to unbutton his coat and looked at Seth with a grin. "What do you say? I think oatmeal cookies are pretty hard to resist." He shrugged out of his coat and tossed it over the arm of the couch.

Seth nodded. This would be a great time to get to know Katie's mother and her friend. Although weary, he knew sleep wouldn't come easily tonight. A miracle had taken place in his life because of Katie's encouragement. He'd never have agreed to sing for anyone else.

If only she were awake so they could have talked about the night. If only she could have sung with him. He wanted to go into her bedroom and just look at her while she slept. He'd noticed the roses on her bedside table and smiled. She'd blushed when she'd mentioned them tonight. What did that mean?

Jane turned toward the kitchen, and Samuel and Seth sat in the fireside chairs. Samuel spoke first. "Well young man, I don't remember when I've enjoyed the song "God Bless America" more than I did tonight."

"Thank you, sir."

"Oh, you don't need to 'sir' me. Just call me Samuel like everyone else does. It's never been Sam or Sammy, even when I was a little boy. My mother didn't shorten names."

Seth stretched out his legs and crossed them at the ankles. He ran his hand through his hair as he spoke. "That's interesting. My mother was the same way. When friends called my brother Pete instead of Peter, she always found a gentle way of correcting them. I didn't have to deal with it because no one tried to shorten Seth."

Katie's mother poked her head around the door. "Hey. Wait till I come in there. I don't want to miss anything. The coffee's almost done and I'll only be a minute."

Samuel stood. "I think I'll go and see if I can carry the tray." He headed toward the kitchen.

Seth got up and looked into the fireplace. It wasn't cold in the room, but the fire was inviting. He wished Katie were here. He turned to the mantle and picked up the picture of John and J. J. He concentrated on J. J. This had been Katie's son. Anger gripped his heart at the thought of her loss. Anne had said she shouldn't have more children. Was that still true?

He put the picture back as Jane and Samuel came into the room. Samuel put the tray on the coffee table and turned to Seth. "How many cookies do you want? I'm starting with three because I've eaten Jane's cookies before, and you can't stop at one. Or even two." He grinned and took the cup of coffee Jane handed him.

"I didn't eat much at dinner so I'll have three too."

Katie's mother frowned. "Oh, Seth. I could have made you a sandwich. I can still do it if you'd like." She started to turn toward the kitchen.

He stopped her. "This is all I need. I love oatmeal cookies, and these look great." No one spoke for a moment. Seth sighed and relaxed. He glanced between Samuel and Katie's mother as he sipped the coffee.

What kind of relationship did Jane and Samuel have? He'd ask Katie tomorrow.

Katie's mother broke the silence. "Isn't it strange that Katie had decided to participate tonight and then couldn't after all? Her fall puzzles me." She placed her empty plate on the floor by her feet. "There are some things I'm going to ask God when I get a chance." Seth saw the distress in her eyes. He'd had some of those same feelings and questions. Before he could speak, Samuel did.

"Yeah, me too. It makes me sad for her. Do you think she's resentful over it?

Jane shook her head and smiled. "No." She turned to Seth. "As soon as you told her to not worry and that you'd do it, she quit fretting and concentrated on being well enough to go with us tonight."

Seth was restless and stood. "I never expected Katie to be there."

Jane shrugged. "She wouldn't take no for an answer. She wasn't going to miss it." She looked down at her hands and back up at him. "Seth, your talents are amazing, and your choice of songs touched hearts. That's not the norm at a political fundraiser."

He thanked her and walked back to his chair but didn't sit down. Should he say what was on his heart? He took a deep breath and plunged in. "I realize I've only known Katie for a month, but . . ." He shook his head. "It's hard to explain. I feel as if I've known her for years. She's an incredible lady."

Katie's mother nodded. "When I saw the roses and read your note, I knew this wasn't a casual friendship. At least on your side. I didn't realize you young people knew the language of flowers. I thought it was just our generation who sent those messages." She smiled at Samuel.

Seth rubbed the back of his neck and sat. "My mother loves flowers, and Peter and I learned what the colors meant at a fairly early age. I still love the look on Mother's face when Dad brings her flowers. Did Katie understand or did you interpret them for her?"

"I told her. She loved them. I also think she loved the message they sent."

His knuckles were white from gripping the arms of his chair, and he moved them to his lap. "I know this is moving quickly, but I can't seem to slow my feelings down. From the moment I met her she has been on my mind. I feel like a callow youth in the first throes of love. Whew. Doesn't that sound dramatic?"

"I'm thrilled over the changes in Katie." Jane's voice was tender as she spoke. "Meeting you is a sweet gift from God for her. I couldn't be more delighted. I've been waiting for her to awaken from her grief." She set down her coffee cup and stifled a yawn.

Seth immediately got to his feet. "It's time for me to leave. Please tell Katie I'll call tomorrow."

Samuel stood and picked his coat up off the couch. "I need to be going too."

Jane helped him into his coat. "Come for breakfast tomorrow morning before you drive back home." She smoothed the fabric over his shoulders, and let her hand linger for a moment.

Seth hid a smile. Theirs was definitely more than a casual friendship. Samuel's answer was short but definite. "Great. What time?"

Jane tried to stifle another yawn but gave in to it and covered her mouth. "Whew. I'm more weary than I thought. Around nine would be good. How about you Seth? Do you want to join us?"

He said he'd like to but had several meetings on his schedule for the morning that couldn't be changed. They said their goodbyes and Samuel and Seth left together.

As he started his car, Seth regretted he hadn't gone in to Katie's room to say a silent good night. He'd call between meetings tomorrow.

He looked at the stars. A month ago he would have been thanking his lucky stars. Now he thanked the Lord. What a change.

Chapter 36

"Katie, wake up, it's after five." Her mother's hand gently touched her shoulder as Katie opened her eyes. She stretched.

"Wow. It feels like I've slept forever. It's still Thursday, right? The fundraiser was just last night?" At her mother's chuckle and nod she pushed the covers back and struggled to sit.

"Here, let me help." Her mother pulled the duvet farther down and helped Katie slide her legs over the edge of the bed. She moved the wheelchair close and Katie smoothly transferred into it.

"Thanks, Mom." Katie moved the wheels back and forth and jiggled on the chair in a little mock dance, then giggled. "I had a dream about dancing and ooh, it was so fun. That's what I'm really looking forward to."

Her mother laughed. "Well, now you had better get ready for dinner. We'll hold the dance afterward."

Katie grinned and took a deep breath. "It smells like you've been cooking."

"Yes. Lasagna."

"Great. I'm hungry." Katie's stomach growled as she turned the wheelchair and rolled toward the bathroom. She laughed again. "See?"

Her mother spoke before walking out the door. "You did say Anne would be here around six thirty didn't you?"

"Yup, and she said she'd call if anything came up and she couldn't make it."

"Okay. Well, yell if you need me. I'll leave the door open so I can hear you." Her mother turned and walked down the hall.

Left to herself, Katie took her time getting ready for the evening. Keeping her injured leg dry while taking a shower presented no problems since her showerhead was on a movable rod and she could adjust its height. The built in bench was long enough for her to stretch out her leg. She relaxed for several minutes in the warm steam.

Did Seth shower at night or in the morning? Oh, brother. What was she thinking? She grabbed the shower gel and told herself to get a grip. As she lathered, the scent surrounded her and she breathed deeply. Would Seth like this smell? That thought made her sit up straight and get down to the business of getting ready for the evening. Seth wasn't coming for dinner, but he'd be there later. She smiled.

Dinner was delightful. Afterward, Katie's mom insisted she'd do the cleanup alone, so Katie and Anne moved to the living room. Anne chose a chair by the fireplace and Katie transferred to the sofa. She struggled to get comfortable, and Anne arranged pillows behind her back and under her leg.

"How does that feel? You're not too tired? Does you leg hurt?" Anne reached for the throw at the end of the sofa.

Katie grasped her hand to stop her. "I slept almost all day, and I have hardly any pain in my leg, so quit fussing. Sit down and tell me all you know."

They both laughed, because that's what they used to say when they were getting ready for a good gossip session in "the old days." Anne went back to her chair and got comfortable.

Katie remembered what she'd wanted to ask Anne. "Have you seen any more of Doctor Joseph Browne?"

"He was at the fundraiser last night, and I spoke to him briefly after you left." Anne looked down at her hands.

What was she hiding? Katie leaned forward. "Did you go talk to him or the other way around?"

Anne looked up and grinned. "I know what you're getting at. Don't create a situation out of nothing."

"Well, that doesn't answer my question. Did you go talk to him or did he come over and talk to you?"

Anne paused. "He came over to me. And yes, I was glad he did, but you know he's a client, and that's all there is to it."

"He won't be a client forever. I liked him, Anne."

"You only met him once. How could you like him?"

Katie shrugged. "I got a good feeling about him. He seemed to have a special relationship with his daughter." Katie looked up at the picture of John and J. J. on the mantle and back at Anne. She sighed. "I admit that it doesn't hurt as much any more. Time does heal, but sometimes I feel guilty for not missing them as much as I used to. Why can't life be less complicated?"

Before Anne could say anything, Katie's mom came in from the kitchen. "I just put the coffee on. Do either of you need anything?"

"No, Mother. Come and sit down." Katie looked at her watch. She realized Seth would be there shortly and her heart skipped a beat. At that moment, they heard the doorbell ring. Her mother jumped up to get it.

Katie propped herself a little higher on the sofa and smoothed her hair. It was taking forever for Seth to greet her mom and take off his coat. She wished she'd been able to get up and open the door. He saw Anne first and greeted her, then looked at Katie on the sofa. His eyes crinkled as his smile widened. Did she see love in those eyes?

He raised an eyebrow. "Have you recovered from last night? I don't need to ask. You look beautiful and rested."

Katie knew her smile was huge but couldn't help it. Did it matter if her mother and friend could tell how happy she was to see him? This moment had been in the back of her mind since she had awakened from her nap, and now here he was. He radiated health and charm, and the nicest part of all was that he was here to see her. "I'm doing great, thanks." She lightly tapped her leg. "There's hardly any pain, and I slept most of the day." There was room at the end of the sofa, and she pointed to the space. “You can sit there if you want to.” He avoided her leg and sat down. He’d taken his shoes off, and he looked comfortable and at home. At home? Her heart picked up speed at the thought.

Her mother had gone into the kitchen and now came back carrying a tray with the coffee carafe and cups. Seth rose and took it from her. After setting it on the coffee table, he put his hands on his hips and raised his eyebrows. “Where are the cookies? Katie promised me cookies.”

Katie’s mom laughed. “They’re still on the counter. You can get them if you’d like.”

He started toward the kitchen. “That’s the only reason I came tonight.” All three of the women laughed.

Katie bit her lip. All of a sudden she was torn between wanting to be alone with Seth, and then again, glad she wasn’t.

* * *

Seth sat at the end of the sofa with his coffee and cookies. He enjoyed listening to their take on last night’s event, but he longed to be alone with Katie. He brushed his fingers over the sock-covered toes of her right foot. She wiggled them in acknowledgement and went right on talking. He wanted to transfer her from the sofa into his lap, and remembered carrying her from the car to bed last night. She’d looked so beautiful lying there asleep when he’d come back with the wheelchair.

Had she heard him call her, “my darling?” How long was her mother going to stay with her? He wished he could ask.

When he noticed Katie stifle a yawn, he stood. “I’d better be going. It’s late and Katie’s tired.”

Anne and Jane carried the dishes out to the kitchen. Seth touched Katie’s hair. He wished they’d been able to have some private time but was thankful he’d gotten to see her. Her mother wouldn’t be staying forever. He could wait. As long as it took. He smiled at her, kissed his finger and placed it on her forehead.

She grasped his hand and held it. “Thanks for coming tonight.”

"I thought the day would never end. Kept looking at my watch all day." He glanced toward the kitchen, leaned down and lightly kissed her lips. "I've been wanting to do that since I walked in the door."

Katie's hand was still in his and she held it to her cheek. The sparkle in her eyes brightened. "Seth, I . . ."

Jane and Anne chose that moment to walk back into the room. What had Katie been about to say? He reluctantly let go of her hand and moved away. "I'll get our coats, Anne." As he turned, he glanced at Katie's husband's picture on the mantle. Was she really ready for a relationship with someone else? Please, God. May the answer be yes.

Chapter 37

Friday and Saturday were lazy days. Katie talked to Seth several times on the phone but he didn't stop by. She rested and got stronger each day. On Sunday morning, Katie and her mother had a leisurely breakfast and afterward her mother got ready to leave. As she was walking out the door she stopped and turned.

"Are you sure you don't need me to stay longer, dear?"

Katie shook her head. "I'll be fine. I'm almost as good as new."

Her mother fidgeted with her suitcase handle. "I really can stay you know."

"Mother."

"Okay. I just don't want you to feel abandoned." She moved into the elevator and blew a kiss. "Love you."

"Love you too."

The house seemed quiet and somewhat lonely after the door closed behind her mother. Katie maneuvered the wheelchair into her studio and contemplated her guitar. She hadn't picked it up since her fall. Who would have thought a nasty accident would have had such a miraculous ending. On Friday, the doctor had told her that not only was his surgery successful, but that the new injury had benefits they hadn't anticipated. Maybe now the rest of her could heal, too, and she could get on with her life.

Katie picked up her instrument and checked its tuning. After making several adjustments to the strings she played a simple worship chorus then moved on to Bach. Next she played a waltz. Oh yes, soon she'd dance!

It seemed as if she'd only played for a few minutes when the doorbell rang. A glance at the clock showed an hour had passed. She propped the guitar against its case and used her crutches instead of the wheelchair to answer the door. She looked through the peephole. Seth. She opened the door and moved back so he could come in. "Hi."

He cupped her cheek with his right hand, then moved his thumb under her chin and turned her face up. They gazed at each other for a moment, and Seth stepped closer and took her in his arms. She snuggled against him. His leather jacket was cold from the air outside, and she shivered. "Sorry. Leather's cold, isn't it?"

Katie smiled up at him and tugged lightly on the zipper. "Do you intend to stay awhile?"

"Oh yes, if you'll let me." He shrugged out of his jacket as she turned to walk with the aid of her crutches toward the living room.

He followed her, rubbing his hands together to warm them. She turned on the fireplace, then sat in one of the wing back chairs. Seth raised an eyebrow in question and motioned toward the sofa. "We could be more comfortable there, and your leg could be elevated."

"What a great idea." She reached for the crutches.

"You won't need those. Here, let me move you." He carried her to the sofa, arranged one of the pillows behind her back, then sat down and placed her legs in his lap.

"Is this comfortable?" He indicated her bulky boot.

She nodded. "Surprisingly I haven't had a lot of pain."

"I'm glad." He leaned back and turned his head to the side to look at her. "When did your mother leave?"

"This afternoon, around two thirty. What did you think of Samuel?"

"I liked him. They seemed comfortable with each other. Has this been going on for a long time?"

"Well, I know they've been friends for awhile but I get the feeling it's getting a little more serious. I liked him too. Mother has been alone a long time. I'd love for her to marry again." She sighed.

"Why the sigh?"

"I keep wondering if she put her life on hold because of me. Why didn't I notice? It feels as if I've been in another world."

Seth gently massaged her good foot through the sock she wore. "In a way you have. Life as you knew it stopped with John and J. J.'s deaths."

She closed her eyes and squeezed them with her thumb and forefinger. A tear made its way down her cheek.

"Darling, I'm sorry. I didn't mean to make you cry." He lifted her up onto his lap. Katie buried her face in his shoulder and sobbed. He held her and stroked her back while she cried.

Eventually the warmth of his hand caressing her back soothed and surrounded her with a sense of peace. Darling. He'd called her darling. It sounded so good. His touch, his smell, how she fit in his embrace, all of it seemed so right. She moved her cheek against his sweater and realized it was damp from her tears. She took a shuddering breath and pulled slightly away. What must he think of her? She was a basket case. She ran her hand over his shoulder. "Sorry. I drenched you."

"I love being drenched." He gave her a tissue from the box beside the couch and pulled her back into his arms. Seth rubbed his cheek against her hair and they sat in companionable silence for a little while.

"Katie?"

"Hm?"

"Are you okay?"

"Uh huh." She shifted but didn't lift her head. "Sorry for the outburst."

"Don't be sorry. It's okay. I'm not afraid of a few tears."

Katie smiled against his shoulder. She couldn't believe how good it felt to be in his arms. "Seth?"

"Yes?" He cupped her cheek in his hand. Katie moved her face against it and was warmed by his caress and concern.

"I like this." Katie couldn't believe she'd said it, but she meant it. This was good. Somehow the time seemed right.

He hugged her closer. "I like this too. In fact, it feels so right."

She smiled. "You took the words right out of my mouth." At that, he lifted her chin and kissed her. Both her hands crept around his neck as she kissed him back. Her lips molded to his as he pulled her closer. Feelings of confusion vied with the thrill of being held in his arms. These lips, so different from John's, pulled an unexpected thrill from deep within her. She pushed feelings of confusion to the back of her mind and relished the joy bubbling up in her heart. Reluctantly, Katie ended the kiss and nestled into his shoulder.

"Katie? Darling?"

She tipped her head back so she could see his face. "Am I your darling, Seth? Is this too soon?"

He smoothed her hair. "It's not too soon for me. It seems as if I've known you for years. And yes, as far as I'm concerned, you are my darling."

Katie smiled. "I love you, Seth." There. She'd said it, and the sky hadn't fallen in. Her heart was racing and by the astonishment on his face, it was obvious she had surprised him. She put her hand over his heart. Had it speeded up?

He covered her hand with his. "Can you feel it? It's all yours."

She nodded. "I didn't plan to tell you that I love you. It just came out of my mouth."

They talked quietly. Katie loved the security of his arms. She loved the smile in his eyes and the slight rasp in his voice. How had this happened? They'd known each other less than two months. Was he really as perfect as he seemed? She prayed it was true.

Soon Katie needed to move her leg to a more comfortable position, so Seth lifted her back onto the sofa and arranged pillows under her again. This time he sat so she could lean against him and snuggle into his arms.

"Does lifting and carrying me around make you feel like a 'he' man?" She chuckled.

"You mean like 'you Jane—me Tarzan?' I wouldn't know. I've never manhandled a woman before." He chuckled. "You don't object? I know you're independent. It wasn't all that long ago you told me you could take care of yourself."

Katie thought back to the evening he'd called to check up on her. "I'm surprised you came around again after that phone call. If I remember right, I was rather annoyed."

"Rather? Ha! How about very. I'm glad I didn't give up." His hand rested along the back of the sofa and he moved it to touch her hair. "Oh girl, you are so special."

The touch of his hand on her hair and the tenderness in his voice sparked a feeling of wonder. Wonder. What a charming word.

Chapter 38

Katie awakened Monday morning with feelings of both joy and apprehension. Had last night really happened? Had she actually told Seth she was falling in love with him? Had she imagined the look of delight that crossed his face as she blurted it out? She whispered a prayer as she threw back the duvet and stretched.

"Thanks God, for second chances. I didn't even know I wanted a second chance at love."

She sat up and thought about the little intimate gestures Seth constantly used that showed he was aware of her. Like the way he moved his foot last night until it touched hers and then left it there. Or how, when they were eating, he didn't just hand the soda to her, but held it for her to drink from the straw, then set it down. They'd turned on the television to watch a program they both enjoyed, and Seth had picked up her hand. She liked how he threaded his fingers through hers in an intimate way.

In fact, she couldn't think of anything about him she didn't like. She even liked his watch. Oh, boy. She was in trouble.

She reached for her crutches, got out of bed and moved across the room to pull up the shades. The days were getting longer so it was light now before eight o'clock. She sat on the window seat and looked down at the backyard. Spring was less than a month away and oh, how welcome it would be.

It had snowed during the night and two neighbors were leaning on their shovels talking. A Currier and Ives scene if she'd ever seen one. She loved this city. Her home. What was Seth's home like?

Was that Seth's car coming down her side street? She glanced over at the loveseat. Where was her robe? She usually tossed it over there. In the bathroom? She moved as quickly as she could and checked behind the door. Oh good. There it was. She turned to the sink to brush her teeth, then ran a brush through her hair. She was tying the belt of her robe when the doorbell rang. Whew. Finished. She anchored the crutches more firmly under her arms and headed down the hall. No need to check the peephole. She opened the door.

He looked so good. His tanned cheeks were slightly flushed from the cold, his hair mussed from the wind, and a mischievous smile sat on his lips. He raised his right hand holding a cardboard tray with coffee for two and then the left with a bag. "Breakfast?"

She moved aside to let him enter. "Love some."

He stopped. "Love?" He bent forward, and she instinctively raised her lips to his for a feather-light kiss.

Good thing he had his hands full because Katie wanted to move into his arms. Goodness, she wasn't even dressed. She shut the door and followed him to the kitchen. He looked good from this direction too. She smiled to herself.

Seth set things on the table, hung his jacket on the back of a chair, then pulled one out for Katie and she slid into it. He raised an eyebrow. "Plates?"

She nodded. "In the cabinet to the right of the sink. Silverware is in the drawer to the left." She opened the bag and breathed deeply. "I love bagels. And they're still warm." She reached for the plates but he set them on the table and took her right hand.

"Morning, Katie." He crouched to her level. "I'd like to be able to say that to you every morning." His voice was warm and rich and filled with love.

She reached out and cupped his cheek with her left hand. As she scanned his face she wondered how this man had become so dear in such a short while. "I've hardly dared to believe in second chances, but now . . ."

He turned his face into her hand and kissed her palm, then moved the hand he held and placed it against his chest. "Feel that?"

She nodded. His heart was thudding.

He kept her hand pressed to his heart. "Every time I think about you or hear your voice or even hear a guitar playing, my heart starts to beat faster. Nothing could have prepared me for this." He breathed deeply. "If someone had told me three months ago that I'd meet someone as special as you, I'd have laughed in disbelief. Now I can't imagine my life without you." He stood and gazed down at her. "I can't tell you how often each day I thank God that I met you, Katie."

Hearing him declaring his feeling for her was wonderful, but the fact that he added God to the mix made her heart sing. She struggled to her feet and moved into his arms, her chest squeezed with emotion. Her arms crept around his neck, and he pulled her close. He bent and kissed her, lingering just a little then breaking the kiss to pull her tightly into his arms. She loved the feel of him, solid and secure. This was so right. God still worked miracles.

Epilogue

Seven Months Later

"I do." Katie could barely get the simple words past the thickening in her throat. Was she emotional? Yes. Did she have doubts? No. This man was a special gift from God, just for her. The previous months had been wonderful. Time spent making plans, long conversations, sharing dreams. She glanced down at their clasped hands. His were so strong and yet she knew how gentle they could be. She met his eyes and let her love shine from her gaze. His answering smile melted her heart.

After the official kiss, they turned around. Before them sat their families and the few close friends they'd invited to share this day. Most were clapping, and several wiped tears from their eyes. Beside her, Anne sniffed. When Anne tried to hand the bouquet back to her, Katie shook her head and turned to Seth.

The organist started playing. Katie had a moment of uncertainty. Would her newly healed leg be able to do this? His strong right hand grasped hers, and doubt fled. Seth bowed, Katie curtsied and he pulled her into a dancing embrace. She heard gasps then laughter as the organist played a Strauss waltz and they danced down the aisle and out the door.

CPSIA information can be obtained at www.ICGtesting.com
Printed in the USA
BVOW05s1234171114

375462BV00001B/4/P